THE
PROMISE
OF
Lightning

THE DELANEYS OF CAMBRIA, BOOK 2

LINDA SEED

Linda Seed

This is a work of fiction. Any characters, organizations, places, or events portrayed in this novel are either products of the author's imagination or are used fictitiously.

THE PROMISE
OF LIGHTNING
Copyright © 2017 by Linda Seed

The author is available for book signings, book club discussions, conferences, and other appearances.

Linda Seed may be contacted via e-mail at lindaseed24@gmail.com or on Facebook at www.facebook.com/LindaSeedAuthor. Learn more about Linda Seed's novels at www.lindaseed.com.

Cover design by Teaberry Creative.

BY LINDA SEED

THE MAIN STREET MERCHANTS

MOONSTONE BEACH
CAMBRIA SKY
NEARLY WILD
FIRE AND GLASS

THE DELANEYS OF CAMBRIA

A LONG, COOL RAIN
THE PROMISE OF LIGHTNING
LOVING THE STORM
SEARCHING FOR SUNSHINE

THE RUSSO SISTERS

SAVING SOFIA
FIRST CRUSH

THE
PROMISE
OF
Lightning

THE DELANEYS OF CAMBRIA, BOOK 2

Chapter One

Drew McCray hated weddings.

First, they didn't mean anything. You could take vows in front of a church full of people, and your wife could still run out with all of your stuff, leaving you with nothing but a broken coffeemaker and your memories.

Second, you had to smile and make nice with a bunch of strangers—or people who were worse than strangers—and eat overcooked pasta while the band played the Chicken Dance.

You didn't want to get him started on the Chicken Dance.

So he was already predisposed to be grumpy as hell six months before, when his sister had announced her engagement and asked him to be in the wedding party. He'd hidden the grumpiness for her sake, though. That is, until she called eight days before the ceremony and told him about Wedding Week.

"What's Wedding Week?" he asked her. He was standing in his workshop with a half-built sloop set up on pallets in front of him, his cellphone to his ear, the smell of sawdust in the air.

"It's going to be fun!" Julia assured him, her voice annoyingly perky, especially at this time of the morning. "We're going to have the rehearsal and the rehearsal dinner, of course. And a party for the out-of-town guests. And the bachelor party. And kayaking! You love kayaking."

He did love kayaking, but he wasn't going to love doing it with Julia's future in-laws, given his complicated and troubled past with the Delaneys.

That was a long story, and one he didn't much like to think about. But the gist of it was, if he had a choice between spending an event-filled week with them or stabbing himself in the eye, he'd have to seriously think about how much he needed his binocular vision.

"Damn it, Julia. I can't go to Cambria now. I'm busy. I'll go for the wedding, like we'd planned."

"You're not busy," she said.

"Well, that's … how do you know if I'm busy?"

"Because when I talked to you yesterday, you said that you didn't have much going on this week. You said the boat you're working on isn't a rush job, and you didn't have any special plans, and you were just going to have a relaxing week."

Had he said all that? Thinking back on it, he guessed he had. But when he'd said it, he hadn't realized his sister was luring him into a trap—one that involved a bachelor party, kayaking, and probably even the damned Chicken Dance with a bunch of people who probably were hoping his kayak would sink to the bottom of the Pacific Ocean.

"Seriously? That's what yesterday's phone call was about? You were grilling me for information so you could spring Wedding Week on me?"

"Well …"

"I probably can't even get a flight on such short notice."

"I checked online, and there's a flight from Victoria to San Luis Obispo tomorrow morning on Delta." She sounded pleased with herself.

"Tomorrow morning," he repeated. Then he was silent, brooding over the imminent loss of the quiet, uneventful week he'd had planned.

"Oh, come on, Drew. I know I should have told you earlier, but you'd have figured out a way to get out of it. And I need you there. You're my brother, and I love you, and Dad isn't here anymore, so …"

He closed his eyes and tipped back his head, letting out a sigh.

How was he supposed to say no, now that she'd played the Dead Father card?

"Will you do it?" she prompted him.

"Julia …"

"Please?"

What else could he do? She was his sister. His fathers were gone—both his biological father and the man who'd raised him—and his relationship with his mother was difficult at best. Julia was all he had left.

"Of course I'll do it."

"Oh! Thank you, Drew. Thank you! I'll email you the flight information, and the itinerary for Wedding Week, and—"

"There's an itinerary for Wedding Week?" He was already regretting having caved.

"It's not a colonoscopy, Drew, it's some parties and kayaking. It's going to be fun!"

"Can I just have the damned colonoscopy instead? Because—"

"Drew. I'm happy. Let me be happy."

And that settled it. Of course he wanted her to be happy. And of course he wouldn't intentionally do anything to take that happiness away.

"Send me the information," he said, then hung up the phone and slid it into the back pocket of his jeans.

Fuck.

He shot a glance at Eddie, the big tabby cat who'd adopted him a few weeks before. "I'm screwed, Eddie, aren't I?"

Eddie just meowed.

Drew regretted that leaving early meant he'd have to put a hold on his current boat project—a custom sloop he was building for a local guy on Salt Spring Island.

When life got to be too difficult or too impossible to fathom—when family problems or the demands of an inheritance he didn't know what to do with overwhelmed him—Drew built boats.

The boat-building had started as a hobby when he was a kid living in Montana with his parents and his sister. When Drew was about twelve, his father—or, at least, the man he'd then believed to be his father—had begun building a twelve-foot fishing boat from a kit in the family's two-car garage.

After about a week of standing tentatively by while Andrew McCray began the painstaking process of laying out plans and patterns and cutting panels of wood out of teak, Drew asked if he could help.

What followed was a period of time Drew looked back on as one of the best in his life. He and Andrew worked side by side on the boat for months, when they weren't occupied with work or school. Drew had learned about the tools, the materials, and, most importantly, the art of craftsmanship—the satisfaction of striving for excellence not because he'd be graded or judged on the end result, but for the sake of the thing itself.

And he'd learned about his dad, because they hadn't just worked; they'd talked about things they somehow hadn't been able to discuss with each other before. Andrew talked about his work as a repair technician for the telephone company, telling stories about his coworkers and his frustrations with his boss. Drew talked about school and his teachers and the girls he liked, and whether he should pursue football when he got to high school or let that slide so he could focus on his grades and still have time to be a kid and mess around with his friends.

When the boat was finished, there had been fishing trips on Ennis Lake. It embarrassed him now to think that sometimes he hadn't wanted to go; at the time, he'd considered it childish and boring to have to spend time with his father when he could have been with his friends.

Now, he would have given ten years of his own life just to have his dad back long enough for one more day out on the lake beneath the puffy clouds, with the sounds of the birds and the insects in his ears.

He couldn't have that, but he did have work that was a direct legacy from his father.

Drew had been building custom boats for a living since shortly after he'd graduated from high school. He'd started as an apprentice at a shop in Bozeman that made drift boats that could navigate the rivers of Montana.

While he was doing that, he was building a boat in his parents' garage in his spare time. The first time he took the boat out onto the lake, another fisherman asked about it—and then offered to buy it.

He built another one and sold that, and another after that. Eventually, he realized he no longer needed to be anybody's apprentice.

At the height of his business—before his ex-wife, Tessa, drove him into bankruptcy—he was renting workshop space five times the size of his parents' garage, and he employed three people, including two builders and one sales guy.

The business was easy enough to move from Montana to Salt Spring Island, off the coast of Vancouver, when he'd needed a change of environment. Only now there were no regular employees, and there was no sales guy. There was only Drew, building boats small enough that he could manage alone or with part-time help that he brought in on an as-needed basis.

At first, working on such a small scale came from necessity. When Tessa had left him, she'd cleaned out the bank accounts and maxed out the credit cards. He couldn't afford to pay anybody, and he couldn't afford advertising. But now that money was no longer an issue—or at least, the *lack* of it wasn't an issue—he kept doing what he was doing because it was peaceful, and because working alone amid the smells of sawdust and varnish gave him time to clear his head.

And right now, he really needed time to clear his head, because he was about to face more family complications than he knew what to do with.

While the idea of staying here and hiding out with his boats and his solitude was appealing, he didn't want to disappoint his sister.

So he packed his stuff, scrambled around to acquire a cat carrier that would fit under an airline seat, left his home and his quiet island, cursed the gods for his circumstances, and caught the flight Julia had picked out for him.

If it all went as badly as he expected, he could always fake his own drowning during the kayaking trip.

Megan Scott thought, not for the first time, that she might have too many pets.

There was Bobby, the Maltese she'd had since she was in college; Sunshine, a golden retriever she'd adopted after he'd been hit by a car and then abandoned; Mr. Wiggles, an angora cat whose owner had wanted to put him down over a treatable health condition; Jerry, a three-legged hamster; and Sally Struthers, a guinea pig she'd agreed to provide a foster home for, but who'd charmed her way into becoming a permanent part of the family.

The thought that she'd gone overboard with the furry friends usually struck her at two times: when she was cleaning up after them, and when her boyfriend, Liam, was complaining about them.

Which he was doing now.

"I get having a dog. Who doesn't like to have a dog to come home to after work? But, Jesus. This place is like a petting zoo." Scowling, he lifted Mr. Wiggles from his spot on the sofa and deposited him onto the floor, then sat in the space the cat had just vacated.

"Liam, you're a rancher," Megan pointed out to him, not unreasonably. "You're around animals all day."

"Yeah, but not in the house." Mr. Wiggles was rubbing up against Liam's leg, and Liam nudged him away with his foot.

"Okay, I can admit that it's a lot for the space I've got. But I've had Bobby forever. And the rest …"

The rest of the animals all had been in dire circumstances when Megan had met them. What was she supposed to do? Let them suffer? Let them be put down, dying alone and unloved when they still had so much life left in them? She was a vet, for God's sake. She'd taken an oath to protect the welfare of the animals in her care, to ease suffering. What else was she doing by providing a home to her pets, if not easing their suffering?

"Yeah, yeah," Liam said, having heard it all before. "I guess it would make more sense if you had a bigger space."

That part, at least, was hard to argue with. Megan's house

was a one-bedroom, one-bathroom cottage that barely could accommodate her own needs, let alone those of her animal companions.

"It is a little tight in here," she admitted. The house had been built in the 1920s, a time when people had lower expectations in terms of square footage.

"If you'd consider moving in with me …"

Here we go.

Liam had initially broached the subject of the two of them moving in together months before, shortly after Liam's brother Colin had become engaged. Megan supposed it was an issue of brotherly competition. She had been using various arguments to put him off, and she pulled out the best of those now.

"But, Liam, you live with your parents."

He shrugged. "We've talked about this. I only live with them because it's convenient to be there at the ranch. We can get our own place. Hell, we can have a place built on the property. Someplace big enough for your dogs and your cat and your damned guinea pig." He grinned. "Your hamster can have its own room."

He wasn't exaggerating about the hamster room. Liam was a Delaney, and the Delaneys had serious money—enough that she'd be able to have whatever features she wanted in this hypothetical new house of theirs.

The only problem was, the main thing she wanted out of any new home was that Liam not be in it.

She'd been seeing Liam for two years, and over the past six months or so, she'd slowly come to the realization that she wanted to break things off.

She just hadn't figured out how to do it.

An outsider observing the situation would have thought that the problem was Liam's personality. He was temperamental and prickly, quick to anger and perpetually irritated. But what the outsider wouldn't see was that Liam was also kind, honest, loyal, and willing to sacrifice anything for those he loved.

He was also sexy as hell.

That last part was what had gotten her into trouble, had gotten her hopelessly enmeshed in a relationship that just wasn't working.

As for why it wasn't working, that was more simple than any question of his temperament, or their compatibility, or the collective sum of his flaws and attributes.

What it came down to was that Megan's heart just wasn't in it. And that wasn't something you could overcome through compromise; it wasn't something you could smooth over with the help of a relationship counselor.

Her heart knew what it wanted, and it didn't want Liam.

She'd been working her way up to telling him for months now, but she hadn't been able to do it. And now, she really couldn't do it until after the wedding. She was in the wedding party, and so was he. The potential awkwardness of both of them going through the activities of Wedding Week fresh from the emotional savagery of a breakup was something she couldn't even contemplate.

So, she would have to wait. But as the wedding drew closer, Liam was becoming more and more determined to persuade her to take their relationship to the next level. Was that because he really wanted it? Or did he sense her pulling away? Was this his last-ditch attempt to grab onto her before it was too late?

She looked at him, at the way he was sprawled comfortably in her living room, his long legs stretched out in front of him, his arms spread along the back of the sofa, and she felt a genuine, warm bloom of affection. She loved him, she really did.

She just didn't love him the way he needed her to. If she

could have, she would have. God, it would have made things so much easier if she could just marry him, have his babies, live on the Delaney Ranch for the rest of her days in comfort, with a clear view of her place in the world.

She just couldn't do it—and if she tried, it wouldn't be fair to either one of them.

"Hey, Liam? I'm pretty tired. I think I'm just going to call it a night." They'd gone to dinner at Robin's and then had come back here, and from the looks of him, he intended to stay awhile. But right now, she just wanted to be alone, wanted to watch TV in her sweatpants and not think about the state of her love life.

"Yeah, I'm pretty tired, too," he said agreeably. He got up and headed toward the bedroom.

"Um … Liam?"

"Yeah?" He turned back toward her.

"I think I'm going to just … you know. Sleep alone tonight. If it's okay. I've got an early morning."

And, oh, the look on his face. He looked like a kid who'd just opened the Christmas present he'd always wanted, and then had learned that it was intended for someone else.

He rallied admirably, though.

"Oh. Sure. Call me tomorrow?"

"I will."

He went to kiss her, and she offered her cheek. And if he couldn't read that one—couldn't see that it meant trouble—then he wasn't really trying.

"Is everything okay?" he asked.

"Yeah. Yeah. I'm just …"

"Tired," he supplied.

"I am."

"Well … call me." He went out the front door and closed it behind him. When he was gone, she exhaled in relief.

If she weren't such a wimp, she could fix this. Could let him go, so he could find someone who really did want all of the things he wanted.

After the wedding. I'll wait until after the wedding, but no longer.

She scrubbed at her face with her hands, then felt Mr. Wiggles rubbing against her pant leg.

"He's gone, you can get back on the sofa," she told him.

The fluffy white cat leaped up onto the cushions, turned around a few times, and curled up into a ball of fur, purring contentedly.

Megan wished there were something or someone in her life that could make her purr like that.

Chapter Two

The trip was miserable. Drew was crammed into a tiny seat through three flights, with stops in San Francisco and Los Angeles, Eddie yowling in his carrier under the seat most of the way, earning Drew the scornful looks of his fellow passengers.

He could have paid for first class since receiving his inheritance—he could have paid for a private jet. But he'd been raised middle-class, raised to look for the best deal, to go for the bargain.

Old habits.

Drew had a trim build, so he avoided the dreaded spill-over into his seatmates' space, but he was also tall, so his knees pressed uncomfortably against the seatback in front of him all the way from Canada to California.

By the time he got to the airport in San Luis Obispo, he was tired, grumpy, and not in the best frame of mind to consider the rigors of Wedding Week.

He got his rental car, piled his luggage into it, maneuvered out onto the road, and took the first opportunity to pull over briefly near a patch of grass where Eddie could stretch his legs and pee.

Wedding Week had been his mother's idea, he'd be willing

to bet his sizable net worth on it.

Julia was a down-to-earth woman, and her fiancé, Colin Delaney, had never struck Drew as the kind of guy who would care about putting on a showy wedding. But Isabelle? Well, that was a different story.

Drew and Julia's mother wasn't materialistic—not exactly. Hell, she probably could have maneuvered her way into marrying a billionaire back when she'd conceived Drew with a very rich man who was not her husband. But she hadn't done it, opting instead to preserve her marriage to the man she'd vowed to love until death.

So, it wasn't that.

If she was behind Wedding Week—and he was certain that she was—it was more likely to be about how the Delaneys would perceive her. She wanted to be a driving force behind this event, and not someone who, for the second time, had been marginalized by a powerful family.

And, God, how much nerve had that taken? Who was she to the Delaneys? She was the woman Redmond Delaney had enjoyed a secret affair with back in the day—an affair that had resulted in Drew's birth. How hard must it have been for her to push her way forward now, all these years later, to assert her place in the family order?

He almost had to admire it. Or, he would have, if it didn't mean he'd have to spend an entire week with his biological family—who were also about to become Julia's in-laws.

Drew's relationship with the Delaneys was problematic at best. The Delaney family's attitudes toward him ranged from acceptance (Sandra) to neutrality (Breanna) to benign condescension (Colin) to outright hostility (Liam).

Of course, Drew himself hadn't helped matters. When he'd learned that Redmond had left him a fortune, he'd traveled to

Cambria to meet the family he'd never known. He'd gone into the thing with the attitude that the Delaneys had rejected him, had denied his existence and had shut him out from the time of his birth.

The truth was more complicated. Drew's biological father had never claimed him, that much was true. But the rest of the family had been as surprised about Drew's existence as he'd been about theirs.

Still, anger had a way of spilling over onto anyone within range, and Drew's anger had oozed thickly onto every Delaney he met.

To put it simply, he'd been kind of an asshole to them.

Now he had to go out there and make nice for his sister's sake. He'd do it for her, but that didn't mean he was going to like it.

He drove the rental car up Highway 1 toward Cambria, the vast, blue ocean to his left, the rolling hills to his right, their waist-high grass baked golden by the summer sun.

The temperature reading on the car's dashboard said seventy-two degrees. Seagulls soared overhead, cawing in the breeze.

This stretch of the Central Coast was beautiful, he could admit that.

And now he owned a sizable part of it, a fact that, two years later, he was still struggling to comprehend.

When Redmond Delaney had died, Drew had been dead-ass broke, dodging creditors and avoiding debt collectors, barely able to pay his rent or buy food.

So it had been surreal to learn that Redmond had left him a large percentage of his estate—a fortune so vast and varied, including cash, land, investments, and shares in the family corporation, that Drew could barely conceive of the scope of it.

This turn of events had been a lot to cope with—so Drew had coped mostly by trying not to think about it.

He'd paid off his debts and had bought a new truck for cash, but otherwise, the money and assets had mostly just sat there, appreciating at a dizzying rate. Colin—Drew's future brother-in-law—had urged him to get a financial adviser, to educate himself about money management, to talk to a lawyer. Hell, to do anything other than what he was doing, which was nothing.

But every time Drew tried to think about what his first step should be, he felt paralyzed. So, he continued to live in the same rental cottage on Salt Spring Island where he'd lived when the news had come. He continued to fly economy class. He continued to buy two-for-one cans of beans at the grocery store.

The only thing that had changed, really, was the way other people treated him.

Since news of his wealth had broken a couple of years before, he'd gotten a constant stream of phone calls, e-mails, and even in-person visits from people who wanted things. The kinds of people they were and the kinds of things they wanted varied, but it all came down to the same thing.

Money.

His ex-wife wanted to get back together. Financial advisers wanted him to invest with them. Luxury car and boat salesmen wanted to sell him things. Distant relatives wanted loans. Charities wanted donations. People he hadn't seen or heard from since he was a kid wanted to rekindle friendships.

And Drew had sealed himself inside a protective bubble, no longer knowing what to think or who to trust.

It had occurred to him more than once that maybe the Delaneys could help him, if he'd let them. They'd been dealing with the responsibilities of unimaginable wealth for generations.

By now, they probably had some idea how to do it.

As he drove over the boundary into Cambria, the highway lined with towering, green pines, he wondered if maybe he shouldn't put his awkwardness and resentment aside and reach out to the Delaneys, since he was here anyway.

There might be something to that idea, if he could set aside his defensiveness, his anger, his hurt at having been lied to his entire life.

It was probably time.

He took the exit for Moonstone Beach, found the pet-friendly hotel where he'd made his reservations, and pulled into the parking lot. The place was across a two-lane road from the beach, and he was greeted by the sound of the pounding waves and the smell of salt air.

The sky was a flawless blue, and tourists walked in pairs along the wooden boardwalk across the road, atop the craggy bluffs that hugged the beach.

It wasn't exactly a hellhole, and it seemed to Drew that it might be hard to keep his pissy attitude going in a place like this.

He lifted the cat carrier out of the car and went to get checked in.

When Megan finally did break up with Liam, she knew that part of her would miss him. But an even bigger part of her was going to miss his family.

Like his sister, Breanna, for instance.

"Whose genius idea was Wedding Week, anyway?" Breanna demanded as she and Megan were checking the final plans for the bachelorette party. "Why would anybody want a wedding to last a whole damned week? It should be one day—two, tops. Vows, food, cake, and you're out of there."

Breanna, who'd been enlisted to help with a whole slew of

wedding and pre-wedding tasks, looked frazzled, and she shoved her thick, dark hair away from where it had fallen into her eyes.

"But the bachelorette party's going to be fun, don't you think?" Megan said.

Breanna wrinkled her nose in thought. "Yeah, it will be. Even if we're not having strippers."

The question of strippers vs. no strippers had been debated, batted around, and analyzed by pretty much all of the women involved, before Julia, the bride, had come down on the side of discretion and good taste. Megan, herself, could have gone either way, but Breanna had lobbied hard for men in G-strings, and the loss had been a difficult blow.

But that didn't mean there wouldn't be plenty of alcohol and humiliation. They'd booked Ted's, a dive bar a block off of Main Street, for a private party that would include catered food, an open bar, a dart tournament, and, once everyone was drunk enough to release their inhibitions, karaoke.

"I swear to God, if I can't have strippers, then I'm at least going to get my mom to sing," Breanna declared, and the thought made Megan smile.

Sandra Delaney, matriarch of the family, was known more for her ill-tempered grousing than for singing. The idea of her standing in front of the crowd, microphone in hand, belting out the theme song from *Titanic* was almost enough to lift Megan out of her sour mood.

The mood hadn't escaped Breanna's notice, and she gave her friend a pointed look as the two of them sat at the kitchen table at Megan's house, lists of guests and plans for the party spread out in front of them amid two tall, sweating glasses of iced tea.

"I know what's up with me," Breanna said. "I'm dreading Wedding Week. But what's up with you?"

What could Megan say? How could she tell Breanna that she'd be breaking up with Liam as soon as the festivities were over? Breanna liked Megan, but she loved her brother. It wasn't hard to imagine which one of them would get Breanna in the wake of the split.

"I just … It's nothing," Megan said. She didn't sound convincing, even to herself.

"Bull," Breanna said. "It's something, and I can guess what. My brother's been acting like an ass again. What did he do this time?"

Megan wanted to hold back, wanted to avoid getting into this. But the fact was, Breanna was pretty much her best friend here in Cambria. Before she could stop herself, Megan was spilling everything about her feelings, her fears—and her plans to end the relationship.

"It's not that he's done anything. He hasn't. Things have been fine. They're … fine." She doodled on the corner of the guest list with a pen to avoid making eye contact with her friend.

"But?" Breanna prompted her.

"But … I'm tired of 'fine.'"

Breanna raised her eyebrows and focused on Megan silently for a moment. Then she said, "This is a wine discussion, not an iced tea discussion." She got up, went to Megan's refrigerator, and hunted around inside. She emerged with an unopened bottle of Chardonnay. "Thank God you're prepared," she remarked. She found a corkscrew, opened the bottle, poured two glasses, and brought them back to the table.

"Okay, tell me what you meant by being tired of 'fine.'"

Megan knew she should filter herself, because this was Liam's sister, his family. But little by little it all came out: the way the relationship had progressed too fast when Liam had moved to Cambria from Montana to be with her when they'd only been dating for a few months; the way Sandra just seemed to assume that Megan and Liam would eventually get married; the way Liam seemed pissed off all the time, but wouldn't talk about it with Megan; and most of all, the way she couldn't feel the magic.

When Megan and Liam had first met, through her work treating some of the animals on the Delaney Ranch, she'd thought she felt something—some spark of lightning in her blood that said they were right for each other. But more and more, she wondered if maybe she'd imagined it. Maybe she'd just wanted it to be right so much that she'd manufactured an electric charge that wasn't there.

She loved Liam, in her way, but he was just a good man. He wasn't magic—at least, not for her. And she was afraid that if she didn't do something soon, she was going to end up married to him, stuck in a relationship that wasn't working for her, just going along with the expectations and the momentum. And she couldn't let that happen.

When she finished, she felt the hot sting of tears behind her eyes, and she took a slug of Chardonnay to chase the feeling away.

"Well, damn it," Breanna said.

"Yeah," Megan agreed.

Breanna didn't say anything else for a while, and Megan wondered which way it would go. Would Breanna turn cold and accuse her of setting out to break Liam's heart? Would she accuse Megan of being selfish or unfaithful, of being shallow or somehow not good enough for her brother?

If that happened, well, Megan supposed it was just something she'd have to deal with. It would hurt to lose her friend, but if it was going to happen, it might as well happen now rather than later.

"How long have you felt this way?" Breanna said.

"A while."

"So, you're going to break up with him." Breanna fixed her gaze on Megan's face.

"I … yeah. I have to."

Breanna sighed and leaned back in her chair. "Well, you're going to have to wait until after the wedding. Otherwise …"

"I know. Otherwise, Liam will be hurt and pissed off, and we'll still be forced to go through Wedding Week together, and Colin and Julia's big event will be all about me and Liam."

"That pretty much sums it up," Breanna agreed. "Maybe you'll get lucky and he'll hit on one of the wedding guests."

"He won't," Megan said. Liam was a lot of things—temperamental, volatile, impulsive and emotional—but he wasn't a cheater. Liam Delaney was loyal, and he was honorable. Breaking up with him would have been so much easier if he hadn't been.

"No, he won't," Breanna agreed.

They both thought about that, the gloom of impending heartache in the air between them.

"If you can't be my friend anymore after this, I'll understand, but … but I hope …"

Megan couldn't say the rest. Emotion was cutting off her words.

"Well, this sucks, because I really wanted you to be my sister-in-law," Breanna said, wiping one fat tear from her own cheek. "But you're always going to be my friend. Just … This sucks, that's all."

"It does."

Bobby, sensing that Megan was upset, got up on his hind legs and put his front paws on her leg, letting out a little whine. She scratched between his ears.

"Now, let's get back to what's important," Breanna said.

"How are we going to get my mom drunk so she'll sing *Copa-cabana?*"

Chapter Three

Drew had hoped to have a quiet evening to himself before he had to deal with the Delaneys. But he hadn't been at the hotel more than an hour before Julia called with the first of many Wedding Week obligations.

She swore that wasn't what it was, but if it quacked like a duck and walked like a duck, Drew knew better than to think it was a giraffe.

"It's not a big deal. It's just dinner with the family," she insisted. She said *the family* as though it were a simple matter that they were not only her own future in-laws, but Drew's relatives as well.

His part in it hadn't caught up yet with what was in his head and his heart. He knew he'd have to get there eventually, for his own good as well as everyone else's, so he let out a long breath and resigned himself to having a meal with them.

"*Just* dinner with the family?" he said.

"Well …"

"Julia, what?"

"It's just dinner. But it's maybe not just family. Or, not just the Delaneys. There are a lot of people in from out of town, and we couldn't just leave them on their own, so …"

He braced himself. "Who, then?"

"Uncle Joe and Aunt Marcy and the twins," she began.

"Okay." He liked Uncle Joe, and Drew hadn't seen him in a while. "Who else?"

"Some of the guys from the Montana ranch. And Mike, of course." Mike was the contractor Julia used in her landscaping business, and he was also her best friend. "And ..."

Here it came.

"And who?"

"Well ... and Mom."

Of course, Drew knew that Isabelle would be at the wedding and at many of the events leading up to it. But he had hoped that he might be able to get a day or two into the trip before dealing with her. The reasons for his discomfort were threefold:

1. She'd lied to him his entire life about who his father was, and he hadn't quite brought himself to forgive her yet.

2. This was, as far as Drew knew, the first time she'd been confronted with a room full of Delaneys since she'd carried on her secret affair with Redmond more than thirty years before. That was likely to create tension at the dinner table. And:

3. She'd been the one who had conspired to keep Drew hidden not only from his biological father, but also from most of the people who would be in the room this evening.

It seemed unlikely that they would all swap stories and hug like schoolgirls.

Though he supposed anything was possible.

"Remember that you're doing it for me," Julia said plaintively.

He rubbed his eyelids with his fingers. "What time do I have to be there?"

Drew didn't dislike all of the Delaneys. In fact, most of

them were okay, if you could get past the circumstances.

But he disliked one particular Delaney—Liam—enough that it all averaged out.

So he was a little dismayed that it happened to be Liam who answered the door when Drew, a bottle of wine in his hand, rang the bell at the Delaney Ranch farmhouse.

"I didn't know you were coming," Liam said, his eyebrows gathered in irritation. He said it in the same tone one might say, *What is this snake doing in my bathtub?* or, *Who crapped on the carpet?* He made no move to step aside so Drew could enter.

"Well, I'm here." Drew stood a little taller, puffing himself up the way animals do when faced by a predator. "You going to let me in?"

"I don't see why I should." Liam's face was grim, his lips pressed into a hard line.

"Maybe because the bride invited me. And maybe because I'll knock you on your ass if you don't."

Could Drew knock Liam on his ass, if it came to that? Probably not. Liam wasn't quite as tall as Drew, but he had a lifetime of physical work behind him, making him strong and wiry. Plus, Liam had a history of brawling, while Drew hadn't been in a fight since he'd been girl-slapped by Brian Cooper in the fifth grade.

Come to think of it, Brian Cooper had made him cry. But Liam didn't need to know that.

In response to Drew's baseless threat to knock him on his ass, Liam turned a little bit red in the face and took a step toward him. Drew was just wondering if he'd actually have to fight when a pretty, dark-haired woman in tortoiseshell glasses peeked out at Drew from behind Liam's shoulder.

"Liam? What's wrong?" The woman put her hand on Liam's arm, and something about the easy, casual touch told

Drew that this was the vet Liam was involved with.

"Not a damn thing." Liam's gaze was still fixed on Drew, steely and unyielding. "I'm just about to take out the trash."

Liam took another step toward Drew, and now they were both on the front porch, standing nearly chest to chest, with just inches of space keeping them from actually butting into each other. The brunette, who was tall for a woman but who was still a good four inches shorter than either of them, shoved her way in between them, facing Liam.

She put her hands on Liam's shoulders and whispered something to him, something that sounded like, *Don't do this.* Liam, who had been looking past her at Drew with his fuck-off scowl in place, settled slightly and looked at her.

"You should go back inside," he told her.

"No, *you* should." Her tone was firm but gentle, like a grade-school teacher scolding her favorite student. "Go on." Her hands still on his shoulders, she turned him around and gave him a little shove toward the open door.

"Goddamn it, Megan," Liam protested.

"What's your mother going to say if you get into a fistfight on her front porch?" the woman asked.

That was what finally caused Liam to grudgingly go into the house, leaving Drew alone on the porch with the woman who quite possibly had saved him from grave bodily harm.

When he was gone, she held out her hand.

"Megan Scott."

"Drew McCray."

Her eyes widened. "You're Julia's brother. And …"

"And Liam's bastard cousin, yeah." He shifted his stance, the bottle of wine sweating in his hand. "Thanks for calling off Cro-Magnon Man."

Her expression turned from mild curiosity to scorn. "I'm

pretty sure I heard you threaten him. That might have had some-thing to do with his attitude."

Of course she was going to be on Liam's side. She was sleeping with the guy, after all—though Drew couldn't imagine why.

"That was right before he called me trash, wasn't it?"

Inside the open door, a crowd of people were milling around with plates and drinks in their hands. Julia spotted him and came out onto the porch, bringing a much-needed shot of sunlight.

"Drew! You're here! Oh, I'm so glad!" She threw her arms around him and pulled him into a tight hug. "Have you met Megan? Come on inside! I want to tell Sandra you're here."

As Drew went into the house with Julia, Megan stood on the porch and watched him go. Everything Liam had said about the guy was starting to make sense.

For two years, Megan had been hearing stories about Drew McCray, most of which were intended to justify Liam's intense dislike for the man. Megan had thought Liam was being un-reasonable—as he'd been known to do—but now, she was start-ing to think maybe he was on to something.

This was Liam's home, after all. And McCray had come to the door already looking for a fight. What kind of guest behaved that way? What kind of man showed up at another man's home and threatened to hit him?

Despite Megan's mixed feelings about Liam, her natural sense of loyalty kicked in. Sure, she was planning to break up with him. And yes, their relationship was hanging on by its meta-phorical fingernails. But that didn't mean she was going to let some guy walk in here and be hostile to the man she'd once loved.

She straightened her spine, turned toward the house, and marched inside to tell Drew McCray exactly what she thought of him.

Once Julia swept Drew into the house, there was too much going on for him to think about the confrontation with Liam— or the one with Liam's girlfriend.

The big front room of the farmhouse was full of people, some of whom Drew knew, some he didn't. He exchanged a hello and a handshake with Liam's brother Ryan, who, Drew had to admit, had always been decent to him. He saw his uncle and aunt, and spent a few minutes catching up on what they were doing, and what he was doing, and how long it had been.

Everybody seemed to have paper plates full of food and glasses of this or that—wine, beer, iced tea. Across the room, Drew saw Orin Delaney, the man who'd turned out to be Drew's uncle and who would soon be Julia's father-in-law. Drew made his way through the crowd, said a few perfunctory words to the man, and shook his hand.

"You've got to come into the kitchen and say hello to Sandra," Julia said, her hand on Drew's shoulder, guiding him.

Sandra, by most people's reckoning, was the most formidable of the Delaneys. She stood only five feet tall, which brought her up to Drew's shoulder, but her presence made it seem like she filled any room where she happened to be.

In the kitchen, Sandra was shuffling around in jeans, a San Francisco Giants baseball jersey, and sneakers, her graying hair caught back in a ponytail. She was barking orders to a handful of people as she stirred something on the stove. "Breanna, you get the rolls out of the oven and set them out to cool. Gen, the salad looks like it's been attacked by a pack of starving wolves. You go on and make up some more. You'd think nobody's had a meal for a week. *Hmph.* By God, Michael, I'd think you could put out some silverware without so much complaining. Get to it, boy."

Despite the grumbling and the scowling, Drew knew from his previous dealings with Sandra that she was happy and in her element when she was ordering around a group of people—especially when she was feeding them.

When she caught sight of Drew standing in the doorway to the kitchen, she stopped what she was doing and turned, her hands on her narrow hips, to appraise him.

"Well, there you are, boy. If you thought you could come to Cambria and just hide out in some damned hotel without coming out here to get a meal, then I'd say you were wrong." She looked him over, from his shoes (work boots) to his hair (russet, a little too long, slightly mussed). "Well, I guess you better put that damned bottle down and get over here so I can get a good look."

Feeling awkward, Drew set the bottle of wine down on the big butcher block table in the center of the room and went to stand in front of Sandra.

Without warning, she reached out and pulled him into a firm hug. "It's good to see you," she muttered, her voice low so only he could hear. When she pushed him away, he saw moisture in her eyes. She blinked, put the stern look back on her face, and returned her attention to the pot she'd been stirring.

When Drew had been here a couple of years before to discuss his inheritance and meet this mystery family of his, Sandra had been the most matter-of-fact about his presence, and, now that he considered it, about his very existence. She hadn't been warm—he didn't think he'd ever seen her be warm to anyone—but she'd taken him in and accepted him when others had viewed him with suspicion.

Still, this show of emotion came as a surprise, and he found himself overtaken by a little of it as well.

He was just about to ask Sandra how she'd been—or, at least, whether he could do anything to help with the meal—when the kitchen door swung open and Megan Scott came in, her eyes hot with indignation.

"Drew? I don't believe we finished our conversation." She delivered the line with the controlled anger of someone who was about to go to battle with a hostile customer service rep.

Drew felt his defenses slide back into place.

"I kind of thought we did," he said.

"If we could have a word?" Megan stood with her arms crossed over her chest, her lips tight.

"I'm busy," Drew said, and turned away from her.

"You're busy."

"I was just about to help with this …" He looked around the kitchen. "Salad. I was just going to help Gen, here, make this salad."

"Don't bring me into this," Gen said.

"You need some help, Sandra?" Drew asked.

"Don't bring me into it, either, boy. A woman wants to have a word with you, I'd say you best go have a word. Now go on, get."

Drew mentally flailed around for an alternate excuse. "But I haven't even seen my mother yet.…"

"She's still at her hotel," Julia put in, from where she'd been gathering paper plates and napkins to take out to the buffet table. "Should be here in half an hour."

Well, shit.

"You got any more excuses, or are you going to go talk to the woman?" Sandra demanded. She raised her eyebrows at him meaningfully.

Drew brooded a little, but decided there was no getting out

of it.

"Fine."

He followed Megan out of the kitchen, down a hallway, and into what appeared to be Sandra's sewing room. They stood in a little room cluttered with a sewing machine, plastic bins full of buttons, tape measures, scissors, and thread, and bolts of cloth. Megan closed the door and turned to him.

"What's this about?" Drew said, as though he didn't know.

"I want to know what your issue is with Liam." She glared up at him.

He shifted his stance uncomfortably. "I figure my problem with Liam is between me and Liam."

"You threatened him."

"He was being an ass."

"So are you."

He started to say something, then stopped. He rubbed at the stubble on his chin and looked at her ruefully. "Yeah. Shit. I guess I am."

The turn in the conversation seemed to take her by surprise, and she blinked at him a few times.

"All I'm saying is, you didn't have to—"

"I know. I get it." He held up a hand to stop her. "It's just … I don't know how much you've heard about my history, but it's not exactly a picnic at the beach, me being here."

"No. I guess it's not." The anger seemed to have leaked out of her, and she gave him a look of sympathy.

That might have been worse than the anger. No man wanted a pretty woman's pity.

"You should apologize to Liam." Her voice was softer now.

"Like hell."

"Drew—"

"Like hell," he repeated. "But I'll keep my distance, if he'll do the same."

He pushed past her and left the sewing room without letting her get in another word.

Megan stood alone in the empty sewing room, thinking about what had just happened.

She knew it hadn't been her business to confront Drew about his treatment of Liam, but she couldn't seem to help herself. If there was one thing her parents had taught her, it was that you stand up for your people. And Liam was still her person, at least for another week.

She'd stormed in here assuming that Drew was a rude jerk, just like Liam had told her he was. But she wasn't sure he was as bad as all that. He seemed like a guy in an uncomfortable situation who didn't quite know how to handle himself.

It sucked when you were all set to have a good rant, and the person you were ranting at ruined the whole thing by admitting to being wrong.

The sensation was unfamiliar to her, because Liam would *never* admit to being wrong, even though he often was.

And maybe Liam had been wrong this time. That thing he'd said about taking out the trash? Now that she thought about it, the remark had been especially unkind considering Drew's uncertain place in the family.

If there was a good rant to be had, it was possible she'd directed hers at the wrong person.

Chapter Four

The weather was good, so the party—which wasn't even technically a party—had spilled out of the house and into the front yard, where Liam and Colin had set up patio chairs and a barbecue grill. Their father, Orin, looking ruddy and stout and somewhat embarrassed by the attentions of the crowd, cooked hamburger patties on the grill while groups of people stood around and talked. Michael and Lucas, Breanna's boys, threw a football on the grass with Alice and Avery, Joe and Marcy's eleven-year-old twins.

The mood was casual and festive, and Drew probably would have been enjoying himself under other circumstances. As it was, though, he was gauging how long he had to stay for the sake of good manners before he could quietly slink away to his hotel.

His mother hadn't arrived yet, so that was one box he hadn't checked off—and would have to before he could go.

He stood on the front porch drinking a beer and talking to Colin, the groom-to-be, while he waited. If there was any Delaney he really had to get along with, it was Colin, since the man was going to be his brother-in-law.

Colin was okay, by Drew's estimation. He was a lawyer and the Delaney family's money manager, and in fact, a couple of years before, he'd been the one to track Drew down from the bunker he'd crawled into to hide out from his creditors. By the time Colin was done with him, Drew had enough money and assets to buy most of his creditors.

Not that he'd want to.

Colin was smarter and a little more polished and sophisticated than the rest of the Delaneys—traits that had intimidated Drew when he'd first met him. But now, after a couple of years of slowly getting to know him, Drew was forming a tentative friendship with Colin. Which was good, because he'd likely be showing up at Thanksgiving and Christmas dinners for the next God-knew-how-many years.

Now, Colin was leaning against the porch railing with a glass of white wine in his hand. He was wearing a blue and white striped button-down shirt and a pair of linen pants that looked freshly pressed, in contrast to Drew and the rest of the Delaneys, who had gone for jeans or shorts and T-shirts. Colin's dark hair looked like he'd gotten it cut at an expensive salon, and his face was impeccably shaved.

"Did you see the documents I sent you on the Bay Area property?" Colin asked. He was keeping his voice casual, but Drew suspected it took some effort not to show his annoyance.

"Yeah, I saw them. Didn't read them, but I saw them."

"Drew ..."

"Just do whatever you think is right. I'll vote however you want."

Colin turned and looked out over the yard, likely in an attempt to keep from throttling Drew.

As part of Drew's inheritance, he'd received a sizable share of the family corporation, which required him to vote from time to time on matters involving investments, property management, and other issues of importance.

But Drew didn't know shit about investing or property management. Colin did. Why shouldn't he let Colin call the shots? He'd done all right so far. Better than all right.

The way Drew saw it, none of the Delaneys really wanted him making these kinds of decisions anyway. It wasn't his family legacy the way it was theirs. The shares were his, and the money, too, because of his blood, not because of anything he'd done to earn it. Why pretend otherwise?

Colin turned back to him, little lines of tension at the corners of his eyes.

"Drew, I can teach you what you need to know. I can—"

"Yeah."

"If you're afraid you'll make the wrong decisions, or that you'll make a mistake, that isn't—"

"Yeah, I got it," Drew said, growing irritated. They'd had this conversation before.

Colin wasn't a man who was easily angered, unlike Liam. He shared a more even temperament with his brother Ryan. But now, facing yet another brush-off from Drew regarding the family business, Colin looked like he was beginning to lose his patience. He stretched his neck, leaned his butt against the porch railing, and sighed.

"I'm going to tell you this because you're my cousin and you're also going to be my brother-in-law. You're family, like it or not, so what I'm about to say, I say with all due respect, and with only your own best interests at heart."

"Okay," Drew said.

"You've got to pull your head out of your ass."

Drew opened his mouth to reply, then closed it again.

"I know that when you first got your inheritance, you were dealing with a lot," Colin went on. "It was a shock. I get that. You didn't know what to do, so you didn't do anything. Fine.

Makes sense. But it's been two years, Drew. What have you done with the money? Have you invested it? Have you talked to one of the financial advisers whose names I gave you?"

"Well, I—"

"No, you haven't," Colin finished for him. "You don't want to live some flashy lifestyle, that's fine. I get that, too. We're not really about that here, anyway. But every day you sit on your ass and do nothing is a lost opportunity."

Drew was beginning to feel defensive, the way he had with Liam. But he couldn't very well offer to knock Colin on his ass.

"Look." Colin leaned toward him, his face intense, his voice low to avoid being overheard. "The business—it means something to us. It means a lot. Generations of our family have built this, and we care about it. Every time you refuse to read a document, it's like you're rejecting us, rejecting the family."

That, at least, got Drew's attention. Was that how they saw it? Hell, was that how he *meant* it? On some level, it might have been. It was no secret that he'd had a hard time learning that he was a Delaney. If a person really stretched their imagination, they could maybe see a little of why Liam was so pissed.

"That's ... I don't mean it that way. It's not ... you know. Rejection."

Colin nodded, his face tense. "What we've made here? It's worth more than just, 'I'll vote however you want.' The least you could do is read the documents."

Having said what he had to say, Colin walked down the porch steps and went to see whether his father needed any help at the grill.

Drew was sulking in a corner, wishing that his mother would just get here already so he could say hello to her and then run. He wasn't a fan of parties in the first place, and this one had featured not one but two people telling him he was an asshole.

The fact that they both might have been right didn't help much.

But he had beer, and that did help, at least a little.

He was on his second one, getting the beginnings of a welcome buzz, when Sandra walked up to him and thrust a paper plate full of food into his hand.

"Boy, you'd better eat this. You're thinner than you were when I saw you two years ago, and you were too skinny then." She appraised him critically, her eyebrows drawn together like two caterpillars who'd suffered an unfortunate collision.

"Thanks, but I'm not that hungry."

"You got a problem with my food?" she snapped at him.

"Uh … no."

"Well, good. Go on and eat it, then. You haven't had a bite since you've been here."

Drew wondered how she knew that, when she'd been in the kitchen through most of the party and he'd been outside or in the front room. But then he decided not to question it. He'd always heard that Sandra Delaney was spooky that way—she knew everything that went on under her roof, and much of what went on beyond it.

He gave a sullen shrug, sank down into the folding chair that had been set up in a far corner of the front room, and began eating some potato salad. It was very good potato salad.

Sandra grabbed another folding chair, put it beside Drew's, and sat down. "You didn't invite me to sit with you, but it's my damned house, so I figure I've got a right to do it anyway." She let out a grunt as she sat. "Been on my feet since this morning. If I'm not due for a rest, I don't know who the hell is."

He looked at her out of the corner of his eye as he ate. In his limited experience with Sandra, he'd never known her to tire, even after long days of caring for everyone in her sphere. He doubted she was tired now, even though she had a right to be. It was more likely that she'd come over here because she had something to say to him.

He hoped he wasn't about to be told off a third time at the same party. That would be harsh—though not unprecedented.

"Have a good talk with Megan, did you?"

At least she hadn't wasted time.

Sandra had a reputation for knowing everything, but she didn't have a reputation as a busybody. Still, he was just getting to know her. Maybe that was a facet of her personality he just hadn't learned about yet.

"Sure," he said. He focused on his potato salad.

"She seemed a little worked up."

"Did she?" He tried some of the baked beans.

"Don't toy with me, boy," she said in a growl that had probably served her well when her children were young. Then, in a softer voice: "I'm not asking because I'm nosy, or because I want to get into your business. I'm asking because I know it's hard for you to be here. *Hmph.* And I wanted to make sure you're getting along okay."

He might have been suspicious of the Delaneys since the day he'd met them, but Sandra's words felt real. They felt true. He looked at her—really looked at her—and decided to give her something true in return.

"Liam and I got into it a little when I got here." He shrugged. "Megan wanted me to apologize to him."

Sandra let out a delighted hoot. "Well, I figure that's gonna happen the day they start selling ice cream cones in hell!"

Drew grinned. "Yeah, well."

He let his gaze drift across the crowded room, to where Liam and Megan were standing with drinks in their hands, talking to Mike.

Megan was lean, with long, glossy hair and a way of holding herself that suggested both confidence and ease. She was standing closer to Mike than to Liam, and she leaned in as Mike said something into her ear, then threw her head back in laughter.

Liam's face darkened slightly, then he put his arm around her waist and drew her close to him—apparently jealous, even though Mike was balding and nearing sixty. Megan said something to Liam before disengaging herself in a move so smooth he probably didn't even know he was getting the brush-off.

Drew didn't hear Sandra talking to him until she gave his ankle a kick with her sneaker-clad foot.

"Ow!"

Sandra was giving him a look that was half scowl, half grin.

"Why, boy, do you have a thing for Liam's girl? Because that's the kind of thing that leads to emergency room visits and new dental work."

"What? No. Of course not. Why would you say that?"

Why would he have a thing for a woman who apparently didn't like him much? Why would he have a thing for someone he'd just met less than an hour before? And why would he have a thing for any woman foolish enough to take up with Liam?

"I say it because I'm not an idiot." She let out a *hmph*. "And because I'm not blind. Your eyes haven't left that woman since she came in the room."

He ran a hand through his hair and turned to Sandra. "I wouldn't do that. I might not get along with Liam, but he's family. I guess. Sort of. And guys don't do that to other guys in their family. Even if I did have a thing for her. Which I don't."

She held his gaze for a long time, then nodded. "Well, all right then. You know what, boy? I don't mind the sound of that."

"Of what?"

"Of you calling us family." She gave his jean-clad knee in a brisk pat-pat with her hand. "I'd best get back to the kitchen."

Isabelle finally arrived at the Delaney Ranch, which, for Drew, was a good news–bad news situation. It was good news, because once he had a chance to see her, he could finally leave. But it was also bad news, because these days, seeing his mother was pretty much always bad news.

"Drew! Oh, come here, give me a hug." Isabelle leaned in on a cloud of White Shoulders perfume and gave his cheek a kiss that was sticky with red lipstick. "My goodness, where have you been?"

"Where have *I* been? I've been here, waiting for you, for more than an hour."

"Oh, I didn't mean that. I meant, what took you so long to get into town?"

He started to tell her that he'd only learned about Wedding Week the day before, but she cut him off.

"Oh, you're here now, that's the important thing. Here's the itinerary for this week." She pulled a folded piece of paper out of her oversized purse and handed it to him.

"Do we really need an itinerary?"

"Of course we need an itinerary. How else do you expect everyone to know where to go and how to dress, and … Well. Look it over. Tomorrow's golf for the men, and the bachelorette party for the ladies."

"Golf?" Drew held the piece of paper in his hand, feeling helpless. "I don't golf."

"Nonsense. Just because you never have, doesn't mean you can't. I have you scheduled as part of a foursome with Colin, Liam, and Ryan."

Drew's stomach sank. Golfing with Liam was likely to end with somebody wearing a nine-iron like a hat, and Drew didn't especially want it to be him.

"Aw, hell. Can't I go with Matt?" Drew wasn't exactly close to his stepfather, but they got along well enough that neither of them was likely to give the other one a concussion.

"Matt's not coming into town until Saturday. He couldn't get the time off work."

Drew wondered how Matt had managed to get out of this, if Drew himself couldn't. He imagined the fight Matt and Isabelle must have had, and then decided he was better off not imagining it at all.

He wished Matt were here, and not only so that he would have a semi-friendly face in attendance. Looking at the thinly veiled tension around Isabelle's eyes and in the fine lines around her mouth, Drew figured his mother probably needed her husband. She was fully made up and a bit overdressed for the occasion, and she'd recently had her hair done—all sure signs that she'd felt it necessary to gird herself for battle.

"Mom? How are you doing with … you know. With all this?"

He saw a spark of something in her eyes—a sign, maybe, that he'd truly seen her, had recognized her for who and what she was, just for that brief moment. But then that spark died as she pasted a for-company smile on her face.

"Why, I'm fine, Drew. Just fine. Your sister's getting married. I'm thrilled."

Chapter Five

Megan didn't want to sleep with Liam, but she didn't want to have that conversation with him. At least, not until after the wedding, when they could air out the problems in their relationship without causing drama that would take the focus off of Colin and Julia.

So when the party was wrapping up and Liam suggested going home with Megan, she had to think fast.

"Breanna's coming over tonight," she said, without any rationale in mind for why that might be the case. "I'm sorry. We've had it planned for days."

"Well, hell. What for?"

"Wedding stuff," she blurted out.

"What kind of wedding stuff?"

"Girl stuff. Girl wedding stuff. If you really want to hear about it, I could—"

"No." He shuddered theatrically. "I can't think of anything I'd less like to hear about than girl wedding stuff."

"Well, all right then." Megan felt an inner wave of relief.

"Let me at least drive you home. I could just—"

"Oh, jeez. I told Breanna we'd go over there together. Besides, you're already home. It wouldn't make much sense for you to have to leave when Breanna's going over there anyway."

He was clearly unhappy, but he put on the brave face of someone who hadn't been laid in a while but who was trying to act like it didn't matter.

"Fine," he said. "But I'll see you tomorrow, right?"

She frowned. "Tomorrow I've got work, and you've got golf with your brothers."

"Ah, fuck. I forgot about that. I don't even golf. I could get out of it."

"But I can't get out of work. And anyway, Colin does golf, and he's probably looking forward to it. And he's the groom; this is his Wedding Week."

"Fuck," Liam said again.

She kissed him on the cheek—because that, at least, was something she could do with sincerity—and ran off to find Breanna.

"You're coming home with me," Megan said, grabbing Breanna by the arm and yanking her into the hallway outside the kitchen, where she'd been busy helping Sandra clean up.

"What? Why?"

"There's no time to explain. But if anyone asks, it's about wedding stuff. Girl wedding stuff."

"*Is* it about girl wedding stuff?" Breanna's dark, curly hair was pulled back into a ponytail, but a loose tendril had drifted into her face.

"No! Of course not! But that's what you need to tell Liam if he asks you."

Breanna raised her eyebrows in question.

"Please?" Megan begged. "Oh, God. Here he comes."

Liam walked up to them, looking even more irritable than usual. "Bree? Megan says—"

"Oh, good. I've been looking for you," Breanna said. "I've got to go to Megan's tonight, and I was wondering if you could keep an eye on the boys."

"Well … I …"

"Please? It's wedding stuff, and it really can't wait."

Liam looked as though he'd enjoy an unmedicated root canal more than he would enjoy an evening of babysitting. But he also looked like a guy who didn't want to say that in front of his girlfriend.

"I guess."

"Thank you!" Breanna raised up on tiptoes and gave Liam the second friendly kiss on the cheek he'd received in the past ten minutes. He didn't seem to enjoy this one much more than the last.

When he was gone, Breanna looked pleased with herself.

"Well, that worked out pretty well for you," Megan observed.

"If I'm going to play along with your alibi, I might as well get a kid-free night out of it. Get your stuff, and let's get out of here."

They headed toward Megan's house, but it was still early, and Breanna didn't want to waste a night of babysitting by going straight there. So instead, they took a detour to De-Vine, a wine bar on Main Street that Breanna particularly liked.

Rose Bachman, a close friend of Ryan's wife, was behind the bar, her hair dyed in shades of pink and blue, a silver barbell glittering over one eyebrow.

"Hey, ladies. What can I get you?"

Rose, whose status as the mother of a toddler had not diminished her fashion sense, wore a black tank top emblazoned with the image of two skeletons embracing.

"What's good?" Megan asked.

"It's wine. It's all good," Rose replied.

Megan settled on a glass of Opolo sparkling wine, and Breanna ordered the J. Lohr Signature Cabernet. When they were settled in at the bar with their drinks, Megan launched into it without preamble.

"He was jealous. Of Mike. You know, Julia's friend? The old guy?"

"We're talking Liam, then?" Rose asked, wanting to get caught up.

"Yes, Liam," Megan said. "I was chatting with Mike—who's really nice, by the way—about dogs. Because he's thinking of getting a dog, and I was giving him some advice on breeds. And Liam didn't like it!" She shook her head in disgust. "What is his problem?"

"His problem is, you're about to break up with him, and he's not stupid. He knows it's coming," Breanna said.

"Well … I'm not breaking up with him for *Mike*," Megan said.

"But you are breaking up with him," Rose put in, for clarification.

Megan winced. "After the wedding."

"Ouch. Are you sure?" Rose asked.

"Yeah." Megan picked up her glass by the stem and twirled it in a slow, clockwise motion. "Yes. It's overdue. I have to. I really hate this."

"In that case, you need more wine." Rose reached over the bar and topped off Megan's glass.

Megan sipped, and then said, "Hey. What do you guys think of Drew McCray?"

"I met him for about a minute once when he was in town before," Rose said. "Seemed kind of pissy. I liked him."

"I'm reserving judgment," Breanna said. "But Mom likes him. And you know Mom."

They all nodded, acknowledging Sandra's uncanny instincts. If Sandra liked somebody, that meant something.

"Why are you asking about Drew?" Breanna wanted to know.

"Oh … no reason. I just met him at the house earlier. Liam got into it with him."

"Uh oh," Rose said.

"It's just …" Megan twirled her wine glass a little more. "Whenever Liam's talked about him, he's made Drew seem like this awful person. And he didn't seem like an awful person."

Rose and Breanna exchanged a look.

"How *did* he seem?" Rose wanted to know. "Did he seem hot? Scrumptious? Delightfully delectable?"

"What are you talking about?" Megan demanded.

"Oh, nothing. Just the way you kind of *sparkled* when you asked about him."

"I did not!"

"You did," Breanna said. "Oh, shit. You did. And then you blushed."

"No, I—"

"Oh, crap, Megan. Are you hot for Drew? Because Liam's going to—"

"No!"

But she *was* blushing; she could feel it. She put a hand to her cheek to hide the rising color.

"Oh, man," Breanna said miserably. "You and Drew. Poor Liam. I mean, he's kind of a jerk, but he's still my brother."

As though summoned, Liam walked in the front door of De-Vine, saw the three women, and froze in surprise.

"Oh. Hey. Mom sent me to pick up some champagne for the … ah, shit. I'm not even sure. For one of the Wedding Week things. The rehearsal dinner, I guess."

"Right," Rose confirmed. "She called ahead. Here, let me go in the back and get it." She vanished into the back of the store while Megan and Breanna sat at the bar awkwardly.

"We just … stopped in," Megan told him. "On the way to my place."

"All right," Liam said. "Hey, if you think you and Bree will be done with your thing in time, I could still come over after you're—"

"I'm staying over," Breanna put in quickly. "Girl sleepover. We planned it a while ago."

He looked crestfallen. "Oh."

Rose came back out carrying a box full of wine bottles. She put the box on the counter and rang up the sale.

Liam paid, hefted the box, said his goodbyes, and went out the door and onto Main Street.

"Dead man walking," Rose announced in grim tones.

Megan leaned over and slowly banged her head against the surface of the bar.

Drew went back to his hotel feeling spent. He wasn't much for parties in the first place, but a party at the Delaney house— one that featured his mother as a bonus attraction—had left him feeling wrung out.

He took a long shower followed by a slow walk on the beach. The evening was growing dark, and the tourists had mostly retreated to their hotel rooms along Moonstone Beach Drive, so he was alone with his thoughts.

One of those thoughts was that Liam's girlfriend maybe had a point. Liam had acted like a dick when Drew had shown up at the house—he had, in fact, acted like Liam—but that didn't mean Drew was right to take the bait. He could have been more mature. For one thing, he could have kept it in mind that he, himself, had acted like a dick on his last visit, and maybe that's why Liam wasn't more welcoming to him.

Thinking that Liam's girlfriend hadn't been altogether wrong led Drew to think about the woman herself. No, he hadn't enjoyed being confronted in Sandra's sewing room. But he had to admire anyone who saw what they believed to be an injustice and who stood up and said something. Most people didn't. Most people just quietly stewed.

Megan had Liam's back. Drew wondered if Liam appreciated that, or if he even knew it.

What had Liam ever done to deserve a woman like that? Well, he was richer than a small country, for one thing. That tended to afford a man opportunities with women.

Except, Megan didn't seem like someone who would be interested in a man for his net worth. Drew had become well acquainted with that kind of woman in the time since he'd inherited Redmond's fortune. He'd had plenty of opportunities, though he'd been smart enough not to take them.

He'd only spent a few minutes with Megan, but his instinct told him that she did what she did because she meant it, not because there might be a profit in it.

Of course, his instincts had been known to be wrong. Take his marriage, for instance.

By the time he got back to his hotel room, with sand in his shoes and the smell of the ocean on his clothes, he was feeling a little better about things.

He fed Eddie, cleaned out the litter box, and refilled the cat's water dish.

Tomorrow, he had golf with the Delaney brothers. He didn't golf—never had, in fact—but he guessed that didn't matter. It was a chance to reach out to the Delaneys and maybe smooth some ruffled feathers.

It was time.

And if that didn't work, he could always beat the crap out of Liam with his driver. Then, the day wouldn't be a complete loss.

Chapter Six

They went to a golf course in Paso Robles for a nine a.m. tee time. The course wasn't Pebble Beach, but it wasn't bad, either. The greens were as lush as the local water restrictions would allow, and the course offered a view of graceful, low hills dotted with grape vines heavy with fruit waiting to be turned into wine.

Isabelle, with Colin's help, had organized a kind of informal tournament, with the members of various foursomes competing for bragging rights. A group that included Mike, Orin, Drew's uncle Joe, and one of the ranch hands was set to tee off right before them. A little later were some guys Colin knew from the law firm where he used to work.

It didn't take a genius to guess that the lawyers probably had the edge where golf was concerned. Fortunately, Drew wasn't out to win; his simple goals were merely to avoid getting in a fight with Liam or falling into a water hazard.

Drew and Colin had driven to the course together in Colin's rental car, and Liam and Ryan had paired up in Liam's truck. Because Colin was the only one of them who owned his own golf clubs, the rest of them had to rent clubs at the pro shop before they loaded up their carts and drove out to the first hole.

Colin teed off first, and even though Drew didn't know a damned thing about golf, it seemed to him that Colin just looked good—it wasn't hard to imagine him playing alongside some minor PGA pro. The ball flew farther than Drew would have thought possible, though it did veer slightly to the right of the green.

"Well, shit," Liam grumbled, glowering over the pure grace of Colin's shot. "I hope you don't expect me to do that."

"It's not that hard. Here, I'll show you." Colin came up behind Liam and tried to move his brother's arms into the correct position, but Liam glared at him.

"You better back the hell off," he said.

"Fine." Colin raised his arms in surrender and stepped away.

Liam must have had some natural athletic ability, because he didn't do too badly. He did miss the ball entirely on his first swing, but then he managed to get it halfway down the fairway on the second try, a little bit off in the rough but not so far that it wasn't salvageable.

"Not bad," Colin observed, giving Liam a smack on the shoulder.

Ryan had played before, and while he wasn't as good as Colin, he did seem to have some idea what he was doing. His ball made it farther than Liam's and landed smack in the middle of the fairway.

That left Drew, who had never picked up a golf club before let alone hit anything with one. He figured his male pride didn't preclude him getting a little advice.

"Hey, Colin? Little help?"

Since Drew had rarely asked for Colin's help with anything, the man seemed not only willing but eager to oblige.

"You've got your grip all wrong. You've got to put your left hand here, like this." Colin used his own hand on his own club to demonstrate. Drew adjusted accordingly.

Colin led him through a couple of practice swings and then teed up the ball for him.

Drew's first ball veered off into the trees, so they all called it practice and let him do another one. The second one was only marginally better; Drew clipped the top of the ball, and it rolled off the tee and down the fairway maybe fifty yards at best before coming to a rest.

"Good shot," Liam observed. "If you're playing against an eight-year-old girl."

Drew calculated his choices: He could get into it with Liam here and now, maybe challenge him to a fistfight and decide this thing once and for all. Or, he could be a good sport. He went with the last one.

"I don't know," he said. "I'll bet there are more than a few eight-year-old girls who could take me."

Liam had been trying to pick a fight, and Drew could see on his face that he didn't quite know what to do now that it hadn't worked.

Colin clapped Drew on the back. "You'll get there. Now, I'm thinking you need your three-wood for the next shot."

Drew continued not to take the bait that Liam put out there, and eventually, Liam began to drop his defensiveness and relax a little. As the morning went on, Liam started to chat with his brothers as though Drew weren't there—which was just fine with him.

Liam must have been thinking about everything surrounding Colin's impending nuptials, because around the fourth hole, when they were all standing around the green waiting for Colin to putt, he said, "Do you think Megan wants to get married?"

The question hit Drew right in the gut, though he wasn't sure why. Maybe because of his own bad experience with marriage. Maybe because the idea of Liam settling down with a woman, maybe having some kids, was surprising. Or maybe because of the reaction Drew had experienced to Megan—a reaction that didn't necessarily mesh well with the image of her married to Liam.

"You probably ought to ask her," Ryan said, not unreasonably.

"Yeah, yeah," Liam said. "But right now, I'm asking you what you think."

Ryan considered the question. "She ever said anything about it?"

"Not lately." Liam scowled. "We used to talk about that sort of thing sometimes. Back when I first moved out here from Montana. But we don't talk about it much anymore. Which is weird, I guess, because we've been together two years now. I know she wants kids someday."

Colin sank his putt and came to stand beside Liam while Ryan took his place on the green.

"You thinking of popping the question?" Colin asked.

"No. Ah, hell. Maybe." Liam scratched at the back of his neck. "The thing is, she seems kind of … different lately. Not unhappy, exactly, but … not happy, either. I wonder if maybe all this wedding stuff is making her wonder why we haven't gone there yet."

"Instead of you wondering, maybe you two ought to have a conversation," Ryan suggested again, since the idea hadn't seemed to take the first time.

Liam was silent as they all watched Ryan putt. He missed the hole, took another shot, and got it in.

"It's just ... women want commitment, right? Isn't that what they're always saying?" Liam seemed truly baffled by the eternal question of what women want.

"I think it depends on the woman," Drew suggested. It was a risk to jump into the conversation, but Liam just shot him an irritated look and didn't remark on it.

"What a woman wants is for a man to have a damned conversation with her," Ryan put in.

"What I was thinking," Liam said as they walked back to their carts, as though Ryan hadn't spoken, "was to maybe ask her. You know, to marry me. This week, even. At the reception."

It was clear from the expression on Liam's face that this was what he'd been asking them about all along. He wasn't looking for advice on the needs and desires of women. He was asking Colin if it was okay to propose at his reception.

The three of them stopped and stared at Liam until he started to squirm under the pressure.

"It was just a thought," he said.

Colin got into the driver's seat of his cart, and Drew got in beside him. "If that's what you want, it's all right by me," Colin told Liam, who was standing on the grass beside Colin and Drew's cart. "Let me run it by Julia first, though, in case she feels like you're hogging her limelight."

"She won't think that," Drew said. He knew his sister well enough to know that she'd be delighted by the idea—though Drew, himself, was less delighted.

"No, she won't," Colin agreed. "But I still have to ask her."

"Well, just ... mention it, see what she says," Liam told him.

They headed off to the next hole, with Drew feeling vaguely sick. He told himself it was because his instinct said Megan didn't want to get married—maybe didn't even want Liam at all. He'd seen the way she'd untangled herself from him at the house the day before, the way she'd dodged Liam's kiss.

The sick feeling—it was a natural reaction to knowing a guy was about to get his ass handed to him by the woman he loved.

That was all it was.

After the tournament—where Drew came in last—he thought that he might drive down to Morro Bay and rent a boat for some fishing. He always felt most like himself when he was alone out on the water.

But first, he checked his phone to make sure the world had managed all right since the last time he'd looked at it.

He had a few voice mail messages: the usual pleas from people who wanted him to buy things or donate money. He deleted them.

He also had a string of text messages from Tessa.

Drew, please call me right away.

Please, it's urgent.

This is a LIFE AND DEATH EMERGENCY, Drew. CALL ME!!!

His every instinct had told him to delete the texts and pretend he never got them. But he'd loved her once.

Against his better judgment, he called.

"Drew! Thank God." She sounded out of breath.

"What's going on, Tessa?"

"I didn't think you were going to call! Drew … How have you been?"

"Tessa. What's the emergency?"

"Can't we just take a minute to talk first? It's been a while, and—"

"I'm hanging up now."

"Wait!"

It turned out her "emergency" was that she had applied to rent a new apartment in Bozeman—something bigger and better located than her current place—and she didn't have the money for the deposit.

"That's your emergency?" His face began to grow hot, and he was clutching his phone so hard it was in danger of shattering. "You need money for an apartment?"

"You make it sound like it's nothing. Like it's no big deal. But I've already given notice at my place, and I'm going to be homeless in a week if I can't come up with the money."

He gritted his teeth to keep from screaming at her. "You might use some of the money you stole from our joint accounts," he said.

" 'Stole.' That's how you see it."

"That's how it was."

"It's only a few thousand dollars, Drew. What is that to you? It's nothing. You have so much."

He was standing outside the main house at the ranch after Colin brought him back. He looked up at the canopy of an oak tree above him, at the gentle light filtering through.

"We're not married anymore, Tessa. It's not my job to provide for you."

"Well … we could be. Married again, I mean. Oh, Drew, if you'd just give us a chance, we could—"

He hung up on her.

After that, he was too dispirited for fishing. He got into his car and drove back to the hotel.

The Wedding Week schedule had Drew down as one of three designated drivers for the women attending that night's bachelorette party. His evening would be his own until he got a call from Julia that the party was over. Then he would go over to Ted's in his rental car, which seated four comfortably or five a little less comfortably, and provide safe and sober transportation to whoever needed it.

Ryan and Mike—the other two designated drivers—were planning to hang out and have pizza at Ryan's place until it was time for them to perform their duties, and Ryan called Drew to see if he wanted to join them.

Drew liked Mike, and he kind of liked Ryan, too, despite the fact that he was a Delaney. Besides, the book he'd brought wasn't that good. So he fed Eddie, then headed over to Ryan's house on the Delaney Ranch property.

When he got there, Ryan's wife, Gen, had already left for the bachelorette party. Mike was sprawled on Ryan's sofa with a bottle of Coke in his hand, a bag of Doritos open on the coffee table in front of him. Ryan was putting out a platter of corn chips and salsa while they waited for the pizza.

A guy Drew didn't know—thirtyish, blond, with glasses that made him look studious—was sitting in an armchair next to the coffee table.

Ryan made the introductions. "Drew, this is Will Bachman, a friend of mine. Will's offered to help with the driving. He claims it's for the sake of safety and good citizenship, but it's actually so he can have a kid-free evening for a change."

Will offered a wave. "Actually, that's not accurate. Rose's mother is watching Poppy tonight at our house while Rose is at De-Vine. I came so I could have a mother-in-law–free evening."

Drew wandered into the living room and took a seat. "Rose is your wife? From the wine shop?" He tried to reconcile the idea of the tattooed, purple-haired woman from the wine bar whom he'd met last time he was in town, with her facial piercings and her edgy fashion sense, with this somewhat geeky-looking guy on Ryan's sofa.

"A couple of years now," Will confirmed. "We have a two-year-old."

He seemed to be saying the last bit by way of explanation for his overall frazzled look and the dark circles under his eyes.

Of course, Drew already knew Mike. He raised a hand to the man in greeting. Mike was in his late fifties, with a balding head and a shape that suggested the Doritos in front of him were his main source of nutrition. Drew knew from Julia, though, that Mike could heft a sixty-pound bag of concrete like it was weightless.

Ryan offered Drew a Coke, which he accepted in lieu of the beer he would have preferred. Once he was settled, the other three resumed the conversation they'd been having when he'd arrived. The topic was marriage, weddings, and women.

"You couldn't make me get married again if the woman was made out of beer and hundred-dollar bills," Mike said. Like Drew, Mike had been through a divorce that had left him emotionally and financially traumatized.

"Unless your ex agreed to take you back," Drew said.

"Yeah, unless that." Mike shook his head sadly at his own pathetic state. "Only woman I've ever loved. Only woman I ever will love. I'm a goddamned Hallmark card, if the card is about divorce and loneliness and wanting to kill yourself."

"I like being married," Will said. "I like being a father. It's messy and loud and expensive, and the terrible twos are awful. And I can't remember the last time I got a full night's sleep, but …" He drifted off. "What was I saying?"

"I think Colin's going to like being married, too," Ryan said. "He's suited to it."

"You think Liam's suited to it?" Drew asked. He hadn't wanted to bring up the thing with Liam and Megan, but he couldn't help himself. It had been on his mind.

"Ah, hell, who knows?" Ryan said. Drew got the impression he was avoiding the question.

"Why, is Liam thinking of getting married?" Will asked.

"Might be," Ryan said mildly.

"He said he was. At golf yesterday. He said he was thinking about it." Drew took a swig of his Coke.

"Dumb bastard," Mike remarked, shaking his head in sympathy.

"He said that?" Will sat forward in his chair. "Really?"

"Yeah. Why?" Drew said.

Will's eyebrows rose, and he pushed his glasses more firmly onto his nose. "No reason. It's just …"

"It's just what?" Ryan said.

"Nothing," Will said. "Liam doesn't seem the type, that's all."

At that moment, the doorbell rang.

"It's the pizza. I'll get it," Will said, looking relieved.

Drew wondered what the man was trying not to say, and why he was trying not to say it.

They ate the pizza, and then watched an episode of *The Walking Dead* on Netflix. Drew waited for his opportunity and approached Will when Ryan sent him into the kitchen for another round of soft drinks.

"You want one of these?" Will asked, standing in the glow of the refrigerator light with a couple of cans of Dr Pepper in his hands.

"No, thanks."

"They've got Diet 7-up. That must be Gen's."

"Sure, hand it over." Drew didn't want the drink, but he took it to give himself an excuse for why he'd come into the kitchen in the first place. He looked into the pantry, picked up a box of crackers, and then put it back.

"Hey, Will?"

"Yeah?" Will looked at him questioningly. With his tousled, sun-kissed hair, his lean build, and the glasses, the guy looked like a surfer who might be able to explain particle physics, should the need arise.

"Is there some reason Liam shouldn't ask Megan to marry him? I'm just asking because it seemed like you—"

"What? No." Will shook his head rapidly. "No, no."

"Really? Because you looked like maybe you knew something about it."

Will looked deeply dismayed, like a guy who just realized he'd done something that might cause his wife to withhold sex for a week or more. Which, it turned out, he was.

"If Rose finds out that I leaked it, she's going to kill me."

"Leaked what?"

Will peeked out the kitchen door and into the family room like a secret agent on a clandestine mission. "Don't tell anybody I told you this."

"Told me what?"

"Ah, jeez."

"Will. What?" Drew fixed him with a stare that he'd seen TV detectives use to sweat suspects.

"Megan's planning to break up with him."

"She's … Wait a minute. Are you sure?"

"Yeah." He leaned back against the refrigerator miserably. "She told Rose, and Rose told me. She thinks it's just not working, but she wants to wait until after the wedding, because she doesn't want to cause wedding drama."

"Oh. Shit."

Drew felt such a range of feelings that he could hardly make sense of the contrasts. He was glad Megan wasn't going to marry Liam, though he denied to himself that he was glad. He felt sorry for Liam, who was working his way up to a proposal. He felt apprehension about the train wreck that would ensue at his sister's wedding if Liam did propose and Megan said no. And he felt confused, because just yesterday, Megan had defended Liam like a mother bear with her cub. Did a woman do that when she was planning to break up with someone? Had Will gotten the story wrong?

"Listen, if Rose finds out I told you ..."

"No," Drew said absently. "No, I won't say anything."

"Good. Because I like sex. And I like being allowed inside my own house." Will grinned at him and went back into the family room to check on how the zombie apocalypse was coming along.

Drew stood alone in the kitchen, thinking about what to do and whether to get involved. After a few minutes staring vacantly at Ryan and Gen's granite countertop, he decided that he shouldn't do anything.

If Liam was about to get humiliated at the wedding when his proposal was rejected, well, the man was a dickhead anyway, and he had it coming.

Drew just had to hope that Liam and Megan had the sense to keep their feelings to themselves for the sake of Julia and Colin.

Of course, Liam had never kept his feelings to himself about anything, as far as Drew knew.

Shit.

He didn't care about Liam's feelings—much. But he did care about Julia's. And a screaming fight at her wedding reception probably wasn't what she had in mind for her big day.

He was still thinking about it later that night, after a few more snacks and a few more TV shows, when it was time to pick up the women from the bar.

Chapter Seven

Megan was drunk.

She didn't really think she'd had that much—a couple of mojitos and a beer or two—but she didn't usually drink, so her tolerance was low. She wasn't very familiar with what it felt like to be drunk, having experienced it so few times in her life. But she was pretty sure she was there now, because of the way the room was spinning.

In terms of raucousness and bad behavior, the bachelorette party had been about a six on a scale of one to ten. There weren't any strippers, so that helped keep the number at a reasonable level. Nobody had danced on a table. But Julia had sung a boozy rendition of "I Will Always Love You"; one of the guests—thankfully, one who was single—had made out in the corner with a guy from the caterer's; and at least two of Julia's friends had ended up hugging the toilet and moaning.

Megan had conducted herself well enough, though she probably wouldn't have complained so loudly about Liam, who'd texted her throughout the evening, if she'd been sober.

"Damn it! There he is again!" she exclaimed to Breanna at about one a.m., looking at the display on her cell phone.

The dart tournament had just broken up after Ted, the eponymous owner of the bar, had taken away their darts for the sake of public safety, and people were starting to think about calling for their rides home.

"What's he want this time?" Breanna's speech was slightly slurred, but maybe it wasn't. Maybe it was Megan's hearing. Was it possible for someone's hearing to become slurred as a result of drinking too much? Was that a thing?

"He wants to know when we'll be done, so he can pick me up. I don't want him to pick me up!"

"Because?" Breanna prompted her.

"Because then we'll have drunk sex! Or, drunk-sober sex, since I'll be the only one who's drunk. But I don't want to have drunk-sober sex! Because I'm going to break up with him in a few days, and that would just be ..." She searched for a word.

"Sleazy?" Breanna suggested.

"Yes!" Megan pointed a finger at her. "Yes! That's it. Sleazy."

She was so pleased at having selected just the right word that she forgot what she'd been saying.

"He probably wouldn't mind," Breanna said. "It could be goodbye sex."

"I don't want goodbye sex." Megan leaned against the bar miserably. "I just want the goodbye."

Breanna put a hand on Megan's shoulder. "Maybe you should tell him sooner instead of later, then."

"I can't. Look at Julia."

They both looked at the bride-to-be, who was holding an open bottle of champagne in her hand and hugging everyone she could get her free arm around, her thick, auburn hair askew, a mock bridal veil made of paper napkins atop her head.

"Yeah. I kind of see your point," Breanna said. "If Liam throws a table at the reception, it's going to kind of burst her bubble."

Megan thought about how to respond to Liam, then thought about it some more. It seemed that her mental processes were running at about half speed due to the alcohol. Her phone chimed, signaling another text from Liam.

I'm coming over there now. Just sit tight.

"What is wrong with him?" Megan moaned to Breanna. "He's so needy. So … so clingy. He's never been clingy before. Why is he clinging now? Right now, when I need space?" She threw her arms out to her sides to indicate the space that Liam wouldn't give her. "I just need some damned space, Bree!"

"That's why he's clinging," Breanna said wisely. "Because you're trying to get space, and he's scared that you're about to do exactly what you're about to do."

Right about then, the door to Ted's opened, and Drew McCray appeared in the doorway, looking all tall and ginger-haired and sober. She seemed to remember that he was one of their designated drivers for the evening. Even in her impaired state, she seized on him as an answer to the immediate Liam problem.

She got up off her barstool, crossed the room, and launched herself in Drew's direction.

"I need a ride! Home! I need … You're driving, right?"

It sounded to her as though she'd inadvertently asked the same question three or four times, but somehow, he hadn't answered yet.

He looked at her with amusement.

"Hi, Megan. You have a good time?"

"I don't have time for small talk! Liam's on his way! We have to go!" She grabbed his arm and pulled him toward the door.

For some reason, he was resisting her efforts to drag him out of the bar. The amusement on his face changed to concern and not a little confusion.

"Hang on a minute. What's going on?"

Well, this was an alarming development.

As soon as Drew walked into Ted's, he was confronted by an obviously drunk Megan Scott, who was rambling on about something that had to do with Liam and needing to escape from him.

He knew the two of them were headed straight off a cliff, but what was this? Was she afraid of him?

"Can we please just go?" she asked again.

He doubted he would be able to get much of anything coherent out of her right now. All he'd been able to gather was that Liam was headed here, and she didn't want to see him. The cause of keeping the two of them separate seemed like a good one, so he nodded.

"Sure. But I've got to take as many people as I can fit into my car. Let me just grab a few more drunk women, and I'll be right with you."

A few minutes later, after much boozy hugging and the gathering of purses, Drew pulled out of the parking lot at Ted's with four women crammed into his car: Megan, his aunt Marcy, one of Colin's law firm friends who was staying on Moonstone Beach, and Julia's friend Gianna, who'd come out here from Montana.

Megan was sitting in the front passenger seat, and as Drew's car moved from the parking lot into the street, a big pickup truck passed them going the opposite direction, toward Ted's.

"It's Liam!" Megan exclaimed, and then ducked under the dashboard as though trying to dodge gunfire.

If she was, in fact, scared of him, Drew wanted to find out why and do something about it. But it didn't seem like the kind of thing he could ask about in a car crowded with people.

Once Liam had passed and they were out onto Main Street, he said, "I think you're safe to sit up now."

"Are you sure?" She said it in a stage whisper, as though Liam were there in the car with them.

"Pretty sure."

She sat up and rearranged herself, as though she'd suddenly realized she might have damaged her dignity by diving for the floor.

If any of the women in the back seat had noticed Megan's little drama, they didn't mention it. They were heavily involved in a conversation about the karaoke experience they'd had that evening, and were debating the merits of Celine Dion vs. Mariah Carey in terms of their music's singability. Celine Dion seemed to be winning, mainly because of Mariah Carey's unreachable high notes.

"There something going on you want to tell me about?" Drew asked mildly.

"No." Megan sounded both drunk and miserable. "Only that I don't want to have drunk-sober sex, and if I tell Liam that, he's going to ask why. And if I were sober, I could figure out how to get around telling him the reason, but I'm not sober, so I'll probably just blurt it out that I'm waiting until after the wedding to break up with him. Oh, God. I was right. I did just blurt it out."

Gianna leaned forward from where she was squeezed into the back seat between Marcy and the lawyer. "You're going to break up with Liam Delaney? What for? He's gorgeous."

"He is," the lawyer agreed. "He's got that manly cowboy thing going on. *Grrr.*"

Drew wasn't sure what the growling sound signified, but he was pretty sure it was at least R-rated.

"And the brooding, tortured-soul thing is kind of hot," Marcy agreed.

Drew's aunt was at least ten years older than Liam, and Drew had to cope with the startling new information that she was a cougar. That was news he just didn't need.

Megan twisted around to look at the other women. "The tortured-soul thing only seems hot because you don't have to deal with it day after day. At some point you have to stop being tortured, you know? Otherwise, it's just poor-me this, poor-me that. I mean, I know he's sad because his uncle died, but that was two years ago!" Then, she gasped and slapped a hand over her mouth. "Oh, crap. Drew. I forgot that Liam's uncle was your father. I'm so sorry."

"Don't worry about it."

"But—"

"Really. Don't worry about it."

Six months or even a year ago, the remark might have wounded Drew. But by now, he was beginning to come to terms with the fact that he would never meet his biological father. It was a sore point, yes. But it wasn't a raw, open wound anymore like it once was. There was hurt, but he could deal with the hurt.

"You mean Liam wasn't a tortured soul, or whatever you called it, before Redmond died?" he asked.

"Who knows? I didn't know him before Redmond died." Megan turned around and faced forward again. "But I sort of doubt that he went around spreading sunshine and happy thoughts."

Drew let out a guffaw. He doubted it, too.

The streets of Cambria were mostly empty at this time of night, with the bars and restaurants closed and the locals and tourists bedded down for the night. Drew drove through the quiet, dark streets to Moonstone Beach, where he dropped off the lawyer and then, a few hotels down the road, his aunt.

Then he got back onto Highway 1 and turned off on Main Street, where he deposited Gianna at the door of her B&B. It wasn't the most direct route; he'd passed by Megan's neighborhood on the way here, and logically, he should have taken her home after the Moonstone Beach run. But he wanted to be alone with her, and so now he had to double back to head toward Happy Hill.

If Megan noticed his awkward route, she didn't comment on it.

He told himself that the reason he wanted to be alone with her was so he could talk to her privately and make sure she was okay. He didn't like the way she'd ducked under the dashboard to avoid Liam. He wanted to make sure there wasn't something going on there that required his intervention.

And that really was part of the reason. But the other part was something undefinable, something that defied logic.

He just wanted to be around her.

He hadn't spent much time in Megan's presence, and the time he had spent had mostly involved her telling him off. But something inside him grew all warm and soft when she was near, and he hadn't felt that since back when he'd met Tessa.

Back when he'd been in love.

Not that he felt anything resembling love for Megan. How could he, when he didn't even know her? He only knew that he wanted to have that warm, soft feeling some more, and she was the one who could make it happen.

When they were alone in the car and headed up Charing Lane and into her neighborhood, he stole a look at her. "Are you okay? I mean … the thing with Liam. You seemed afraid of him, and the way you were hiding …"

Her eyes widened, and she seemed genuinely surprised. "What do you mean?"

"Well, everybody knows he's got a temper, and—"

"No! God, no." She let out a humorless laugh and waved her hands in front of her to signal her dismissal of the idea. "Liam's not abusive, if that's what you're thinking."

That was a relief, because if that had been the case, Drew would have had to kick his ass. And as much as he wanted to do that, he didn't know if he could manage it.

"Well, that's good."

"He seems like an ass. Right? I know that. I do know that." Her voice was foggy from the alcohol. "But he's not like that. He's …" She seemed to be searching for a way to explain it. "Liam's got a lot of feelings. And sometimes he doesn't know what to do with them. But I'd rather be with someone who's got a lot of feelings than with someone who doesn't have any, you know?"

"I guess," Drew said.

"It's just …"

"What?" He turned onto her street and slowed the car, wanting to prolong the drive.

"He's a good person," she went on. "And when he loves somebody, he *really* loves them. With everything he's got. And that's great. That's wonderful. A miracle, even. But … he's so wrapped up in being angry, in being wronged …" She shook her head and didn't finish.

Drew could sympathize with Liam on that, because much of the time, he himself was all wrapped up in being angry and wronged. But understandable or not, that kind of thing wasn't easy for significant others to deal with. If Megan needed evidence of that, she could just ask Tessa.

He couldn't believe he was about to defend Liam, but it seemed wrong not to.

"You know, sometimes people need time to process things. He and Redmond were close, everybody tells me, and it's only been two years. When someone you love dies, two years is nothing."

"Right, but …" She shrugged and slumped back against the seat.

He waited her out. If she was going to tell him all of it, she'd do it in her own time.

"That's not even the biggest problem," she said finally.

"Then what is?"

"He keeps asking me to move in with him."

"And?"

"And I always thought that when the man in my life asked me to move in with him, I'd feel elated. Over the moon. Beyond excited, you know?"

He pulled up at the curb outside her house, parked the car, and turned off the engine.

"So, what *did* you feel?"

"Existential dread."

"Well, that's not good."

"No."

Drew felt bad about Liam's impending heartbreak—the guy was a dick, but he was still a guy, and Drew felt a certain male kinship with him on the subject. But you had to love a woman—or anyone, for that matter—who casually threw the phrase *existential dread* into conversation.

"You've got to tell him," he said.

"I will. Soon. After the wedding."

Drew weighed his options. Telling her what Liam and his brothers had discussed during golf that day would be a betrayal of confidence. On the other hand, not telling her what they'd discussed would be like watching a train wreck when he could have thrown the switch to move one of those trains to another track.

"It can't wait until after the wedding. You have to tell him right away. Tomorrow. Or, I guess it would be today, technically."

She turned in her seat to look at him in the darkness of the car's interior. The moon was bright, and he could see the outline of her face in its silvery glow.

"I can't tell him yet. We're going to be spending so much time together for the wedding, and if he's pissed at me … and you know he's going to be pissed. And hurt."

"Ah, God, Megan …"

"What?"

She didn't seem drunk anymore, or at least, she'd sobered up enough since leaving the bar that she seemed fully present with him, fully aware.

He dived in.

"He's going to ask you to marry him. At the reception. Most likely with a microphone in his hand, in front of everybody. And you can't let it get that far. Because then you'll either have to crush him in front of everybody he knows, or you'll have to say yes when you really mean no." And neither of those options seemed viable to Drew.

"Oh … crap." Megan slapped a hand over her mouth in surprise. "Why would he do that? If I haven't been willing to move in with him, what makes him think I want to *marry* him?"

Drew shrugged. "He probably thinks that you said no to moving in with him because you want the full boat. Commitment. The ring, and all that."

"He said that?"

"Sort of. Plus, I'm a guy, and it's what I would think."

"Crap!" She ran her hands into her hair and held them there, atop her head, as though she were trying to keep it from flying off.

All at once, Drew felt sorry for Liam.

Getting dumped was bad. Getting dumped by someone you hoped to marry was worse. But as he looked at how her skin seemed to glow in the moonlight, the way her hair fell down onto her shoulders in a glorious cascade, he thought that getting dumped by Megan Scott—no matter the circumstances, no matter how or when she chose to do it—would be a blow from which the man was unlikely to recover.

Drew doubted that he, himself, would.

Chapter Eight

It was two-thirty in the morning, Megan was sitting in the car of a man she barely knew, and she'd just learned that her boyfriend was a ticking time bomb.

Funny how things happened.

She was probably still a little drunk—though less than she had been when she'd left the bar—because she should have been thinking about Liam, but instead, she was thinking about Drew.

This close to him in the car, she could smell some leftover hint of a light, spicy aftershave and his warm skin. His long body was folded into a car that was too small for him, making him seem somehow vulnerable. When he spoke to her, the timbre of his voice ran straight down her body to her toes.

Maybe she was still more drunk than she thought, because she wanted to reach out and lay the palm of her hand on his face.

This wasn't good, not at all.

"I'd better go," she said. "Liam's probably going to show up looking for me."

"What, like a stalker?"

She winced in both sympathy and regret. "No, like a guy who wants to make sure I got home safely. I kind of ditched him back at the bar." Plus, he probably wanted to get laid, since she'd been putting him off for a while. She didn't tell Drew that, because there were things he just didn't need to know.

She didn't want to sleep with Liam, not anymore, not now that her heart wasn't in it. Plus, it was too late, and she was too tired.

When it came to the relationship, she was tired in a way that had nothing to do with the hour or the alcohol.

"Give me your phone," Drew said.

"What?"

"Your phone. Hand it over." He put out his hand, waiting.

She dug her phone out of her purse, unlocked it, and gave it to him.

Drew went to the text messages, clicked on Liam's name, and began composing a message.

Sorry we missed each other at the bar. Caught a ride with a designated driver. Got home safely. Gianna's sleeping on my couch.

Drew showed her the screen and looked at her questioningly.

"Send it," she said. Drew had solved her sex problem without her ever having told him she had a sex problem. She supposed he must have intuited it. He was a guy, after all.

Drew hit SEND, and the text went off into the great unknown.

He sent it to help Megan deal with her dilemma, but he sent it for his own reasons, as well.

The idea of Liam coming over here and maybe sleeping with Megan made him sick to his stomach, though he couldn't say why it was his business.

It had something to do with the way Megan was looking at him. It had something to do with her obvious misery at the situation she'd found herself in. It had to do with the fact that Liam was pretty much a prick.

But it also had to do with the way she looked with the moonlight coming through the car windows, and the way her hair had shone when he'd seen her in the bar. It had to do with the sound of her voice in the car as she told him things he had no right to know. It had to do with the tingle he'd felt when her fingers brushed his as she'd handed him the phone.

God, he was an asshole.

Liam was his family—in a way. And he was a guy in love. Guys acted stupid when they were in love, so maybe Liam deserved a pass. Maybe he deserved a little compassion from a man who was, if nothing else, his blood cousin.

Drew needed Megan to get out of the car before he kissed her. Because he knew he was going to kiss her, he knew nothing would be able to stop him if she didn't go inside now.

"Okay. Well ... we're here," he said, feeling awkward.

"Right." She opened the car door and got out, and it occurred to Drew that a gentleman would walk her to her front door.

He got out and came around the car to meet her, and they walked together up the front steps to the little cottage. He stood there with his hands in his pockets as she found her keys in her purse and unlocked the door.

"Thanks for the ride. And for listening." She leaned over, rose onto her toes, and kissed him on the cheek.

It was an innocent kiss, a kiss one might give to one's mother.

But it caused an electric charge that went straight to his groin.

Jesus.

He took a deep breath of the chilly night air and nodded. "You're welcome."

The moment she was inside, he fled like a scared rabbit.

Something told him he should get the next flight home, go back to building the boat he had up on pallets in his workshop, and forget any of this ever happened, forget Megan Scott even existed.

But something else—something stronger—knew he wasn't going to do that.

"You're an idiot," he murmured to himself, not for the first time.

The Wedding Week event for Tuesday was a whale-watching cruise out of Morro Bay.

Drew felt a cold dread just looking at the page his mother had given him. A day of being around Megan, knowing that he had to keep his distance from her, would be excruciating.

He called his mom in the morning to see if he could get out of the whale-watching thing, but she reacted with horror to the very suggestion.

"My goodness, Drew! You came all the way from Canada for this wedding, I would think you'd want to at least parti-cipate."

"I am participating. I'm in the wedding party."

He could almost see her pressing her mouth into an angry line, fine wrinkles feathering out from her lips.

"This is important to Julia."

"Julia won't mind if I don't take a damned whale-watching cruise. Hell, she won't even notice." But he knew that wasn't true. She'd notice, and she'd miss him.

"Well, do what you want," Isabelle said, in a voice that sug-gested exactly the opposite. "But I would think you'd have enough love and respect for your sister to at least make the effort."

That sealed it. After thirty-some-odd years of manipulating Drew's emotions for her own gain, Isabelle was an expert at it. There would be no such thing as free will for him for the next week, and there was no sense in pretending otherwise.

"All right, I'll be there."

"Good."

And then, hesitating, he asked, "Mom? How are things going between you and the Delaneys?" The situation—Isabelle having been Redmond Delaney's illicit lover so many years ago—was more awkward than a three-legged race on a tightrope, and Drew had no sense of how the various parties were handling it.

"Oh … fine," Isabelle said vaguely.

"Fine?" he repeated. "What, exactly, does 'fine' mean?"

She let out a puff of exasperation. "Sandra barks at me, and Orin seems embarrassed by me."

"Sandra barks," he told her. "It's what she does. And Orin seems embarrassed by everything, including, but not limited to, the fact that he stands upright and breathes in and out. Don't worry about it. It's just how they are."

"Well," Isabelle said.

From experience, he knew that *well* didn't mean, *Well, you might be right,* or even *Well, I'll think about that.* What it meant was, *Well, you're full of shit, but I'll be polite and refrain from saying it.*

And for all he knew, Sandra and Orin really did dislike her as much as she thought they did. Isabelle had kept a Delaney child away from them, away from the brother they loved. She'd had her reasons, God knew. But the reasons didn't change the damage that had been done.

Drew himself held out hope that some level of repair with his mother might be possible, at least on his end. If he'd been able to stay at home on Salt Spring Island working on his boats and staying out of all this, he would have. But since he was here, he figured he might as well do what he could to stick things back together with duct tape and Super Glue.

So, against his better judgment, he agreed to go on the whale-watching cruise.

The truth was, he hadn't given in only for Isabelle's sake. As much as it might be hard to see Megan with Liam, it was the kind of sore spot that a person just couldn't help touching and poking at.

God help him, was he really thinking of trying to steal his cousin's girlfriend? The fact was, he couldn't seem to *stop* thinking about it. That wasn't going to help him mend things with the Delaneys. No, it wasn't going to help at all.

Chapter Nine

Megan's cheek was pressed against a café table at Jitters, a coffeehouse on Main Street, and she moaned in time with the pulsing throb in her head. Breanna, sitting in a chair across from her, looked pale and clammy from a bout of vomiting earlier in the morning.

"Whose idea was it to have a bachelorette party?" Breanna whined. Her dark hair, usually so thick and lustrous, was unwashed and pulled back into an untidy ponytail.

"I think it was yours," Megan said.

"No, it wasn't. The strippers were my idea, and we didn't even have any. So, really, none of this was my fault."

Lacy Jordan, a barista with silky blond hair and legs so long they might have belonged to a thoroughbred colt, brought two strong coffees to their table—Breanna's black, Megan's with copious amounts of sugar and cream.

"Here you go, ladies." Lacy sounded unnaturally chipper. "I hope it helps."

"Bite me," Breanna said.

"It doesn't usually come with the service, but if you insist …" Lacy batted her eyelashes and grinned.

"I don't even drink!" Megan complained. "At least, not that much. And I didn't have that much last night! So why do I feel like my brain is being shoved through a dull meat grinder?"

"Tolerance," Lacy said wisely. "You don't have it. The obvious answer is to drink more."

"Bite me," Megan said.

When Lacy had retreated behind the counter, Megan lifted her head off the table, which caused the pounding to intensify. She sipped her coffee and pondered whether an IV drip of espresso would be helpful.

She wasn't sure what she felt worse about: the physical effects of the alcohol she'd consumed the night before, or the fact that she'd had a vivid erotic dream about Drew McCray. How was she supposed to see him today for all of the various infernal Wedding Week events when she would certainly be picturing all of the things he'd done to her in her subconscious the night before?

And oh, God, had he been good. Masterful. Commanding yet gentle, and so very thorough in his attentions to the most intimate parts of her body.

Why was she dreaming about Drew? Even if she were available—which she wasn't yet—it would be stupid and reckless to jump into something with another man so soon after coming off of a long-term relationship. Who did that? Stupid people, that was who. People who were gluttons for emotional torment.

"How did you get home last night?" Breanna wanted to know. "I was talking to Jennifer Crittenden, and when I looked up, you were gone."

"I got a ride with … with one of the designated drivers." She couldn't bring herself to mention his name.

"Oh. Did you go with Drew?"

She could feel heat rising into her face, and she avoided making eye contact with Breanna in the futile hope that her friend wouldn't notice.

"You're blushing. Why are you blushing?" Breanna's hand smacked over her open mouth. "Oh, God! Tell me you did not hook up with Drew. You haven't even broken up with Liam yet. If you cheated on my brother …"

"No," Megan moaned. "Of course I didn't."

"Then what?"

"Because I sort of did. Subconsciously. I had a dream …"

Breanna's eyebrows shot up. "You had a naughty dream about Drew? Well, what are you waiting for? Tell me. How was he?"

"*Amazing.*" She said the word in a stage whisper. She could feel the response in her nether regions just thinking about it. But it wasn't the sex itself she remembered best from the dream. It was the *longing*. The aching need. She hadn't been happy with Liam—not really—for so long. The part of her that felt longing and aching need had mostly been shut down.

But last night, she'd been open for business.

"Really," Breanna said. "Tell me more."

"I'm not going to tell you all the sex details from my dream."

"Aww." Breanna looked disappointed. "Why not?"

"Because I shouldn't have even been having that dream in the first place!" Megan threw her hands into the air in exasperation. "I'm in a relationship! For a little while longer, anyway." She felt miserable, partly because of the hangover and partly because of the stench of infidelity and betrayal that was clinging to her every pore.

Breanna let out a short laugh. "Oh, come on. You don't need to feel guilty over a dream. If we were all held responsible for the things we did in dreams, I'd have been locked up for murder a long time ago." She considered this. "And, I'd have a lot of explaining to do to any number of celebrity wives."

"Yeah. I know, but …"

"But what?"

Megan couldn't say the rest. She couldn't say what really had her feeling like a horrible person—the fact that she *wanted* the dream to be real. Not that she wanted to launch into a relationship with a man she barely knew. But would a brief but intense fling be so wrong?

It would. Yes, it would.

"It's going to be awkward when I see him today," Megan complained.

"You know what's going to be awkward?" Breanna said. "Going on a boat with a hangover. Whoever planned the sequence of events didn't consider the fact that the entire female contingent on today's cruise is going to have their heads hanging over the railing, puking into the water."

That did seem like a distinct possibility.

"At least Liam will be there," Megan said. It wasn't that she was eager to spend time with him, given the circumstances. But Liam would provide a kind of buffer between herself and Drew during the event, something she really needed.

"No, he won't," Breanna said. "Didn't he call you?"

"I've had my phone off." Specifically to avoid Liam's calls.

"The foreman at the ranch is out sick today, so Liam's filling in. He's not coming on the cruise."

Megan blinked at her in surprise. Liam had to come. She might not want to talk to him, but she needed him to show up for the cruise. If he didn't, she might have to talk to Drew. And if she talked to Drew, she might somehow give away the fact that she was thinking erotic thoughts about him.

That wouldn't do at all.

She lay her head back down on the table and gave in to the rhythmic throbbing.

Maybe if she were lucky, she'd fall off the side of the boat and get eaten by a shark. Right now, the thought seemed really appealing.

Eddie didn't look good.

The cat always had his issues: He was temperamental in the extreme, picky about his food, and slow to warm up to new people and animals. But today he looked more unhappy than usual. His food bowl remained untouched, and he didn't seem to want to do his favorite activities, such as tripping Drew while he went about the business of getting dressed and brushing his teeth.

The cat was lying in the corner of the hotel room limply, squinty-eyed, his mouth hanging slackly open.

Drew wasn't much on diagnosing cat ailments, but he tried to think what could be bothering Eddie. As far as Drew could tell, Eddie hadn't eaten anything in the room that wasn't meant to be eaten. He hadn't gotten into any kind of accident, and there'd been no other cats or dogs in his orbit to fight with.

"What's wrong, Ed?" Drew crouched down and rubbed behind the cat's ears. Eddie simply closed his eyes in response.

Before Eddie, Drew hadn't had a pet since the golden retriever they'd had when he was in high school. He hadn't been looking for a pet, either. But a couple of weeks before, he'd been in his workshop with the door open to catch the morning breeze when Eddie had sauntered in, meowing at him.

Drew had shooed the cat away, but the next day he'd come back, mewing insistently. On the third day, Drew fed him a can of tuna he'd dug out of the back of his pantry.

Everybody knew that once you fed a stray cat you'd never get rid of it, so Drew had pretty much accepted Eddie at that point. He'd asked around the neighborhood whether anybody had lost a large orange tabby, but Eddie had no collar, and it seemed pretty clear to Drew that the animal was homeless.

Or had been, until now.

At first, Eddie had accepted food, water, and a place to sleep, but he hadn't allowed Drew to touch him. He'd mostly taken up residence underneath a work bench, refusing to come out except to eat or to make his daily treks into the forest surrounding Drew's house.

But gradually, he'd begun to be more bold, coming close enough to sniff Drew's shoes or tentatively brush his leg on the way to somewhere else.

Eventually, Eddie had allowed Drew to pet him, then to pick him up. But he still didn't much like other people, and that was why Drew had elected to bring him on the trip rather than getting a cat-sitter.

But maybe the trip, with all of that time crammed into a cat carrier under the seat of a Delta jet, had stressed him out more than Drew had realized. Maybe he missed his home. Or maybe he was mourning the fact that he was stuck inside the hotel room and couldn't wander outdoors the way he was used to on Salt Spring Island.

Drew peered at Eddie, and the cat gazed mournfully back at him.

Then Eddie let out a strangled, explosive noise that was either a cough or a sneeze.

Not just stress, then.

"Are you sick, buddy?" he asked the cat.

Drew hadn't really wanted a cat, but he'd gotten used to having somebody around, even if that somebody didn't contribute to the rent and wasn't much of a conversationalist.

Seeing Eddie in distress bothered Drew more than he would have expected. The cat needed a vet.

It occurred to him, of course, that Megan was a vet, but Megan would be on the Morro Bay cruise today and would have taken the day off.

Drew pulled out his phone and checked for vets' offices in Cambria. He found two: Megan's clinic, which specialized in large animals like cows and horses, and one other, a place in the Tin Village area that seemed to be more focused on dogs and cats.

If Drew took Eddie to the vet, it would mean that he wouldn't get to Morro Bay in time for the whale-watching cruise, and would miss out on a fun-filled day of camaraderie with the Delaneys and the McCrays.

Drew grinned and stroked Eddie's fur.

"I owe you one, dude."

Drew called Julia and made his excuses about the whale-watching trip. At first, she was upset that he wouldn't be there, but he played up Eddie's suffering, even going so far as to take a short video of the cat's misery on his phone so he could send it to Julia.

Once she'd had a chance to watch the video—complete with one of Eddie's strangled cough-gag-sneeze episodes—she texted that he was off the hook. He'd known she would. Julia had a soft spot for children and animals—anything small and helpless and, preferably, cute.

With that done, he loaded Eddie into his cat carrier and put him in the rental car.

It was a measure of Eddie's misery that he didn't even pro-test being put into the carrier. Usually, Drew risked his eyesight and a certain amount of spilled blood every time he had to take Eddie anywhere. This time, the cat just submitted limply.

Drew drove Eddie to the Tin Village vet's office. Tin Vil-lage was a collection of industrial-looking, metal-sided structures off of Burton Drive that housed a variety of businesses ranging from a hardware store to a cookie shop to various business headquarters for the restaurants and shops on Main Street.

The vet's office was in the center of the complex, its un-assuming door almost hidden behind a pair of potted palm trees. Cutout silhouettes of a dog and a cat adorned a glass panel in the upper half of the door.

When Drew approached the receptionist, she frowned at him in a combination of scorn and concern for Eddie's plight.

"I'm sorry." The woman was upper-middle-aged, maybe fifty, with blond hair shot with gray that had been sprayed into an immovable bob. "We're completely booked up. You should have made an appointment."

"I kind of didn't want to wait," he said. "He seems pretty sick." He held up the cat carrier so the woman could peer in at Eddie through the mesh on its side.

"Have you tried Megan Scott?" the woman suggested. "She mostly works on cattle, horses—that kind of thing. But she takes domestic animals, too."

"I'm pretty sure she's busy today," Drew said.

The woman scrunched up her nose in either thought or sympathy—it was hard to tell. "Right, the wedding. Today's the whale-watching thing."

In a town this small, it was no surprise that the receptionist knew Megan's business. Drew had experienced much the same thing on Salt Spring Island. If he'd been home, his neighbors would already know how many times Eddie had sneezed since eight a.m., and whether the cat had managed to take a shit. Which he hadn't.

The receptionist suggested that Drew try a clinic down the highway in Cayucos and gave him the name and number. He went back to his car, got in, and loaded Eddie into the passenger seat.

He could try the place in Cayucos, sure. But the boat wasn't set to leave for forty-five minutes yet, and Drew couldn't help thinking about how Megan had looked last night in the passenger seat of his car, her skin shining softly in the moonlight.

It wasn't a question of whether it would be self-serving to call her now about Eddie. It was only a question of *how* self-serving.

Eddie let out another gag-like explosion of air and cat mucus.

"You're right, Eddie," he said. "Your health comes first."

Chapter Ten

Drew didn't have Megan's cell phone number, and he sure as hell wasn't going to ask Liam. He considered asking Julia, but her patience with him skipping out of the cruise was going to come to an abrupt end if she knew he was trying to take another one of her guests with him.

He briefly considered which of the Delaneys was most sympathetic to him, and he realized that it was Sandra, despite her crusty attitude. Sandra was not going on the cruise—"If I wanted to watch a bunch of whales jumping around, I'd go to a damned aquarium," she'd told Julia—and so he tried her at home.

"Well, Christ on a Cheez-It, boy, why do you need to call the woman?" she demanded over the phone. "You'll be face to face with her all afternoon on that damned boat. Though it's beyond me why any of you are doing such a fool thing in the first place. You want to look at water, you can see it from the damned beach."

Drew had a sudden insight and he grinned, glad she couldn't see it. "Sandra, are you afraid of the water?"

"*Hmph.*" The sound was neither denial nor affirmation. "I just don't see why you'd want to leave a perfectly good piece of solid ground, that's all. You got a problem with that?"

"Not at all."

"Well, then."

He took another stab at the original purpose of his call. "Um … Megan's cell number? I wouldn't bother her, but my cat is sick."

"Sure he is." She let out a harsh cackle. "You want to make a move on Liam's girl, I guess that's your own business. But I figure you ought to do it like a man instead of bringing a defenseless cat into it."

He considered protesting his innocence and maybe sending her the same video he'd used to placate Julia. But Sandra wasn't much for explanations or excuses.

He waited silently for a moment while she considered the situation.

"It's your funeral," she said at last, and gave him the number.

Megan was in her car on her way to Morro Bay, thinking about how to avoid Drew, when Drew called her.

"Are you in Morro Bay yet?" he asked, without introduction.

"Who is this?" But she knew who it was. How could she not recognize his voice when she'd heard it purring indecent things into her ear in her dream?

"It's Drew. Listen, I know you're taking the day off work for the whale-watching thing, but … Eddie's sick, and the other vet in town is booked up."

"Who's Eddie?" If she'd been able to focus, she'd have understood that Eddie was a pet of some kind, but she couldn't focus, because that voice …

"My cat."

She took a moment to get hold of her faculties, then reminded herself that she was a professional and the welfare of a
helpless animal was at stake.

"What are his symptoms?"

"He won't eat, he's listless. He just lies around with his
mouth hanging open in a way that looks really weird to me. And
he's got a sneeze. Or maybe it's a cough. It's kind of hard to
tell."

"Sounds like he's got an upper respiratory infection."

"You mean, like a cold?"

"Exactly like a cold."

"Well ... that doesn't sound too bad. Except that he hasn't
eaten or had anything to drink since yesterday. He seems really
miserable."

Megan continued driving south on Highway 1. On the one
hand, she'd been hoping to avoid the whale-watching cruise, and
now she could. On the other, the reason she'd wanted to avoid
the cruise was so she could avoid Drew.

She pondered the irony of that while she thought about the
cat and its ailment. She didn't have to take care of Drew's cat.
The other vet in Cambria might be booked up, but there were at
least three vets in Morro Bay he could try, and when you added
in San Luis Obispo, Los Osos, and Templeton, there had to be
at least a dozen.

But he hadn't called them; he'd called her. The cat needed
help, and what kind of doctor would she be if she could simply
ignore an animal in need?

She let out a sigh, flipped on her turn signal, and took the
next exit off the highway so she could turn the car around.

"I'll see you at my office in fifteen minutes."

"Look, Megan, I'm sorry to do this to you. I—"

"Fifteen minutes."

***

Megan told herself to focus on the cat, not the man. Eddie was sick and needed her help, and she couldn't help him if she was thinking about what it would feel like to have Drew's hands on her body.

Those hands had been all over her last night in her dream, but she couldn't think about that. If she thought about it, then she couldn't do her job. Besides, she might start stammering and blushing, and that wouldn't do.

Eddie was lying on the examining table, and Megan checked his eyes, his nose, and his throat. Considering what Drew had told her about Eddie's temperament, the fact that the cat allowed her to poke and probe him without much protest was an indication of his ill health.

"Is he up to date on his vaccines?" Megan didn't look at Drew as she asked the question. Instead, she peered into Eddie's nasal cavity with a scope.

"Yeah. I got him his shots as soon as I figured out he was planning to stay."

"Good. Has he had any of these symptoms before?"

"Now that you mention it, yeah. When he first started coming around, he had the sneeze. It wasn't this bad, though."

She used a cotton swab to take a sample of mucus from the inside of Eddie's nose. This, finally, provoked a response, and with skills honed from years of experience, she deftly dodged a swipe from the cat's claws.

She stroked the cat's head with her latex-gloved hand to soothe him. Then she scooped him up into her arms.

"He's dehydrated," she told Drew. "Let me keep him overnight, and I'll give him fluids and keep an eye on him. It's possible that he's a chronic carrier of a viral infection that's triggered by stress. The trip out here might have been too much for him."

She stroked Eddie's head and felt his gentle purr against her chest.

Drew stuffed his hands into his jeans pockets. "Well, is he going to be okay?"

"Sure. I'll make him comfortable and give him an antibiotic to make sure there's no bacterial infection. He'll be good to go in a few days. You'll have to keep an eye on him in stressful situations, though. I assume you're going to fly him back home after the wedding?"

"That was the plan."

"He might have another flare-up. If he does, you want to watch for dehydration and any trouble with his breathing."

Drew nodded. "Listen, thanks for doing this. I didn't want to ruin your plans today, with the cruise and everything, but ..."

"Kids and pets," she mused. "You never know when they're going to get sick, and they usually don't do it on anybody's schedule. Come on, you can follow me back."

Drew followed Megan as she took Eddie into a room that had been the kitchen back when this place had been used as a house rather than a business. On one wall stood a row of stainless steel cages where hospitalized patients could await their recovery. Because Megan had taken time off for Wedding Week, Eddie was the only patient in residence. The cages stood empty, clean, and gleaming in the overhead lights.

Megan opened the door of a small cage and deposited Eddie inside. She closed and latched the door, turned around, and snapped off her gloves.

He was standing close to her, so close that he picked up her scent—some kind of flowery soap and the sunscreen she'd applied in preparation for the cruise that was even now leaving without them.

He felt her nearness like an electric charge through his veins. He wanted to reach out and touch her, but until the break-up happened, she was still with Liam. And even after the break-up did happen, making a move on her would effectively destroy any chance he had of forging a good relationship with the Delaneys.

Or one Delaney, in particular.

She cleared her throat, and he thought he saw a hint of color rise to her cheeks.

"You can leave him here for a day or two so I can watch him," she said. "I'll take care of him."

"What do I owe you?" He was standing too close to her, he knew, but he made no move to back away.

She shook her head. "Nothing. You're a Delaney, and the Delaneys are practically my family, so ..." She blinked hard as she realized what that implied about her future with Liam. "I mean, they would be, if ... I didn't mean ..."

"I have to pay you," he told her. "This is your business. You're a professional. You deserve to get paid."

"It's a favor. I'm doing you a favor. Or, I'm doing Eddie one."

He hesitated. He knew what he was about to say could get them both in trouble, but he said it anyway.

"At least let me buy you lunch, then."

"Oh, I ... shouldn't. Liam—"

"It's just lunch. To say thank you, that's all. You missed out on the event today because of me and Eddie, so I figure it's the least I can do."

It was only logical. He was just being polite. She was doing him a favor by taking care of Eddie, and he figured he owed her one back.

The problem was, even Drew didn't believe that.

***

Megan had her own set of rationalizations.

She had begged off on the cruise and had come back to work because of a sick cat, not because of Drew. She had refused his offer of payment because of her close relationship with the Delaneys, not because of any personal feelings she was developing for him. And lunch with him was simply a friendly compensation for her time, and not anything inappropriate.

It certainly wasn't a date.

That was what she told herself as she gave Eddie a round of antibiotics and subcutaneous fluids. She set him up with a humidifier to help with his breathing, and then she and Drew went outside and she locked up the office.

Eddie wasn't in any kind of life-threatening danger, so he'd be fine if she went out with Drew and checked back in on him in an hour. Since he was her only patient at the moment, she would bring him home with her overnight so she could monitor him.

Usually when she had animals hospitalized overnight, she had a vet tech on duty to care for them, but with just the one—and a small one, at that—it would be easy enough to do it herself.

She was doing Drew and Eddie a favor, so of course it was reasonable to accept some kind of gesture in exchange.

So, the trill of excitement fluttering around in her chest could just calm the hell down.

They walked side by side toward the East Village, where the tourist-oriented art galleries, wine tasting shops, and souvenir boutiques stood side by side with the pharmacy, the bank, and other businesses catering mostly to locals.

At Bridge Street, they made a left and headed up to The Café, where they ordered turkey and avocado sandwiches and sat in the shade of the back patio to eat.

They started with the easy stuff.

"How did you become a vet?" Drew asked as he dug into his sandwich.

She started at the beginning, with the story about how she'd gotten a toy doctor kit for Christmas when she was six, and instead of practicing medicine on her family members, she'd treated the imaginary ailments and injuries of her stuffed animals and the family cat.

She'd always loved animals, and had pressed her parents for more and more of them until their house had been teeming with a dog, two cats, a hamster, a bird, and three mice.

It hadn't surprised anyone when she'd announced her intention to study veterinary medicine in college. She'd gone to UC Davis, intending to come to the aid of the dogs and cats of the greater Los Angeles area, where she'd grown up.

But something happened to her when she got to Davis. In the rural, green expanses of Northern California, she'd finally felt that she could breathe again after a lifetime of never realizing she couldn't.

She'd fallen in love with the space, the colors of nature, the fresh, smog-free air.

After she'd done an internship with a veterinary practice that worked mostly with farm animals, she'd fallen in love with that, too.

"I dreaded telling my mom that I wouldn't be going back to Southern California after I got my doctorate," she told Drew. "She cried."

But Megan knew she couldn't live her life based on what her parents wanted, so she'd settled up north—first in Sacramento, working for another vet's practice, and then, once she'd gained enough experience to open her own, in Cambria.

"Is that how you met Liam?" Drew delivered the question casually, but he watched her carefully as she answered.

"It is. I started doing work for the Delaneys, treating the cattle and the horses, months before I met Liam. Then, when he came to Cambria for his uncle's funeral, we ran into each other while I was on the ranch to take a look at a dehydrated calf."

What she didn't tell Drew was that they hadn't just "run into" each other. Liam knew how to take care of a dehydrated calf; you didn't spend as much time as he had on a ranch without figuring out that much. But he'd used the calf as a pretense for getting her out to the ranch after one of the hands had told him that the new vet in town was young, female, and hot. Liam had confessed as much once they'd been dating for a few weeks, but it didn't seem helpful to recount the story now.

"The funeral," Drew said.

"Yes. Liam was out here from Montana."

Drew nodded slowly. "Yeah. I was here, too."

"I know. Liam talked about you."

"Not in positive terms, I'll bet."

The subject of how Drew and Liam didn't get along was problematic, because if they thought about that, they would have to think about how much worse the two of them would get on if Liam knew that Drew was here now, with Megan.

Megan picked a piece of lettuce off of her sandwich and changed the subject.

"It was probably the stress of the flight that made Eddie sick," she told him. "I'll bet you flew economy class, right?" He was a Delaney, if not by name, then by DNA, and the Delaneys flew economy. Except for Colin, who had more of a taste for life's luxuries than the rest of his family.

"Yeah, on Delta," he confirmed.

She gave him a wry smile and shook her head. "Your inheritance was, what? In the hundreds of millions?" She raised a hand in a *stop* gesture. "No, don't tell me. It's none of my business. It's just, why economy? Why not first class? For that matter, why not a private charter flight? I know why the rest of the Delaneys don't do those kinds of things. They've got this ethic of regular-person thriftiness. Except for Colin. But you …" She gestured vaguely at him. "You were working-class, and then you came into a fortune. I'd expect you to be throwing it around a little. I know I would."

She knew she was prying, but the question had been nagging at her, and it felt good to get it out there.

Drew sat with the remains of his sandwich on a plate in front of him, his elbows on the table, one hand entwined in his hair. He raised his eyebrows and looked at her in a way that made her insides feel hot and soft.

"You know, I'm not entirely sure." He plucked a slice of pickle off of his plate, popped it into his mouth, and chewed thoughtfully. "I always thought that if I ever won the lottery or something, I'd do what you said. Throw it around a little."

"But?"

"But, I don't know … I guess it still doesn't seem real. Any of it. The money, being a Delaney, finding out my dad isn't really my father …" He shook his head. "It was a shock. At first, I guess I didn't do anything with the money because I was waiting for it to sink in. And it still kind of hasn't. Besides, I didn't earn it."

"But don't you need to invest it, or … I don't know. Whatever somebody does with that kind of money."

"That's what Colin keeps telling me. Over and over." He laughed. "I'm going to give that guy gray hair."

Megan looked at him with wide-eyed surprise. "But how can you ... You must get people calling you, asking for money. Salespeople, charities, long-lost relatives ..."

"Every day," he said. "I've had to change my phone number twice."

"But ..."

"I know it doesn't make sense to you. It doesn't make sense to me, either. But when I think about doing something with the money, I just kind of freeze up. I can't make myself do it. Like if I take a first-class flight it means my dad—the one who raised me—never mattered." He shrugged and looked at the table instead of at her.

"But he did matter." Megan reached across the table and put her hand on top of his. "The inheritance was Redmond's way of saying that you mattered, too, even if he couldn't tell you that."

He looked down at where her hand lay atop his, and they both fell silent. Suddenly, Megan was keenly aware of that touch, that point of connection between them. She felt herself blush, and she pulled her hand away.

Chapter Eleven

The moment she touched him—that was what did it. That was when he knew he was going to kiss her, even if she was still with Liam, even if kissing her would upset both of their families, even if kissing her would upend his world and break his heart and leave destruction in its wake. The only thing that was going to stop him was if she didn't want him, and he knew she did. He could see it in the way she looked at him, and he could feel it in the electric charge of her hand on his.

He couldn't kiss her now, on a restaurant patio full of people, some of whom might know her and some of whom might be willing and even eager to spread the news of it to everyone they knew—including Liam. He wouldn't do that, because he wanted the kiss, when it came, to be wholly positive for her, wholly good.

So, he couldn't kiss her now. But he would, and soon. He knew it as sure as he knew the yearnings of his own heart.

He got his chance about a half-hour later when he took her back to her office. He walked her inside, and she turned to head toward the back room to check on Eddie. As she started to go, he caught her hand in his. She turned to him questioningly, and he pulled her into his arms and kissed her.

Given the fact that he'd decided to do it more than thirty minutes before, and that he'd been thinking about it for all that time, the kiss could have failed to meet expectations. It could have paled in comparison to the way it had felt in his fond imaginings.

But it didn't. It exceeded his expectations in ways that he couldn't have anticipated. The feel of her mouth as she melted against him and responded to him, the scent of her skin, the taste of her lips and her tongue, the way she brought her arms around him and tangled her fingers in his hair—all of it combined not only to arouse him, but also to change his world view.

After Tessa, he'd thought that he would likely never get into a serious relationship again. He would date, yes. He would have women in his life. He wasn't about to close that door. But he'd thought that after the disaster of his marriage and its subsequent dissolution, he would never share his life with anyone, would never make himself that vulnerable to another person again.

But now, with Megan in his arms, with her warm body pressed up against his, something in him recognized something in her. It was as though he'd known her all along and simply hadn't realized it. As though he'd been waiting for her. And now, as he kissed her, he thought, *There you are. I'd have known you anywhere.*

After a long moment, they pulled apart. Drew didn't want to let her go—not now, not ever again.

She looked at him with her eyes half closed, still languid from the luxury of the kiss.

"Oh," she said.

"Megan ..." He didn't know what he was about to say. Was he planning to apologize? Not likely. He wasn't sorry, couldn't ever be sorry. Was he planning to explain himself? How could he explain what he was feeling? And he certainly couldn't tell her what he'd just experienced—that sense of having found some-one he'd been looking for since the day he was born.

So he just left the word sitting there, untouched. Just the sound of her name.

"I ... I'd better go check on Eddie," she said, and disap-peared into the back room.

Megan closed the door behind her, separating her from Drew, and slapped a hand to her mouth.

"Oh, God."

Had she really just done that? Had she really just kissed another man while she was still with Liam? She wasn't that per-son, the kind who did such things. She had a firm self-image, one that didn't include making out with her boyfriend's cousin on the sly.

And yet.

What she'd felt when Drew had kissed her—had she ever felt anything like that with a man before? Had she ever felt that jolt from the top of her head down to the ends of her toes, like her entire body was completely, gloriously on fire?

Oh, she was in trouble.

She reminded herself that she'd come into the room for Ed-die, and she went to his cage, where she found the cat sleeping in relative peace. She opened the cage door and stroked him gently, without waking him.

What was she going to do?

She had to break up with Liam, obviously. And she was going to do that, just as she'd planned. But what then? If she took up with Drew now, everyone would think she'd split with Liam so she could be with Drew. That would ruin her rela-tionship with the Delaneys. And she didn't want to think about how much trouble it would cause between Liam and Drew. The two of them were family, whether they chose to acknowledge it or not. And she didn't want to be a wedge between family.

But, God, was there any way she could walk away from Drew after what she'd just experienced? After what she'd just felt?

Megan's pulse was pounding, and she didn't want to go back out there until it slowed.

She pulled her phone out of her back pocket and texted Breanna.

He kissed me!!!

In a moment, Breanna responded:

I hope you're talking about Liam.

Megan responded with the red-faced emoji of shame.

Oh, boy, Breanna wrote back.

By the time Megan emerged into the front room, she was half hoping that Drew had gone. But there he was, with such a look of hope and yearning on his face that it made Megan want to cradle him in her arms.

Which she absolutely was not going to do.

"I think you should go," she said.

He shifted awkwardly from one foot to the other. "Oh. Did I read the signals wrong? Because—"

"You didn't," she told him. "But I still think you should go."

He looked at his feet and nodded. "I'll check in on Eddie tomorrow."

When he was gone, she felt the loss like an injury, like a physical thing.

Her phone buzzed in her pocket, and she pulled it out to find a new text from Breanna.

You're getting yourself into a mess, it said.

No kidding, she thought.

Drew left Megan's office wondering what he was doing. He didn't want a relationship with anyone, let alone his cousin's girlfriend. But what his brain thought he wanted and what the entire rest of his being was urging him to do were two different things.

He hadn't planned on forging a close relationship with the Delaneys, but he didn't want to make sworn enemies of them, either. If he went after Megan—really went after her in earnest, not just a lunch and a kiss—then not only would Liam have to kick his ass, but Drew would have to let him do it, because he would deserve it.

He needed to talk to someone about all of this, but he didn't have anyone he could confide in. If he told Julia about what had just happened, she'd be pissed that he was stirring up trouble with her future in-laws. He had friends on Salt Spring Island, but no one he talked to about his family situation.

Here in Cambria, the people who were most friendly to him were Delaneys, and he couldn't spill his secrets to any of them.

Except maybe one of them. Especially one of them who'd already guessed about his feelings for Megan.

He considered that option, rejected it, and then considered it again.

What did he have to lose, really?

He got into his car and headed toward the ranch.

Sandra was outside in her garden when Drew got there. She was harvesting tomatoes from vines that were planted in neat rows, each one surrounded by a wire cage that supported the weight of the fat, ripe tomatoes. She was wearing jeans and sneakers, and a wide-brimmed straw hat protected her face from the sun. A pair of gloves and a selection of gardening tools sat on the ground nearby, and she held a five-gallon bucket for the tomatoes. Another bucket stood next to the tools, and Drew saw that it was half filled with weeds she'd pulled from around the foot of each plant.

"Hey," Drew said. He stood there awkwardly, with his hands in the pockets of his jeans.

"Well, hey yourself," Sandra replied.

He approached her and peered into the bucket of tomatoes. "Those look good," he said.

She let out a grunt. "I guess they'll do. A damned sight better than last year's crop, I'll tell you that. Those had blight, and the hornworms got 'em. You let hornworms get a foothold, and they'll eat any damned thing that's not nailed down."

Despite Sandra's tirade about hornworms, she seemed to be in a fine mood—at least for Sandra. Everyone else was in Morro Bay on the boat trip, so things were quiet around the ranch except for the sounds of the birds chasing each other around the fence posts that surrounded the garden.

The sun was warm, and a gentle breeze that smelled of the ocean rustled the grass and the branches of a huge sycamore tree that towered over the house.

"You might as well help me pick these tomatoes while you decide whether you're going to come out with it," Sandra told him, gesturing toward the plants.

"Come out with what?"

"Well, how the hell would I know that, boy? It's your story, not mine."

He positioned himself at a plant near the one where she was working, and began to pick tomatoes.

"Not those." She pointed at the one in his hand. "That one needed a little more time on the vine. There should be a little give when you press on them, like this one, here." She showed him a tomato from the bucket to demonstrate.

He turned his attention back to the plant and began inspecting tomatoes for ripeness. He picked one and held it out toward her.

She gave him a crisp nod. "That's more like it."

They worked together side by side in silence for a few minutes before he told her what was on his mind.

"I … might have kissed Megan. Today, at her office." He kept his eyes on the plant in front of him, avoiding looking at Sandra.

She let out a hoot. "You might have? Well, if you don't know for sure, then you probably didn't do it right, by God."

He shrugged. "I do know for sure. I was just trying to make it sound better than it is."

"Did she kiss you back?" Sandra wanted to know.

"I'd rather not say."

"Well, why not?"

"It would be … ungentlemanly, I guess."

"Well, I suppose you're right." Sandra considered that. "I'm thinking she did kiss you back. I saw how she looked at you back at the house. Plus, if she'd shown you the door, I guess the whole thing would be in the past and you and I wouldn't be having this conversation." She pulled a tomato off the vine and deposited it into the bucket.

"The thing is … I don't like Liam."

"Well, that's about the most poorly kept secret I've ever heard." She cackled.

"But … just because I don't like him doesn't mean I want to hurt him. Guys aren't supposed to do that to each other, whether we like each other or not."

She straightened up from where she'd been bent over a plant and faced him with her hands on her narrow hips. "Seems sensible enough. So why'd you go and do it, then?"

Why had he? Was it simple lust? Lack of impulse control? Hostility toward Liam? Or something else?

"I just … I think she's the one." He hadn't known he was going to say it until it was already out of his mouth.

Sandra froze, a tomato in each hand, and looked at him.

"Well, by God, boy."

"I know what you're going to say."

"I doubt it, son."

He went on as though she hadn't spoken. "You're going to say that I'm an idiot, and I just met her, and there's no way I could possibly know that. And you're right. You're right, Sandra."

She turned back to her tomato plant. "Well, you might be an idiot, boy, so I won't dispute that. But the other part? I won't claim to tell you your business. If you say she's it, then I figure you're probably right."

Drew was so surprised by her words that he almost dropped the tomato he was holding.

"I am?"

"Well, hell, you might be. I've seen stranger things. Why, I knew I was going to marry Orin the day I met him. I told him so, too. He thought I was out of my damned mind, but here we are, going on forty years together." She chuckled. "Serves him right for doubting me."

Drew had always thought of Sandra as an extremely practical woman, someone who would never entertain ideas like destiny or love at first sight. Now, having to adjust his expectations so thoroughly caused him to feel a sense of vertigo.

"You're kidding," he said.

"You ever know me to make jokes?" she snapped at him.

"Well, no."

"All right, then." She nodded. "All I'm saying is, if you think she's the one, well, I figure that's possible. But as poorly as things are going between her and my son, they're still going, and you'd best wait until they're through with each other, or you and Liam are going to get into it. *Hmph*. Though I expect that's going to happen at some point, anyway."

Drew considered that.

"You're not going to tell him about this, are you?"

She looked at him as though he'd suddenly learned to fly. "Boy, do I look like a fool to you?"

"Well … no."

"That's because I'm not. Of course I'm not going to tell him. And if you know what's good for you, then you won't, either."

He must have looked as miserable as he felt, because her expression turned to one of sympathy. "Now, buck up, son. She'll be free sooner rather than later. I figure you won't have long to wait."

But to him, even five minutes felt too long. Even a second seemed like forever.

"I didn't plan any of this," he said. It seemed important to tell her that.

"I know you didn't. Now, what say you stop talking and start working. Those damned weeds aren't going to pull themselves."

Breanna called Megan as soon as she got back from the boat trip.

"Tell me that didn't happen," she said. "Tell me that I was so addled by seasickness and my hangover and having my brain baked in the sun that I imagined that text message."

"Oh, Bree," Megan said miserably.

"Alternatively, tell me that you slapped him and told him to get out."

"I did tell him to leave."

"But no slap?"

"Well …"

Megan was sitting on her living room sofa with Mr. Wiggles curled up on one side of her, and Bobby, the Maltese, on the other. She held the phone to her ear with one hand and stroked the cat absently with the other. Bobby lay his head on Megan's thigh and gazed up at her adoringly.

"Why wasn't there a slap?" Breanna wanted to know.

"I don't know!" Megan wailed. "We were in my office because his cat's sick, and we were talking about the cat, and I was about to check on him—the cat, I mean—and then the next thing I knew, Drew kind of *swooped* me into his arms, and we were kissing, and … and then my knees went weak, Breanna. You hear about that kind of thing happening, but my knees actually went weak. If he hadn't been holding me up, I would have melted."

"So you didn't slap him because you were too weak-kneed," Breanna observed.

"Yes!"

"Megan …"

"I know! I know it shouldn't have happened. And it won't happen again, at least …"

"At least what?"

"At least until I break up with Liam."

"Oh … crap," Breanna said. "So, what I'm hearing is that you're all gooey over Drew now, and you're probably going to start seeing him once you dump Liam. Which is going to make it look like you dumped Liam for Drew. Which is going to make you look bad, and make Drew look bad—which he deserves, I guess, for kissing you while you're still taken. And which is going to crush Liam's heart like a paper cup. Because Liam might seem like this hard-ass tough guy, but he's got a really soft heart. Which is why this really, really sucks."

"I know," Megan said.

"You could just forget about Drew," Breanna suggested. "Just write off the kiss, figure it was one of those things, and cut off anything that's going on with him because it's too messy."

The very thought of it made Megan's chest ache. She scooped Bobby up with her free hand and cuddled him to her for comfort.

"I kind of don't think I can," she said.

"Are you telling me you're gone already?" Breanna demanded. "One kiss, and that's it? You're gone?"

"No, I wouldn't say that. But … I'm maybe kind of partly gone."

She set Bobby aside and, with the phone to her ear, began making her rounds, feeding and checking on Eddie, who was in a cage in the corner of the living room, and her other charges: Jerry, Sally Struthers, Sunshine, then finally, Bobby and Mr. Wiggles.

Breanna sighed heavily. "Well, you might as well tell me about the kiss. It was good, obviously. But I need details."

They talked about that, and about their experience with kisses—both the good and the bad.

"What's going to happen when you see him tomorrow?" Breanna asked.

"Tomorrow's the bachelor party," Megan said. "Guys only. I won't have to see him."

"Yeah, but that's at night. During the day, we've got the Hearst Castle tour."

"Oh … crap."

"Exactly."

Megan couldn't very well skip out on the Hearst Castle thing after she'd missed the Morro Bay event today.

"I guess I'll just … blend into the crowd," she said.

Breanna grunted, a sound that was remarkably similar to Sandra's. "Fat chance of that."

Chapter Twelve

As remarkable and unlikely as it seemed, Liam had never been to Hearst Castle, the behemoth estate of William Randolph Hearst that sat just ten miles up the coast from the ranch. The site was host to some 700,000 visitors a year, but Liam had not been one of them. He and Megan were discussing that as the bus that drove visitors up the winding road to the estate passed by a small herd of zebras.

"How can it possibly be that you've never visited Hearst Castle?" Megan asked, amazed by the revelation.

"Well, why the hell would I?" he asked, irritated. "It's for the tourists. I'm not a tourist."

"No, but it's part of the history of this area. And you're right here. You'd think—"

"Well, you'd think wrong."

Liam looked to where Drew sat on the bus several rows ahead of them.

"What's his problem?"

"Who?"

"McCray. He keeps looking back here with this expression on his face like somebody killed his cat."

Megan didn't look up to see Drew's expression. She didn't have to. It likely mirrored the one on her own face when she thought about what had happened between the two of them the day before.

"No one did," she said. "The cat's doing better. Drew picked him up this morning."

That had been a brief and awkward encounter that Megan had kept as quick and perfunctory as possible. She'd handed Eddie over at the door with a prescription, and had said only the things she would have said to any owner of one of her veterinary patients.

"Give him one of these pills twice a day, and try to avoid stressful situations," she'd told Drew. "Full recovery might take as long as ten days. Let me know if his condition worsens." And then she'd turned and headed back inside, closing the door behind her before he could say anything.

But she hadn't wanted to close the door. She'd wanted to pull him inside and kiss him again. She'd wanted to do more than kiss him. She'd wanted to find out whether the kiss was an accurate indicator of his skill in bed. And that was why she didn't look at him now. Because if she did, he'd know what she was thinking. He probably already knew.

"The cat thing was a metaphor," Liam pointed out now, unnecessarily.

"I know. I was just saying that—"

"I got that," he said. "But my point is, he's staring. And if he doesn't quit it, I'm going to knock the crap out of him."

They were having the murmured conversation over the recorded voice of Alex Trebek explaining the history and features of Hearst Castle to the occupants of the bus. It seemed to Megan, who was sitting in a window seat, that the bus was veering entirely too close to the edge of the winding road, beyond which was a dropoff that led down a steep hill and toward the ocean.

Megan had never heard of a Hearst Castle bus falling off the road and into a ravine, but she supposed anything was possible. Still, looking out the window of the bus and imagining a fiery death seemed preferable to looking at Drew.

"What the hell's he looking at?" Liam asked again.

"He's probably wondering the same thing about you," Megan snapped at him. "Can you just forget about him and focus on the tour?"

They rode for another couple of minutes before Liam said, "I'm just jealous, I guess."

Megan was so surprised by this that she didn't know what to say for a minute. Was it possible that Liam knew what had passed between her and Drew?

"You … what?" she finally managed to say.

"Look … I know I'm not the most sensitive guy sometimes. I know I get all wrapped up in my own stuff, the ranch and the family and all that. But, I don't know." He glanced back at Drew again. "That guy has a thing for you."

For a moment, she forgot all about the bus and the sharp turns and the steep dropoff.

"Why would you say that?"

"Maybe because I'm not blind." He shrugged. "He looks at you the way I did when we first met, I guess."

There was a poignance in it, in the wistful tone of his voice and in the acknowledgment that things had changed between them since those early days when they'd been happily in love.

"Does he?" she said.

"You know he does."

She considered whether to deny that, but decided not to. Liam wasn't a fool. He saw what he saw, and he knew what he knew.

"Well … maybe I've noticed."

She expected him to be defensive, possibly even hostile. But instead, he seemed to deflate a little in his seat.

"I know things haven't been right between us lately," he said. "I know you want more. And I want to give it to you. I want to fix things, Megan."

How could she tell him that she didn't want more from him, that she only wanted to be free? She opened her mouth to answer, but all that came out was, "We're here."

The crowd on the bus stood and began to file out of the vehicle. Megan followed them, her heart beating hard in her chest.

Liam actually seemed to be interested in the tour, which surprised Megan.

"Holy shit. The guest house is more than five thousand square feet. That's just the guest house! Our main house at the ranch is, what, half that?" He looked around at Casa del Mar, the largest of the Hearst Castle guesthouses, craning his neck to see the ornate ceilings. "I mean … fuck."

Megan considered it fortunate that this particular tour group consisted entirely of their party—with no young children around to hear Liam's expletive except for Breanna's children, Michael and Lucas. They'd heard Liam's colorful language many times before and no longer seemed to care about or notice it.

Liam was so wrapped up in the details of the Hearst estate that he seemed to have forgotten about Drew, who was standing off in the crowd near Julia and Isabelle, sulking.

It didn't take much effort for her to interpret the sulk. Liam, who'd grown more possessive lately, was keeping a hand firmly on Megan during the tour—either holding her hand in his, or draping an arm around her shoulders or her waist. Each time Liam made any kind of fresh contact, Megan could feel Drew

scowling and glowering at them in a way that she found both ir-
ritating and arousing.

She began to have her doubts about whether she could
keep this simmering thing she had going with Drew under wraps
until after the wedding. Because if he kept this up, Liam was
going to call him out on it, and once that happened, there would
be no containing the fallout.

As they filed out of the guest house, Drew began to push
through the crowd to come toward them, and Megan acted
quickly.

"Liam, did you see this? They brought it in from a cathedral
in France." She pointed at a marble statue, having no idea
whether what she'd just said was true.

While Liam was looking at the statue, Megan shot a look at
Drew to ward him off.

Why was he acting this way in front of Liam?

But even as she asked herself the question, she had some
idea of the answer. After that kiss, she belonged to him in some
way, and he belonged to her.

If Drew had been here with a woman, Megan would have
been glowering and scowling, too.

Drew wondered what had made him think he could hold it
together while Liam had his hands on Megan.

And his hands were all over her, as much as they reasonably
could be in public. He was either clutching her hand or resting a
hand on her hip, or—God, he hated this one—cupping the back
of her neck in a way that seemed unpleasantly controlling.

Drew wanted to go over there and slap Liam's hands away
from her.

Because he couldn't do that, he kept up a near constant mo-
nologue in his head:

Get your hands off her, goddamn it. Don't you goddamn touch her.

At a particular moment, as they were all following the guide out of the largest guest house, Liam had done the neck-cupping thing again, and Drew couldn't contain himself anymore. He started to force his way through the group to go over there and take Megan away from him, when she fired a look at him that stopped him.

That look said, *Back the hell off.*

Could he have misinterpreted the way she'd responded to the kiss? Was it possible that she still wanted Liam? The thought made something noxious and foul roil around in his stomach.

He didn't want to be this guy, this lovesick stalker who couldn't take his eyes off of a woman who was with someone else, but there it was.

He bided his time until the official tour was over and they were all free to roam the grounds. Everyone in their group spread out, milling around near the Neptune Pool, or ogling the finely manicured gardens, or snapping pictures of the view from atop the hill.

When Liam ducked into the restroom, leaving Megan standing alone outside the door, Drew knew he only had a minute. He swooped in, took Megan by the hand, pulled her into an alcove, and kissed her.

He kissed her to remind her of the first kiss, the one that had been branded so indelibly on his soul. He kissed her to let her know his intentions—he wasn't backing off, not now and not ever, as long as he thought she might want him. He kissed her to defy Liam, that smug prick. But mostly, he kissed her because he needed to, because he couldn't do anything else.

He kissed her thoroughly, completely, his body pressed against hers in the cool shade of the alcove. And then he stepped back, gave her a look of exquisite longing, and walked away.

There, he thought, feeling better. *That ought to do it.*

At the bachelor party that night, Colin got drunk and tried to fix Drew up with one of his law school friends who was in town for the wedding.

"She's great, man," Colin told him, with one arm draped over Drew's shoulders. "Beautiful, smart, funny. I used to date her for a while, back in the day."

"But you stopped dating her, and you probably had a reason," Drew pointed out.

"I did have a reason. She dumped me," he said cheerfully. "I was kind of an asshole in law school, so that just shows her good judgment."

The party was being held at a bar down in San Luis Obispo, mainly because everyone was sick of Ted's. Rather than doing the designated driver thing—because nobody wanted to get stuck with the job—Colin had hired a private bus to take everyone down the coast for the party.

The bar was a few steps up from Ted's in terms of cleanliness and decor, so it was more in keeping with Colin's refined sensibilities. Classic rock blasted through the sound system, and some thirty guys who'd come down on the bus were in various stages of intoxication. Groups of Colin's male friends and relatives were playing pool, throwing darts, drinking, and chatting up the local women with greatly varying levels of success.

"Seriously, you should give Amanda a call," Colin went on.

"I think I'll pass."

"But why?"

Drew scrambled for excuses. "Well, for one thing, I live on an island more than three thousand miles away from her." Amanda practiced law in Boston, and it seemed unlikely that they could conduct a fledgling relationship across the miles—not to mention the international border.

"Drew, for God's sake. You're rich. Buy a jet."

Colin was undoubtedly the only Delaney who would ever offer the advice to just buy a jet. Sandra reused plastic bags and fretted over the high cost of milk.

Drew considered pulling out the *I'm not ready* excuse, but it had been a few years now since his divorce, so that was unlikely to fly with Colin.

So, he opted for the truth—or, at least, part of it.

"I'm kind of hung up on somebody."

Colin's eyebrows shot up, and he smacked Drew on the back. "Really? That's great. Who is she? And most importantly, is she hung up on you, too? I need another scotch. Let me buy you a scotch." Colin signaled to the bartender, who poured a finger of twelve-year-old scotch for each of them. Somebody behind Drew at the bar jostled him, and his drink sloshed in the glass as he picked it up.

"I think she might be," Drew said. "Hung up on me, I mean. Maybe. At least, I hope she is."

"Well, good! Out with it. Who is she?" Colin didn't seem like he was going to let it go, so Drew was almost relieved when Liam came up to the bar and clapped a hand on Colin's shoulder.

"Pool tournament. Come on," he told Colin. Then he shot a glance at Drew. "You too, shithead. Come play pool."

The *shithead* part made sense, but the thought that Liam wanted to include him in the tournament did not.

"You want me to play pool with you?" It might have been the fact that Drew was a little bit drunk, but he needed clarification.

"We're playing for cash, so hell yeah," Liam said. "I'm going to clean your goddamned clock."

Drew didn't especially want his clock cleaned, but it seemed unmanly to say so.

"I'd like to see you try," he said instead.

The first game in the tournament was between Liam and Colin. It became apparent halfway through that Liam hadn't brought Drew over here to take his money. He'd brought him over here to assert his claim over Megan.

"So, I've pretty much decided I'm going to do it," he said as he leaned over the table and lined up a shot. "I'm going to ask her." He shot a side-eyed look at Drew as he said it.

"Yeah?" Colin was leaning against the wall, his cue propped up in front of him. "Well, that's great, man. Good luck."

"I don't need luck. Why do you think I need luck? You think she's going to say no?"

Colin shrugged. "I didn't say that. It's customary to wish people luck at times such as these, since you don't seem to be familiar with the etiquette."

Liam scowled and took his shot. The nine ball bounced off the far side of the table and missed the corner pocket.

Drew listened to all of this and knew it was for his benefit. He wondered if Liam had seen him kiss Megan the day before, but he knew that wasn't possible. If Liam had seen him, then Drew would be nursing a broken nose right about now and planning for the replacement of his missing teeth.

The territorial nature of it all was starting to piss him off. Megan wasn't a possession, she wasn't a trophy he could put on his mantel or a blue ribbon he could wear on his shirt. She was a living, breathing human being, and marriage was a serious endeavor. The idea that Liam would ask her to marry him just to

keep her in line and assert his dominance over Drew was enough
to make Drew want to break a pool cue over the guy's head.

"Are you sure that's a good idea?" Drew said, before he'd
even known he was going to say it.

"What do you mean?" Liam narrowed his eyes at Drew.

"I mean, are you sure she wants to marry you?"

Liam stood up straight from where he'd been bent over the
pool table. "Why? You know something I don't?"

"No. I'm just saying, it would be pretty embarrassing if you
propose at the reception, in front of all those people, and she
says no."

"She's not going to say no. What makes you think she's
going to say no?" Liam was up in Drew's face now, chest to
chest with him in an effort to intimidate him. It was working.
Drew had to fight the natural instinct to back away.

"Because it's what I would say if a dick like you—"

"Hey, hey, hey." Colin shoved himself in between the two
men, one hand flat on Drew's chest, the other on Liam's as he
shoved the two of them apart. "As much as I think it would
make a good story if a bar fight broke out at my bachelor party, I
think you two should calm down."

"Right." Drew put up his hands in surrender. "Right.
Sorry."

"He called me a dick," Liam pointed out.

"Yeah, and you called him a shithead over there at the bar,"
Colin reminded him.

"Well."

"Look. I'll just go over there and talk to Mike," Drew said,
gesturing toward the far end of the room.

Liam nodded toward the pool table, where he'd dominated
the play so far. "Like hell you will. I'm winning."

Drew went back to the hotel that night feeling mostly like shit. Part of it was the alcohol, no question. But part of it was everything that had happened with Liam.

He'd had some time to reflect on the bus ride back into town, and part of what he thought about was that, in his head, he'd accused Liam of using Megan like an object instead of thinking of her as a person. But Drew was doing the same thing, wasn't he? When he thought about taking Megan away from Liam, wasn't it at least partly about winning? About taking Liam's arrogant, bullshit attitude down a notch and proving that Drew was worthy of respect?

He wasn't feeling too worthy of respect at the moment. Megan deserved better than this. He wanted her, yes, and that was real and had nothing to do with Liam. But it was all tangled up with his feelings about his family, and nothing good was likely to come of that.

Drew checked on Eddie, fed him, and cleaned his litter box. The cat looked okay. He still wasn't himself, but he'd made a bit of a comeback since his time with Megan. Drew stroked Eddie's head and his sleek back, and said, "She's pretty great, isn't she?"

He stripped off his clothes, fell into bed, and turned out the light.

A man needed to be clear about his motives, and a man needed to be able to fall asleep at night feeling good about his choices.

He went to sleep promising himself that he wasn't going to kiss her again, or have lunch with her again, or make up reasons to see her again until she was through with Liam.

What if Liam proposed and she said yes?

He tried to tell himself that wasn't possible, but he knew it was.

If she did—if she said yes and threw her arms around Liam at the reception in front of Drew and everyone else at the wedding—he was going to feel something inside of him die. Some essential kernel of hope that love was possible for him, and that it might be possible with Megan.

And if that happened, he was going to shake Liam's hand and offer his congratulations.

He hoped it wouldn't come to that, because he couldn't get her out of his head. The kisses, yes, but also the part when they'd just been together quietly, when they'd just talked.

He hadn't felt comfortable talking to anyone in a long time. After learning about Redmond, and then with his divorce, he'd been so closed up with his grief and his hurt and his sense of betrayal that he'd built up walls of pain and resentment keeping everyone out.

Problem was, they also kept him in.

Just get through the wedding, he told himself.

Chapter Thirteen

When Drew had kissed Megan at Hearst Castle, she hadn't known how to react. Her senses had been so overloaded with lust and surprise and fear that they would get caught that she'd kind of blown a circuit and had been unable to do or say much of anything.

But now, as she lay in bed thinking about the day and everything that had happened, a number of thoughts competed with each other.

One, where did Drew get the nerve to kiss her like that out in public, where anyone could have seen them? Two, she couldn't wait—really couldn't wait—for him to do it again. And three, she seriously had to break up with Liam.

Was Liam really planning to propose at the wedding? God, she hoped not. There was no way that would end well. She would have two choices: Say no with two hundred people watching, which would humiliate Liam, or say yes, endure the happy congratulations of everyone in the room, and then say no later, leaving Liam the task of explaining to everyone what, exactly, had gone wrong.

There was only one solution: He couldn't propose. She either had to break up with him before then, or she had to stop him from going through with it.

If she broke up with him before the wedding, he wouldn't take it well, and Colin and Julia's big day would be marred by the tension and anger and hurt feelings left in the wake of a breakup like roadkill behind a big rig.

"I never should have let it go this long," she said to Bobby as he snuggled up against her on the bed.

She should have cut Liam loose as soon as she realized things between them weren't going anywhere. But there had been so many reasons not to. She hadn't wanted to hurt him. She had thought maybe they could work things out. And she hadn't wanted to be alone.

"I'm a wuss," she said.

Bobby licked her arm.

The next day on the Wedding Week schedule was kayaking at San Simeon Cove. Drew usually enjoyed kayaking; he was generally enthusiastic about anything that involved some kind of vehicle that went on water.

But he couldn't bear the idea of kayaking side by side with Liam, with Megan somewhere nearby wearing a bikini.

He didn't even bother to beg off on the phone with Julia or Isabelle, because they would lay guilt on him and would probably talk him into going. Instead, he got up in the morning, checked on Eddie—who looked to be somewhat improved—fed the cat, and then had a muffin and coffee in the hotel's breakfast room.

Then he decided it was time to address something that had been on his mind for quite a while now.

There was no way Sandra was going kayaking—he couldn't picture it—so he waited until everyone who was going to San Simeon would already be out there. Then he drove to the Delaney Ranch hoping to speak to her privately.

If he was ever going to make peace with the Delaneys or his biological father, or his newfound wealth, he needed some answers, and he was hoping she could give them to him.

The day was bright and clear, with a cool breeze coming in off the ocean. As Drew got out of the rental car and headed up the front walk toward the house, the sycamore branches that arced gracefully over the farmhouse swayed and whispered their secrets.

Usually when he visited the ranch, his own feelings about his circumstances blocked everything else out. But now he cleared his head and took a moment to take in the place. If he'd seen it under any other conditions—as a tourist, maybe, or as someone visiting a friend—he would have been dumbstruck by its beauty. Rolling hills clothed in golden grass; Monterey pines, sycamores, and oak trees dotting the landscape and providing shade; the ocean, blue and calm on the horizon; the barn, picturesque in the distance; and the house, looking serene and welcoming, as though it had been there, exactly where it belonged, since the dawn of man.

It struck him again as bizarre and improbable that he was part owner of this place. That had been a portion of his inheritance from Redmond: ten percent ownership in the property. Redmond had owned a half share, and he'd split that evenly among Drew and Orin's four children. This place was Drew's as much as it was anyone else's—as much as it was Liam's. But Drew felt like an intruder here, and he thought he probably always would.

He walked up onto the front porch and knocked on the front door. From somewhere inside, he heard Sandra holler, "Come in!"

He went into the house and found her in the kitchen, where she so often was, sitting at the big wooden table in the center of the room, drinking from a mug of coffee and doing a puzzle from a Sudoku book.

She looked up when he came into the room and raised her eyebrows in question.

"Well, boy, it don't look like you're kayaking, now does it?"

"Well … no."

"Playing hooky again, are you?" She let out a soft grunt. "Your mother's not going to be happy about that. Or your sister, I'll bet." She turned her attention back to the puzzle and entered a number into a square in pencil.

Drew sat down at the table across from her. "I just … I wondered if I could talk to you a little. About Redmond."

She pushed the puzzle aside and focused on him over the tops of her reading glasses. "Well, now, it's about time."

"It's been on my mind since I got here, and … well. Longer than that." In truth, the subject had been gnawing at him constantly since he'd learned the truth of his parentage.

"What is it you want to know?"

"Well … What was he like? What kind of man was he?" *And what kind of man denies his son's existence?* He didn't say the last part out loud, but the question was there between them, nonetheless.

Sandra focused her usual scowl on him. "You've known about Redmond for years now. And you're just now getting around to asking?" There was no judgment in her voice, just curiosity.

"I guess … before, I told myself I didn't want to know. I told myself that if he didn't want me"—emotion swelled in his throat, and he paused to force it down—"then I didn't care to know about him." Telling someone, finally, the truth about his feelings made him feel something loosen inside his chest.

"I guess I get that. But what's changed?"

He shrugged. "Time, I guess. I've had time to think. Time for all of it to sink in."

"*Hmph.*" She nodded in understanding. "Well, Redmond was something of a closed book, I can tell you that. Lived with him for decades, and I think the number of words he spoke in this house could fit on the back of a damned napkin. Why, when the news about you came out ... Well. Let's just say not one of us ever saw that coming."

Of course Redmond hadn't told anyone.

When Drew had first learned the truth, he'd been enraged at the Delaneys for failing to make contact with him, for letting him live his entire life never knowing where he came from. They'd told him then that they hadn't known until after Redmond's death, but that hadn't mattered. Drew had been angry, confused, and unwilling to accept what they were telling him.

Now, having had some time to let it all soak in, and having gotten to know the Delaneys a little, he could come to terms with what she was saying. They hadn't known. They hadn't found him, because they never knew he was there to be found.

"So I guess you can't give me any insight, then?" If he'd taken the initiative to seek out Redmond when he first found out, then Drew would have been able to speak to the man. Would have gotten some answers, maybe. But he'd waited until it was too late, and now, it seemed, he would never know any more than he did right now—which was damned little.

"Didn't say that." Sandra nodded in answer to a question only she knew. "Follow me."

Sandra got up from the kitchen table, went out into the main room of the house, and began climbing the stairs, with

Drew trailing behind. Upstairs, she made a left down a long hallway and opened the door to the room Drew knew had been Redmond's. She didn't go inside.

"Haven't changed a thing in there since the day he died," she told Drew. "Oh, I clean it every week. Dust, run the vacuum cleaner and whatnot. But I haven't taken anything out of there. I figure it's all pretty much the way he kept it."

Drew just stood there, frozen.

"But … why? Why didn't you pack it all up?"

She scowled. "Well, we're not keeping it as some kind of shrine, if that's what you're thinking. I left it for you." She nodded decisively. "Figured you'd want to take a look someday, maybe find some kind of memento to keep for yourself. I don't claim a man's belongings can give you all the answers to what the hell he was thinking, but if you're looking for clues, this'd be a place to start."

Drew's throat felt thick, not only at the idea of going through Redmond's things, but at the kindness. She'd saved everything for him, all this time.

"I … don't know what to say."

"I don't see as how you need to say anything. Just go on in, and see whatever there is to see."

Drew stepped into the room and looked around, and Sandra closed the door behind him, leaving him alone.

He didn't know much about what kind of man Redmond was.

He knew that Redmond was the kind of person who could spend most of his life sleeping in the same bedroom without ever moving on, without ever feeling that it wasn't enough. He knew that Redmond had kept to himself, because how else could he have kept his son a secret for so long?

But that was pretty much all he knew, and the questions far outweighed the answers. How was it that Redmond had spent most of his life without a woman in it? Why hadn't he met someone else? Why hadn't he gotten married, had children he could claim as his own?

Drew didn't know what he hoped to find in Redmond's room. Maybe nothing. But the way a man lived could tell a person a lot about him. The things a man kept close to him had to offer some kind of clues.

The room wasn't large. It was quite a bit smaller, in fact, than the room Drew himself was using at the hotel. The walls were covered in dark wood paneling, and the floor was rough oak planks covered in a simple braided rug.

Redmond had slept in a full-size bed with an iron headboard and footboard. A red plaid blanket was neatly spread over the mattress, and the pillows looked to have been recently arranged and fluffed. Probably Sandra's doing.

A small side table held a lamp and several framed pictures. Drew sat on the side of the bed and picked up the pictures, one by one. Orin and Sandra on their wedding day, Sandra looking impossibly young and pretty. Orin holding up a trout he'd just caught. The Delaney children standing in front of a Christmas tree, with Ryan, the oldest, looking to be about twelve years old.

And then there was a separate one of Liam, about five or so, smiling a gap-toothed grin.

One thing Drew knew from this room—Redmond had cared about his family. That made it hurt all the more that he hadn't cared enough about Drew to even meet him.

Drew went to the simple maple dresser that stood to one side of the room and opened each drawer. Redmond seemed to have few items of clothing, all of them practical and neatly stored. Levi's 501s. Plaid flannel shirts. Wool socks. White Hanes T-shirts, the kind you bought three to a package.

In the top drawer was a collection of random belongings: a pin from the Rotary Club. A sterling silver ring. A program from a school play Breanna had performed in. Some old prescription bottles, and a couple of greeting cards proclaiming HAPPY BIRTH-DAY! and MERRY CHRISTMAS!

And tucked into a corner of the drawer, he found a stack of yellowed, worn envelopes bound with a rubber band.

Drew pulled the bundle out of the drawer, pulled off the rubber band, and looked at the first envelope in the stack. The envelope was addressed to Isabelle McCray, Drew's mother. It had been marked RETURN TO SENDER in writing Drew recognized as Isabelle's. The envelope was still sealed.

Drew carried the envelopes over to the bed and sat down. He felt certain that it would be wise to be sitting for this. His heart hammered as he carefully opened the first envelope.

Inside was a check for six thousand dollars and a letter carefully written on a piece of white paper.

Dear Isabelle,

I understand why you don't want to hear from me. I don't want to hurt you or your family. But if you could send me news of our son, I would consider it a kindness. Please send a picture. Just one picture. He would be six months old by now, and I've never seen him. A father should know the look of his son.

Redmond

Drew's breath had been taken from his lungs. He clutched the letter, staring at the words. He'd known that Redmond had written to Isabelle, but seeing the letter, seeing what he'd written in his own hand, felt real. It felt like Redmond, for this moment, was here with him.

He'd assumed that Redmond hadn't wanted him, that he'd simply impregnated Isabelle and walked away. Drew had felt so much anger over that, so much pain. But now, what he was seeing was challenging all that he'd assumed.

His mother had been the one who had kept Drew from knowing Redmond. It had been Isabelle.

He opened the other letters one by one. Each one contained much of the same. Usually, there was a check accompanied by a plea to see Drew, or at least to get news of him. A picture. Some indication that the boy was well, and that he was well loved.

Drew didn't even realize he was crying until a tear plunked down onto the letter in his hand, wetting the paper.

He also didn't realize that Sandra had returned and was standing in the doorway. How long had she been there, watching him?

"Must have been hard, reading what's in those letters," she observed, her arms crossed over her body. He looked up, and she nodded once. "I don't know what's in them—never looked at 'em, myself, even though I knew they were there."

Drew wiped his face with his hands, stacked the letters and the checks, and rewrapped them with the rubber band.

"He wanted to see me," he said, his voice rough. "That's what all of the letters are. Him asking about me, asking to see me or at least get a picture. She never opened them. She couldn't even bother to read them."

The focus of the anger that lived in him was shifting from Redmond to his mother. How could she leave him with so many questions, so much doubt?

"I expect she did it to protect her family," Sandra said. "Not saying it was right, but it was probably what she thought she had to do, for you and Julia."

"And for my dad," Drew said. Andrew McCray, the man who'd raised Drew, the only dad he'd ever known, would have suffered a devastating blow if he'd learned that his son had been fathered by another man. And Isabelle no doubt would have faced an enormous amount of upheaval—divorce, shared custody of her children with a man who'd surely have been full of anger and resentment.

"Sometimes you do what you've got to do to protect the people you love," Sandra said. She came to sit on the bed beside Drew. "Even when it's hard, even when part of you knows it's wrong to keep a secret like that. You do the best you can at the time."

"I can see why she did it," Drew said. "I can't imagine what that would have been like—my parents divorced, me and Julia shuttling back and forth between parents." He shook his head at the thought. "But she lied. For my whole life, she lied."

"Well, she did," Sandra agreed. "I imagine that's a conversation you'll be having with her sooner or later."

"I didn't get to know Redmond," Drew said. "I never got to do that, and now I'm too late."

Sandra put her hand on his shoulder, and this simple, warm touch from her was so surprising and so comforting that he wondered if he'd simply willed it.

"You can get to know us," she said. "We're not him, but we're not bad."

He looked at her, and gave her a half grin. "I was, though. The last time I was here, I wasn't exactly gracious to all of you."

"*Hmph.*" She slapped her hands onto her thighs and stood up. "Always time to change that, boy. Gonna take some work to make up for it. I expect you'll manage, though." Her face was arranged in her usual stern expression, but he thought he saw a hint of a smile there, too.

"I'll try."

Chapter Fourteen

Drew had meant it when he'd told Sandra he would try. And trying meant he needed to make a sincere effort to get along with all of the Delaneys—even Liam. Drew had been an asshole to the Delaneys in the past, and he didn't want to be one any longer. And kissing Megan, or moving in on her in any other fashion, would certainly qualify as asshole behavior.

He promised himself anew that he would let her be—at least for now. He knew that the best course of action would be to step away entirely, but he didn't know if he could do that. So instead, he told himself he would keep her at a distance until she had completely resolved things with Liam.

He told himself he would treat Liam the way he, himself, would want to be treated if he were the guy who was about to get his ass handed to him by a woman. It still wouldn't be any fun for Liam, but at least Drew wouldn't carry any of the blame for his heartache.

Drew was feeling pretty good about his decision—until Megan texted him early that afternoon after everyone had returned from kayaking.

I missed you today.

And, ah, shit, there went his resolve.

She missed him?

The thought of her actively missing him made him nearly weak-kneed. Because he'd missed her, too. He'd thought about her out there on the water, her skin smooth and glowing in the sun.

So many feelings—jealousy, lust, longing—warred within him, and he thought it would almost be worth all of the inner conflict just to be anywhere near her.

He answered her text with his own:

I had business to take care of.

A moment or two later, his phone pinged:

What kind of business?

His response was one word:

Redmond.

Drew wanted to kiss her, wanted to do much more than kiss her. But he found that he also just wanted to talk to her, to be with her. He wanted to tell her everything that had happened today, and what he'd found when he'd looked through Redmond's room.

He knew that was a bad sign. Wanting to sleep with someone was one thing. Over the years, he'd wanted to sleep with any number of women. But when your emotions were churned up and all you wanted was to tell the person everything you were feeling, well, that meant you were in more trouble than mere sexual attraction could ever bring.

Are you okay? she asked.

That was an invitation, he knew. An invitation for him to let her in, to open up his heart to her. And he wanted to do it. God, how he wanted to do it.

I'm not sure.

He stared at his phone, waiting for what she would say to him now. Because whatever it was, it was going to set the tone for what happened next. Something distant and vaguely sympathetic, and it meant they would be dancing around each other for God knew how long. Something more intimate—more sincere—and it meant they would be hurling themselves into the abyss of whatever cataclysmic passion each of them was capable of.

Do you want to talk? I can come over.

He stared at the text message with blood pounding in his ears.

So, the abyss it was.

God help him.

They fell on each other the moment she arrived at the door of his hotel room. He opened the door, saw her, and pulled her to him, his mouth covering hers in a kiss that held all of his need, all of his hurt, all of his tentative, fragile dreams.

He devoured her, tasting her, holding her to him as though his very life were at her mercy.

Megan gave everything back to him, clinging to him, gathering fistfuls of his shirt in her grasping hands.

He knew he shouldn't do this—knew he should back away and send her home. But all of his good intentions about the Delaneys and Liam and not being part of the man's heartache had vanished from his brain, annihilated in an explosion of chemistry and need.

Right now, he wanted her no matter who it hurt, no matter what damage it might do, no matter whether the earth itself should vaporize as a result.

"Megan." He breathed her name. It wasn't a question, wasn't a plea. He said the word with the wonder of having discovered the answer to all of life's mysteries.

She took his face in her hands and kissed him with desperate urgency. He tasted her and touched her, claiming her with his hands on her body.

Having realized that they were still standing in the open door of the hotel room, visible to any of the tourists who might be passing by on Moonstone Beach, she shoved him into the room and swung the door closed with her foot. Then he pushed her back against the closed door with a thump as he thrust his hands under her shirt and over her smooth skin.

Her eyes closed and she gasped at the feel of his rough, urgent touch. He pulled down the cups of her bra and grasped her bare breasts in his hands, and she groaned, no longer thinking, no longer reasoning. The peaks of her nipples responded to his touch.

She'd been thinking about him, wanting him, since the moment they'd met, and now, having his hands on her was so much more than it had been in her fantasies. But it didn't feel new. It felt as though her body recognized him, as though it had come home.

In the moment, everything about this felt right, as though it were meant to be. As though she'd always been waiting for him.

She pulled his T-shirt off over his head and kissed his warm skin, running her hands over his chest. Then she stopped and lifted her eyes, just for a moment, and saw him looking at her with such passion, such desire, that she was lost.

"Stay with me." His voice was ragged.

She unbuttoned her shirt, slid it off of her shoulders, and let it fall to the floor. That was all the answer she gave, and all he needed.

In that moment, he was so grateful to her that he felt the rush of it through his entire body, releasing tensions he hadn't known he had.

He took her hand and led her to the bed.

Making love with Megan was not like it had been with Tessa, or with any of the women he'd been intimate with before. He'd enjoyed other women, yes. But this felt like an entirely different type of act than what he'd known.

It was like she'd been made for him, and he knew that was bullshit—the kind of thing you read about in sappy books or heard about in love songs. And yet, that was how it seemed. Like her body, her curves and planes, had been made to fit his.

This didn't feel just like sex—it felt like he was worshipping her, soothing his soul at the altar of her body.

He undressed her, kissed the length of her, ran his hands along her smooth, trembling skin. Slowly, to make this last as long as he could, he touched her with his fingers, the palms of his hands, his tongue.

She tugged at him, trying to pull him up to her as he pressed a kiss to her inner thigh, but he wouldn't be rushed.

"*Ssh*." He soothed her, caressing her with gentle hands. "Not yet."

He ran his tongue up the tender skin of her leg with agonizing slowness, listening to her little gasps of pleasure, her ragged breath. Then he eased her thighs apart and tasted the core of her as she tangled her hands in his hair.

"Oh … God. Oh." Her body began to shake, and then the orgasm ripped through her like an explosion, leaving nothing but devastation in its wake.

"Drew … Oh, my … Please …" She pulled at him again, but he continued to plunder her with his tongue and his fingers until she rose up, up, up again, crying out in an exquisite spasm of pleasure.

By the time he entered her, he was so close to the edge that he was afraid he wouldn't be able to last. So he moved slowly, teasing both of them, until the tension was unbearable. Then he buried his face in a tangle of her hair and gave her everything he had, clinging to her body, moving faster and harder until he, too, felt himself break apart in a blinding spasm of release.

For a minute, he didn't know his name, where he was, who he was, or even how he got here. He didn't know anything but the shining, pulsing pleasure rushing through him. When it finally receded, he seemed to have lost the power of speech.

That didn't matter; he didn't need it. All he needed was Megan, and he clung to her as they both drifted off into a light sleep.

Chapter Fifteen

Later, they talked a little about Liam and Redmond, and about Tessa.

"You're the first woman I've been with since my ex," he told her as they lay side by side under the covers of the hotel bed. He said it lightly, as though it were idle conversation, but to him, it was an important confession, a signifier of what being here with her meant to him.

"The first? And your divorce was …"

"About three and a half years ago."

"But …"

He tried to explain. "I just wasn't … Look. Tessa left me because I was too wrapped up in all of my feelings about Redmond and my dad. I didn't have room for anything but that. For anything but the anger and the hurt. I didn't have room for her." He'd known that, but this was the first time he'd said it just that way, just that plainly. "Then, once she was gone, there was Redmond's death, and the inheritance, and the Delaneys. And I was still all wrapped up in my feelings. Maybe more than before."

"You thought that if you got involved with someone, it wouldn't go well," she said.

"Well, sure. And it probably wouldn't have."

She was silent for a moment as she considered what he'd said.

"She should have stuck. She should have seen you through it. Even if she wasn't happy, she could have been there."

"Yeah, but how long?" He propped his head up on his hand. "I was one miserable bastard for a year and a half before she pulled the plug. At the time, I felt like a real victim, like she'd really screwed me. But now … I guess I can see her point. I couldn't have been much fun to live with."

"If you care about someone, you stick when they're in trouble," she said.

"Yeah, well."

She sat up and leaned her back against the headboard, pulling a sheet up around her body.

"So, what happened with Redmond?" She reached out and put a hand on his shoulder, and the one small gesture made his entire body warm.

When he'd found the letters, he'd wanted so much to talk to her about it. Now that she was here with him, he let all of it pour out.

"Sandra let me look in his room. She'd been saving everything—all of his things—for me. Which is an amazing gesture, when you think about it. So, I looked through his stuff, and I found some letters." He felt himself start to get emotional, and he took a deep breath to bring his feelings under control.

"What kind of letters?" she prompted him.

"To my mom. About me." He told her about the letters, about the checks and Redmond's pleas to see Drew, and the way they'd all been returned to him unopened. "I always assumed he didn't want me. From the time I found out about him, I assumed that he'd stayed away because he didn't want to have anything to do with me. But it was her, not him. She was the one who kept me from knowing him."

"Have you talked to her about it?"

He shook his head. "Not yet. I need to think. I need … She and I barely had any relationship at all for a couple of years after I found out. Now, we're putting things back together slowly, a little at a time. But this? This is a lot to take in. She kept me from my father, Megan. I don't know how we're going to move on from that."

The look she gave him was all tenderness and sympathy.

"She kept you from your father so you wouldn't lose your other father—the one who raised you."

He nodded, his mouth in a tight line. "Yes. I guess."

"And it was more than just you. If she and your dad had gotten a divorce, it would have affected your whole family. You, your dad. Julia."

He thought about Julia, about the close relationship she'd always had with Andrew, and how that would have been damaged if she'd been shuttled back and forth between the homes of two divorced parents. But Isabelle had also been thinking about herself.

"My mother was saving her own skin," he said.

"Yes, sure. But she was saving her family, too."

"I guess." He rubbed at his face with his hands. "Colin says I need to get over myself and move on. Accept things, so I can go forward, you know? He's right. I need to do something about the money, and the property … other than pretending it's not there. And I need to start getting to know the Delaneys better. They're my family."

And that naturally led to a topic neither one of them wanted to talk about—though they knew they had to.

"I guess this—us—isn't going to help your relationship with Liam much," Megan said.

"I guess it's not."

She sat up straighter and held the sheet around her body, facing him. "Look, Drew. I don't want you to think that I ... I know this looks bad, me cheating on Liam, but ..."

He gave her a wry smile. "Does it look worse than me sleeping with my cousin's girlfriend?"

"Yes! It does! And I don't do this. I've never ... But Liam and I ..."

"Don't." He cut her off. "Don't make what happened between us something you're ashamed of. Please." He didn't think he could stand it if he turned out to be a mistake she'd made, or a thing she felt guilty about.

"I'm not doing that. I just want you to understand. Things between me and Liam haven't been right for a long time."

"All right." There it was, her expression of regret again. He didn't want to be something she regretted. He didn't want that at all.

They were quiet, and he lay back and pulled her into his arms.

He'd thought that he didn't want to talk about Liam, but after a while, he couldn't help asking.

"So ... what went wrong?"

She sighed. "Oh, I don't know. A lot of things. He's angry. He's sad. A lot of it has to do with grief over Redmond, I think, but ... I also think some of it's just Liam. I couldn't break through it. I couldn't get through the anger and the sadness to the real him, you know?"

He nodded and stroked her back. As she spoke, he could feel the vibration of her voice in his chest.

"And things between us just moved too fast. We started dating while he was out here for Redmond's funeral, and that was good. That was fine. But then just a few months later, he moved out here to be with me. I didn't ask him to do that! I didn't know where we were going at that point. We were just getting to know each other. And then … he made this *gesture*! And it was a really big gesture." She sat up again and looked at Drew. "You know, nothing puts a relationship on the fast track like moving halfway across the country to be with someone. I just wasn't ready for that, but nobody asked me. It just happened, and I was kind of pulled along for the ride."

He rubbed at his forehead and winced. "You know, that was partly about Julia. About Colin moving out to Montana to be with her. He and Liam switched places. At the time, Colin said it was a win-win. I guess it wasn't a win for you."

"I wish he'd said he came out here to be with his family. Then it might have been okay. But he said he came for me. And it was just all too much."

He didn't want to ask the question, but he needed to.

"Is that why you're here with me? Because you need to distance yourself from Liam? Is this some kind of—I don't know—some kind of gesture of independence?"

She shook her head, and tears pooled in her eyes.

"No. No. This is … God. I couldn't *not* be with you."

It was the answer he'd wanted to hear. It was how he felt, himself. He couldn't not be with her. It was as though the choice had been made for him long ago, by some force beyond his understanding.

"Yeah. I know." She lay on top of him and he kissed her, and at least for the moment, everything else went away.

Everything but the two of them.

***

She was at the door of the hotel room, about to leave, with her clothes carefully arranged and her purse in her hand, when Drew asked the question.

"When are you going to break up with Liam?"

He was standing there looking impossibly appealing, wearing nothing put a pair of jeans. His hair was still mussed from bed. She could see that he was trying to be casual, but she could also see from the tension around his eyes and the way he didn't know what to do with his hands that it was an act.

"I was planning to do it after the wedding," she told him. "You know—to avoid wedding drama."

He nodded, rocking back and forth slightly on his feet.

"I think you've got to do it now. Unless … I mean, if we're going to keep seeing each other. And I hope to God we will."

For a moment, Megan was amazed that he could wonder whether she wanted him. Of course there was no question of whether they would be together. How could he believe there was?

"Of course we will. Drew. Of course."

He relaxed visibly.

"Okay, then … I think you need to do it now."

She leaned in and kissed him once, though it was so hard to stop at just once.

"I will."

"Really?"

"Yes."

He nodded. "Okay, that's … okay."

She said goodbye to him, got into her truck, and sat behind the wheel in the hotel parking lot for a while, just sitting there, looking out at the ocean with the sun still high above the horizon.

After a minute, she got her phone out of her purse and turned it on. She'd turned it off when she'd arrived, knowing Liam would call her, and knowing she wouldn't be able to face the guilt if he did.

When the phone powered up, she did see missed calls and texts from him, as she'd expected. But there were also several others from Ryan, Colin, and Breanna. That was unusual. What was going on?

She checked her texts.

From Ryan:

Call me as soon as you get this.

From Colin:

Megan, I need to talk to you right away.

And from Breanna:

WHERE ARE YOU???

She felt a chill run through her. Something had happened. Something bad.

The way Ryan told it went something like this:

When they'd all come back from the kayaking thing, he and Liam had gone out into the pasture to check on the stock. The mare Liam usually rode had thrown a shoe, and she was out of commission until they could get the farrier out there to fix it. So, he was riding a big, black Arabian that they hadn't had very long.

It was late afternoon, with the sun sinking down below the tree line, when Ryan and Liam were bringing in a pregnant heifer that Ryan thought would deliver that night. The heifer was agitated—part of the reason Ryan was convinced that it was almost time for her to calve—and didn't want to go.

Ryan didn't see exactly what happened, and later, Liam would say that he didn't remember much of it himself. Maybe the heifer spooked Liam's horse somehow. Maybe the horse just wasn't used to Liam. Maybe something else happened—a snake, or a problem having to do with the tack.

Whatever it was, Liam's horse reared up just as he was leaning over to secure the heifer. He wasn't ready for it, and he toppled off the back of the horse and hit the ground hard. That, in itself, probably wouldn't have done much damage. But then the horse brought one of his front hooves down onto Liam's lower leg.

Ryan heard the bone snap from twenty feet away.

Liam hadn't lost consciousness, but the leg was badly broken. There was no bone poking out anywhere—thank God for that—but legs weren't supposed to bend the way Liam's had.

Ryan had called Orin, who'd brought a four-by-four truck out into the pasture.

Ryan and Orin had hoisted Liam up onto his good leg and loaded him into the truck, with Liam spewing a string of obscenities that was extreme even for him.

There had been some discussion about whether to call an ambulance, but Orin decided that by the time it got out there, they could have Liam halfway to the hospital in Templeton.

The drive out of the pasture had been long and arduous because Orin was doing his best not to let the truck jostle too much, in an effort not to torture Liam. But that wasn't easy, as they didn't have the benefit of a road. Orin tried to balance the need to get Liam help quickly with his desire not to make his son wish the horse had killed him.

The results were mixed.

By the time they moved out of the pasture and onto a relatively level road, they'd had to stop once to let Liam open the passenger door and vomit into the grass.

By the time Megan got to the hospital, most of the Delaneys were gathered in the emergency room waiting area, Liam was drugged up on painkillers, and a series of X-rays had shown that Liam had a comminuted fracture of the tibia and fibula—which meant that both of the bones in his lower leg had been crushed.

"He's gonna need surgery," Orin told her as he stood there in the waiting room, blinking and shifting uncomfortably from foot to foot. "I guess things like this happen, especially with a horse you don't know and who doesn't know you. Couldn't have been helped, I suppose, with Liam's mare being sidelined." He shook his head. "It's a hell of a thing to see your son hurt like that." He sniffed slightly and rubbed at his nose. "A hell of a thing."

Chapter Sixteen

Drew heard about Liam shortly after Megan left the hotel room. First Julia texted him, and then Sandra called.

He didn't think he'd ever known Sandra to be shaken by anything, but when he heard her voice over the phone, his first thought was, *Someone's dead.* She had that sound, that mixture of shock and despair.

As it turned out, nobody was dead, but Liam's accident posed the real risk that he might have permanent disability to the leg—pain, lost range of motion, a persistent limp. Liam was a man who did hard physical work. What would he do if he couldn't perform that work anymore? Of course he didn't need to work to make a living—in that way, he was so much more fortunate than others facing similar injuries—but he needed the work for his self-image, for his emotional well-being. Drew didn't have to know Liam well to know that.

"It's all going to depend on the surgery," Sandra told him. "The surgery goes well, then I suppose he'll recover, though it'll take awhile, and he's likely to climb the walls while he's waiting. But if it doesn't …"

"Is there anything I can do?" Drew asked, feeling completely ineffectual.

"Well, you're family, boy, and I figure family belongs at the hospital right now. Liam might not like you much, but he'll appreciate the gesture. So would I."

Drew was silent.

You're family.

He knew this was a potential turning point in his relationship with the Delaneys. Sandra was explicitly inviting him into the fold. If he showed up, then he'd be accepting his role as a Delaney. If he didn't, then he would be rejecting his place in the family in a way that wouldn't be easy to undo.

He'd been rejecting them for the past few years, in ways big and small. But now, he had to decide what stand he would take moving forward—what kind of man he meant to be.

He had to make the call.

"Okay. What's the name of the hospital?"

He showered, dressed, and was walking through the front door of the hospital in Templeton in under forty-five minutes. The Delaneys were gathered in the emergency room waiting area, huddled together on a bank of chairs near the reception desk.

Megan sat next to Breanna, looking sick and miserable. She avoided eye contact with Drew when he came in.

The family had been told about the results of Liam's X-rays and about the fact that he would need surgery to repair the damage. But they were still waiting for the orthopedic surgeon to meet with them to go over exactly what had to happen and when.

There was some discussion of whether to have Liam transferred to a bigger, better hospital—maybe someplace down in Los Angeles. But Ryan had Googled the surgeon to find out whether the guy knew what he was doing, and it turned out he did, so they decided it was best to avoid the trauma and hassle of a move and stay put.

While they waited, Liam was moved from the ER to a regular room, and the doctor arrived after what seemed like hours—he'd been doing arthroscopic surgery on somebody's knee.

The surgeon, a guy in his fifties with gray hair and wire-rimmed glasses, said a lot of words like "crush injury," "complications," and "rehabilitation." Drew felt a little woozy. He could only imagine how much worse Sandra and the others must have felt.

"Does Liam know all of this?" Megan asked in a voice barely above a whisper.

"I told him, but he's on morphine right now, so I'm not sure how much got through." The nametag on the surgeon's lapel said DR. M. HART.

Sandra had been concerned about possible head injuries, so that was one bit of good news: Dr. Hart reported that Liam's CT scan had shown no evidence of concussion.

"Okay. Okay," Megan said. Her eyes were welling up with tears, and Drew felt a rush of complex emotions he could barely sort out. One of them was concern for Liam, certainly. But the sight of Megan crying over another man—never mind that it was a man she'd been with since long before she knew Drew—made him want to hit somebody. But that would be distinctly counterproductive, so instead, he shoved his hands into his pockets and looked at the clean, white tile floor.

In an effort to think of someone other than himself, Drew asked, "Is he in a lot of pain right now?"

The surgeon shook his head. "No. With the pain medication, he's comfortable for now. There's going to be a certain amount of postoperative pain, but we'll manage that with medication as well."

Drew thought about that—about the cycle of pain and painkillers and potential addiction. He didn't know if Liam was prone to that sort of thing, and he hoped not. But he did know enough about Liam to know that he would be impatient with the recovery process. He'd want to get back to work as soon as possible, and that just wasn't going to be as soon as he would like. That part was going to be hard.

Julia was a few feet away, standing next to Colin and listening to the surgeon. Her face was tense, and she gripped Colin's hand so tightly her knuckles were white.

Drew went over to where she stood and put a hand on her shoulder. She looked at him gratefully.

After a while, some of the family went into Liam's room to see him. Drew didn't think he'd be particularly welcome, so he stayed back in a waiting room, where plastic chairs stood in sterile rows facing a wall-mounted TV in the corner.

A coffee urn stood on a table near the entrance, and Drew poured some into a Styrofoam cup just to give himself something to do.

"How is he?" he asked, when Sandra and Orin returned from Liam's room.

Megan was still with Liam, and Breanna had taken her boys to the cafeteria to find something to eat. Julia and Colin sat beside Drew in the waiting room. A few feet away, a family that included a harried-looking woman and three kids ranging in age from about two to ten sprawled across a bank of chairs.

"Well, I guess he's doing okay, considering," Sandra said. Her face looked pale. "He's pissed off at himself for letting it happen. Which is stupid, if you ask me. He didn't tell the damned horse to stomp on him."

Orin looked ruddy and vaguely ashamed—of what, Drew didn't know.

"You all can go in and see him," Sandra told them.

"Ah … no, that's all right," Drew said.

"You came all the way here from Cambria to show some damned support, so get on in there and show it," Sandra barked at him as he stood up from his chair. With hands that were wiry and strong from years of work, she took him by the shoulders, turned him around, and gave him a gentle but firm shove toward the waiting room door. "You, too," she told Colin and Julia.

At least Drew wouldn't have to go in there alone. He held back and let Colin take the lead as they trooped into the cool, white hospital room where Liam lay looking smaller than usual beneath a sheet and a thin cotton blanket.

Colin made small talk with Liam about how he was going to be fine, and not to worry about anything, and Julia said a few things about how she was just glad it wasn't worse.

But Drew didn't say anything, because he couldn't stop looking at Megan.

She was sitting in a chair next to Liam's bed, holding his hand. Drew couldn't take his eyes off that point of contact—Liam's hand in hers. His chest hurt, and he felt a pressure building up in his head.

Megan was looking at Liam with such compassion and love that Drew's first impulse was to leave the room, to run away, to fly back to Salt Spring Island and never come anywhere near Cambria again.

Was it possible that he'd misread the situation? Could it be that she really was in love with Liam, and that all it had taken was a badly broken leg for her to realize it?

He felt a sharp kick to his ankle and turned to see Sandra standing next to him, glaring at him with her particular Sandra scowl.

"You better pull it together, boy," she whispered as Colin and Julia talked with Liam. "You keep staring at that woman, everybody in this room is going to know you're in love with her. Unless you're ready to declare yourself right here and now in a damned hospital room."

He was not.

He took a deep breath to clear his head, then excused himself to use the men's room.

When he was safely hidden away amid the tile and porcelain, he went to a sink and splashed some water on his face, then dried it with a paper towel. He wadded up the towel, threw it into the trash, and stared at himself in the mirror.

Just what did he think he was doing, trying to steal a woman away from a man who was facing surgery and potential long-term disability? Especially when that man was his own family?

"This is stupid," he told his reflection. "This is just stupid. And … and wrong."

But even as he said it, he knew that what really seemed wrong was the idea that Megan might choose Liam over him.

He didn't know if he could go back in there and watch the two of them together and pretend nothing was wrong. If he tried, he was sure to give himself away to everyone the way Sandra had warned him he would.

As he stood there looking at himself, at his guilty face, he had one impulse: to run like hell.

Fuck it.

He'd come to the hospital, he'd shown his face. He'd done his family duty by being here. But now, he had to get out of here before he either started breaking things or declared his love for Megan in front of every Delaney in the place. Neither of those options seemed viable, so he left the men's room and headed past Liam's room, down the hall, and toward the exit.

"Hey. Where are you going?"

Drew turned to see Julia behind him in the hallway, looking at him in confusion.

"I … have to go." It was lame and vague, and there was no way she was going to accept it.

She didn't.

"Go where? Why? To do what?"

Drew stared at his shoes. "Eddie's in the hotel room alone, and I—"

"He's a cat. You give them a litter box and some kibble, and they're fine. What's really going on?"

It was annoying that Julia always could seem to tell what he was thinking. It had annoyed him when he was five and had lied about brushing his teeth or how many cookies he ate, and it annoyed him now.

"Why does something have to be going on? Why can't it just be that I have to check on the cat? Why does there have to be some kind of conspiracy?"

"That's a question—or three of them, really—and not an answer."

Damn it.

"Why do they need me here, anyway? Liam would probably rather have a visit from the guy who delivers his mail than from me."

"That's not the point."

Julia was as bossy with him as ever, but he noticed something else about her, too. She looked beautiful. She'd always been pretty, but something about her imminent marriage to Colin had made her glow. She looked—

Ah, shit. Her imminent marriage to Colin. Drew hadn't even stopped to think about what all of this might mean.

"The wedding," he said. "Is this … I mean, are you going to have to …"

"I don't know." She seemed to sag a little, as though some of that happiness he'd noticed in her had leaked out through a tiny, unseen hole. "Colin and I haven't had a chance to talk."

"If you have to cancel … All of these people in from out of town …"

"I know."

It occurred to him that he might have been acting a little bit selfish, thinking only about his own feelings. And yet, he still couldn't go back into that room and see Megan holding Liam's hand.

"Listen, Jules, I'll be back later. Or … I'll see you all at the house."

"Drew, you can't just …"

But he didn't listen to the rest of her sentence, because he was already walking down the hall and toward the hospital's parking lot.

Chapter Seventeen

Before he'd even gotten to his car, Drew started feeling like a dick for leaving. But he wouldn't let himself think about that. Instead, he drove out of the parking lot, got onto Highway 46, and headed back toward Cambria and his hotel.

As he drove past golden hills dotted with vineyards in the Paso Robles wine country, he chided himself for being so naïve. Had he really believed that he and Megan were in love just because they'd slept together? He was acting like a teenage girl. Sex was just that—sex. It was fun and physical, and that was that.

He didn't know what was going to happen with Julia's wedding, and a selfish part of him hoped—just a little—that it would get called off. Not that he didn't want to see Julia and Colin married, because he did. But it would be a lot easier on him if they sent everybody home and had some county official down in San Luis Obispo do it. That way, he wouldn't have to see Megan and Liam together any longer than necessary.

But another, better part of him pushed such thoughts aside. Of course he wanted his sister to have the wedding she'd planned and that she deserved. She'd been agonizing over arrangements for the event for a year, and had been looking forward to it with giddy excitement. If Liam's injury caused her to postpone the ceremony, she would no doubt handle it with grace. But underneath that, the disappointment would be crushing.

When Drew arrived at his hotel, he fed Eddie and checked on his condition. The cat, who was lounging on the bed atop Drew's pillow, seemed to be improving steadily, though he wasn't over the virus that had hit him at the beginning of the trip. Drew cleaned out the cat's litter box and paid the neglected animal a little attention, scratching him behind his ears and stroking his silky coat.

Then he locked the room and went out for a walk on Moonstone Beach, thinking that the exercise and the ocean air might help him clear his head.

He walked from one end of the wooden boardwalk to the other and then back again as the sun lowered toward the horizon. The weather was mild, and the sky was dotted with fluffy clouds that took on hues of pink and orange as nightfall neared.

As he walked, he couldn't get Megan out of his head.

He should have never gotten involved. He should never have gone there. Surely his experiences with Tessa had taught him something about restraint. About protecting himself from heartbreak.

It didn't help that right now, at the height of the sunset's glory, the boardwalk was loaded with happy couples holding hands, walking arm-in-arm, or pausing to gaze at the ocean and steal a kiss.

Right now, Cambria really sucked.

Just after nightfall, when Drew was back in his room, Megan called him on his cell phone.

He considered ignoring the call, but who was he kidding? Of course he was going to answer it. How could he not?

"Hey," he said. His attempt to sound causal was failing.

"Hey." The tense silence between them stretched out uncomfortably.

"So, how's Liam?" Drew gripped the phone too hard in his hand.

"He's … okay, I guess. Still drugged up, so he's pretty loopy. Sandra and Orin are with him."

The muscles in Drew's jaw bunched up tight. "Well, I guess you'd better get back to him, then."

"What's going on?" she said. "You were there in his room for maybe a minute, and then you were gone. Where did you go?"

"What difference does it make?"

"What do you mean, what difference? Drew? Do we have a problem here?"

How could he tell her what he was thinking, after just one afternoon together? After they'd barely met?

He couldn't tell her that he was in love with her. He'd sound like an ass.

"No problem," he said. "It's just, you seem to have your hands full with Liam."

When she spoke again, she sounded hurt. "You can't be angry with me because I'm showing him a little … what? A little compassion?"

He shouldn't be, and yet that seemed to be exactly what he was feeling.

He decided to take an extreme approach—honesty.

"Seeing you with him … I wasn't ready for it. You were holding his hand, and … it looked like you might still love him."

"I still care about him," she said. "I still care what happens to him and whether he's okay. What kind of person would I be if I didn't?"

He nodded. "Yeah. I know."

He wanted so much to ask her to break it off with Liam, but of course, he couldn't. Not now. Not with Liam injured and facing surgery. But where, exactly, did that leave the two of them?

Drew didn't know what to say, so he didn't say anything. He just held the phone to his ear, relishing that small connection with her, however tenuous.

"They're going to do the surgery tomorrow," she said after a while.

"Okay."

"They're going to have to use plates and pins to stabilize the bones, and he's going to have a long period of physical therapy afterward to get his full range of motion back. That's if everything goes well. If it doesn't …"

She left that thought out there—the thought of what if it didn't.

"All right."

"Drew? I can't end things with him. Not right now."

He'd known it, but it still felt like a gut-punch to hear it.

"You've got to do what you've got to do, I guess." He sounded petulant even to himself, but he couldn't seem to help it.

"Drew …"

He hung up the phone without saying goodbye.

She stared at the phone and couldn't believe it. He'd actually hung up on her.

She felt tears in her eyes, and swiped them away with her fingertips.

"Megan?" Breanna had come out into the hospital lobby, where Megan was sitting in a hard plastic chair.

Megan looked up at her, attempting to look bright-eyed and calm.

"Were you just in with him? How's he doing?" she asked, hoping that if she distracted Breanna, her friend might not notice how upset she was.

Breanna sat in a chair beside her. "Oh, he's higher than the Empire State Building, so I guess he's fine." She put a hand on Megan's shoulder. "Right now, I'm wondering about you. He's going to be fine, you know. They'll fix him up in surgery, and he'll be good as new."

Megan felt a little bit ashamed about the misunderstanding. Breanna thought she was teary-eyed over Liam, which, of course, she should have been instead of pining away over another man.

"Oh … I know." She let out a shaky laugh. "It could have been a lot worse. He could have had a head injury, or—"

"Not that anything could get through that thick skull," Breanna quipped. "Even a thousand-pound horse."

"Right." Megan nodded. "He'll be fine. I know."

"All right, then buck up, and let's go home. He'll be pretty out of it for the rest of the night, and he's in good hands."

"Okay." But the tears started to leak out of her, and she couldn't seem to get up from her chair.

"Unless … Megan, is there something else wrong?"

Breanna sat down next to her and put her arm around Megan's shoulders.

The compassionate touch, which she didn't deserve, was more than Megan could take. She burst into tears, looking down into her own lap so she wouldn't have to meet Breanna's eyes.

"It's me! I'm awful! I'm an awful person!"

"Oh, Megan. No, you're not. You're a wonderful person. Why would you think you're awful? If it's because we couldn't reach you at first when Liam got hurt, then … Why? Were you someplace you shouldn't have been? Because … Wait. Who were you on the phone with a minute ago?" As Breanna rambled on, having a conversation with herself, she suddenly gasped, wide-eyed. "Oh, my God! You were with him! You were with Drew!"

Megan cried harder and began rummaging around in her purse for some tissues. She found some, then wiped at her eyes and blew her nose.

Breanna's expression grew grim and determined. "Come on," she said, taking Megan by the arm and pulling her up out of the chair. "You can't let my mom see you like this. She'll know." She led Megan out of the hospital and toward her car.

When they were sitting safely inside Breanna's Toyota, Breanna turned to Megan. "Okay, spill. What happened?"

"You really do have your mother's gift, you know? That mind-reading thing …"

"Don't change the subject." Breanna pointed one finger at her.

Megan let her head fall back against the headrest, her gaze on the car's beige roof. "Okay, yes. I was with Drew. And I had my phone off. Because we were … busy."

"And by 'busy,' you mean that you two were wrestling naked," Breanna remarked dryly.

"Well …"

"Megan!" Breanna spoke with the frustrated, exasperated tone she often used with her boys. "Why did you have to do that? I mean, I knew you had the hots for him, but why couldn't you wait until you broke up with Liam?"

"I don't know!" she wailed miserably. "He'd found some letters that Redmond wrote to his mom, and he was upset. And I asked him if he was okay, and he didn't know, and so … I went over there. To talk! I just thought we'd talk!" But that was a lie, because she hadn't thought they would just talk. She'd had a pretty good idea what would happen if she showed up at Drew's hotel room, and yet she'd gone anyway. She just hadn't seemed to be able to help herself.

"And you didn't talk," Breanna said.

"We did. After."

"Oh, Megan."

Megan honked into her tissues while Breanna looked at her scornfully.

"Don't judge me!" she said. "Because I'm already judging myself."

In the parking lot around them, people made their way to and from the hospital. Families visiting loved ones, orderlies and cafeteria workers leaving work for the day. The parking lot lights began coming on as the last light of the day faded.

"Okay." Breanna put on a neutral expression. "Just tell me what happened."

So, she did. Megan told her about sleeping with Drew, and about how it had been a revelation. Then she told her about holding Liam's hand in the hospital room, and Drew coming in and seeing her.

"He was jealous, Bree. He said it looked like I still loved Liam. And I do! Just not that way. Not the way he needs me to. But Drew thinks … He thinks …"

"He thinks you're playing him," Breanna concluded. "He thinks he was just a good time. And from the sound of it, he was a *very* good time."

"He hung up on me," Megan said miserably. "Because I won't break it off right now, with Liam in the hospital on morphine."

"Come to think of it, doing it while he's on morphine might be a great idea," Breanna said.

"Bree!"

"Sorry."

As Megan pulled her emotions together, wiped her eyes, and drew in a long, shaky breath, Breanna appraised her.

"You're in love," she said.

"I really think I might be. Is that stupid?"

"Yes," Breanna said.

"Oh, God …"

"I'm joking," Breanna said. "Mostly."

"I didn't want this to happen." Megan felt the tears begin to come again, so she fought them back. "While I was still with Liam. I wasn't looking for this. But … it happened. And it wasn't just sex, Breanna. It wasn't just me trying to distance myself from Liam. It was … "

"Destiny?" Breanna offered wryly. "Love at first sight? Kismet?"

Megan looked at her. "Yes."

"Oh, shit. You're serious."

Megan just sat there miserably.

"Okay," Breanna said. "Let's recap. You've got one man who you've cheated on, but who you can't break up with because he's all injured and pathetic. You've got another man who you're in love with, but who's pissed off because you're already taken. You're all scheduled to be attendants at a wedding that might not happen now. And both of your men hate each other."

"Pretty much," Megan admitted.

"Well … It's not going to be dull," Breanna said.

Chapter Eighteen

Julia called Drew the next day, around ten a.m., to tell him that the wedding would go forward as scheduled—assuming all went well with Liam's surgery.

"I talked to him this morning. He thought it was stupid that we'd consider calling it off," Julia told Drew. "He said, 'Why the hell would you cancel the damned wedding just because of a broken leg?' Then he accused me of using it as an excuse to avoid marrying Colin. Even on pain meds, he seems like his usual self."

"Well, that's good," Drew said. "I guess he'll still be in the hospital and won't be able to come."

"It's possible he might be able to be there in a wheelchair. He's going to love that," she said dryly.

"Okay. Well, that all makes sense, I guess."

Julia's silence was a warning for him to brace himself for an interrogation.

"Where did you go yesterday?" she asked.

"When?" Playing dumb seemed like the thing to do.

"You know when. Unless you fled more than one hospital yesterday."

"I just … had some things to do." Could he have come up with a more lame line than that one?

"Like what? Laundry? Boat-building? Washing your hair?" The sarcasm in her tone made him feel petulant, as though he were a teenager rebelling against his parents.

"Things, Julia."

She sighed. "Well, I know from long experience that you're not going to tell me anything you don't want to tell me. Have it your way." Then, in a change of topic: "Even though we're going ahead with the wedding, we're canceling the rest of the pre-wedding events except for the rehearsal and the rehearsal dinner. Liam said that was stupid, too, but I thought it made sense."

Drew felt a surge of relief at the thought that he'd no longer have to do barbecues and picnics and who knew what else while trying to pretend that he wasn't in love with Megan. At least Liam's broken leg had accomplished that much.

"Yeah, I guess it does," he agreed.

"But that doesn't mean you're completely off the hook. Come out to the house today for lunch."

"Aw, Julia …"

"Just come," she said.

"But—"

"Sandra's expecting you." And then she hung up.

Shit.

Drew got to the house at around noon, fearing that he might find another huge get-together, the way he had on the day he'd arrived.

But Liam's injury apparently had put a damper on things, so he only found a few members of the immediate family—Sandra, Julia, Breanna, and Colin—and his mother.

Isabelle was sitting at the big kitchen table with a binder in front of her, fussing over the canceled events.

"Well, it's a shame that we won't be doing the picnic, because I was so looking forward to it—the grounds here are just wonderful! But, I guess it can't be helped. I called the caterer, and—" She stopped in midsentence when Drew came into the room.

"Well! There you are." She got up from the table and came around to give him a hug that was probably part genuine, part show. He received the hug stiffly.

"Mom."

Sandra was fussing around at the counter, fuzzy slippers on her feet, a utilitarian white apron tied around her middle.

"Well, come on in, boy," she said.

It felt surreal to Drew to have his mother here. But it probably felt even more so to Sandra. After all, it wasn't every day that your dead brother-in-law's secret lover commandeered your kitchen.

It was hard to look at his mother right now, given what he'd read in Redmond's letters. But then again, conflict with his mother over Redmond was nothing new.

Sandra glanced at Drew and then at Isabelle, sizing up the tension between them. When she began to talk about practical matters—scheduling, and Liam's surgery—he got the sense that it was her way of defusing the metaphorical bomb.

"Called the hospital this morning. Liam's doing okay, considering. Surgery's scheduled for three p.m., so I figure we'll have a decent lunch and then go out there. Megan's already with him." She gave Drew a meaningful look. "I'd say you should come along, Drew, but there's not much sense in you driving all the way out there so you can pop into the room for five seconds and then disappear."

Drew squirmed a little under the mild rebuke. "About that. I—"

"Now, don't use up any of your brain power trying to come up with an excuse." She plopped a thick ceramic bowl of salad onto the kitchen table with a *thwack*. "I figure you don't have enough to spare."

Isabelle, seemingly unaware of the undercurrents between Drew and Sandra, piped in.

"Drew, honey, if you're not going to the hospital, maybe you can help me with the final arrangements for the rehearsal dinner. It's tomorrow, after all, and I haven't even finished the place cards yet."

"What the hell do we need place cards for?" Sandra wanted to know.

"Why, I think they'll come in handy," Isabelle said, unperturbed. "Especially since there will be a few guests you don't know very well—Julia's relatives, my friends …"

"Well, I figure that's what introductions are for," Sandra grumbled. "It's why people talk to each other."

Isabelle either didn't hear Sandra's protests or didn't care. It was hard to tell. Either way, Drew was certain there would, in fact, be place cards.

When Julia came into the kitchen and saw Drew, she gave him a hard hug, then said, "So, are you coming to the hospital after lunch?"

"I—"

"He's gonna help your mother make place cards," Sandra broke in. "For the rehearsal dinner."

Drew seemed to be having his entire day—and, indeed, his week—mapped out for him in a way that was beyond his control. "I am?" he said.

Sandra shot him a look. "Well, I figure you are, unless you want to go out to the hospital with us, maybe spend some time with Liam and Megan before the surgery."

She planted her hands on her hips and looked at him with pursed lips.

So, those were the choices presented to him: Watch the woman he was in love with ministering lovingly to another man, or spend time with the mother who had deceived him his entire life about who he was.

Perfect.

"I ... guess I'll come to the hospital," he said.

"Well, fine then. You can ride with me," Sandra said.

"Oh, honey." Isabelle looked at him with disappointment. "I thought we could spend some time together."

He turned to Sandra.

"When do we leave?"

They left after lunch, when they'd all eaten their fill of the chicken sandwiches and salad that Sandra had put together. Isabelle stayed at the house to work on her place cards.

Julia and Colin went in Colin's car, and Drew and Sandra rode together in Sandra's pickup. Breanna stayed behind so her boys wouldn't have to spend hours in a hospital waiting room—a scenario that would do a disservice to the boys as well as to any patients within earshot of them.

Drew figured Sandra had assigned him to ride with her because she wanted to talk about Megan, and he was right. She started in before they were fully outside town limits.

"Well, I figure you haven't changed your mind about the girl," she said as they headed down Highway 1 toward Route 46. "Still wishing she was yours instead of Liam's."

"Sandra ..."

"Now, don't try to deny it. I've got eyes, haven't I? I saw how you looked when you walked into that hospital room and saw her holding his hand. Why, I'd have thought you were the one that'd been crushed by a damned horse."

"Are you going to lecture me about it? Because you can, you know. I deserve it." He slumped down in the passenger seat of the truck.

"Well, I don't see much point," she said.

And then she lectured him anyway.

"I can see that maybe she and Liam aren't exactly a match fated by God in heaven, or any of that happy crap," she said. "They've got their problems. So if somebody"—she looked at him pointedly—"thought he was going to make a play for her, then it wouldn't be completely out of left field."

He stared at the road and waited for the rest. It didn't take long.

"But she's not the kind of woman's going to abandon a man when he's down. And if she were, then you'd be some kind of fool to want her in the first place."

He knew she was right.

He no longer wondered how Sandra knew what she knew about the inner workings of his heart; he'd simply accepted that she did know more than he would have thought possible. Instead, he focused on the substance of what she was saying: By being there at Liam's side, Megan was just being Megan. And if she were any different, there wouldn't be a need for this conversation to begin with.

There was something else special about Sandra other than her near clairvoyance. Somehow, she made him want to open up to her, whether it seemed wise or not.

"It's not just that," he told her.

"What's not just that, boy? You mean something else has got you looking like the dog ate your last Pop-Tart?"

He scrubbed at his face with his hands.

"Yeah. Guilt."

She glanced at him as she drove. "Because you want Liam's girl? Or because you've done something more than just want?"

He groaned. "Sandra, it's kind of spooky the way you do that."

She let out a low chuckle. "Boy, when you've raised four kids, developing a sixth sense is just a matter of survival. Why, if I hadn't been able to tell what Liam was thinking, he'd have fallen off the barn roof and killed himself when he was twelve."

"Well."

Drew rode in silence for a while as Sandra waited for him to come out with it. Finally, he did.

"I thought … I thought I'd be able to wait. She told me she was having problems with Liam. So, I knew that. I knew the two of them were on their way out. So, I thought, I'll just see what happens. And then, at some point, if she's free, I'll get to know her a little, see where things go."

She shot him a look out of the corner of her eye as she drove. "Seems sensible enough. But it didn't work out that way."

"No. I was in Redmond's room yesterday, and I found his letters, and … I was upset. And later, she called me, and …"

He left the *and* out there to signify all of the many things that had happened between himself and Megan, all of the things that he wouldn't tell Sandra or anyone because they defied explanation or description.

"Boy, are you saying you were out of your mind with … what do they call it? Angst? And so you didn't realize where you were putting your pecker?"

"No. No. I'm saying … What I'm saying is that when I was upset, I didn't want to tell anyone but her."

Sandra considered that. "Well, listen, boy. I'm not much for judging others, because I've done some things in my life I'd rather not face the music for, if I can help it. But this is my boy we're talking about, and he's about to get his leg cut into."

"I know."

"Now, you and Megan are going to do what you're going to do, and I don't imagine Liam's going to stop you. I don't imagine I am, either. But now's not the time."

They rode wordlessly for a while amid the oak-dappled hills on the route to Templeton. The sky was a bright, cloudless blue. Here and there on the hills, cows grazed and mooed.

"I'll tell you something else," Sandra began, and Drew braced himself for a lecture about family, loyalty, faithfulness, and honor. "You're telling me you couldn't help your feelings, that you've got something more than just a strong yen for Megan, something that made you do things you otherwise wouldn't. That about right?"

"Yeah. That's about right."

"Well, you might consider that your mother felt much the same way when she met Redmond."

It wasn't what he'd expected to hear. He didn't know how Sandra felt about his mother, but he'd assumed it was some mixture of irritation and judgment, similar to, but much less loaded than, his own feelings.

The idea that she was defending Isabelle took him a moment to process.

"That's different," he said, because he didn't know what else to say.

She grunted. "Is it?"

"Well ..."

"All I'm saying is, you've done your best to ignore the woman since you got here. And I won't say I don't understand it, because I do. But she's your mother." Sandra took the turn that led toward Templeton, and shot a glance at Drew. "And she's only guilty of what you've done yourself, seems to me."

"She had a child from an illicit relationship, passed that child off as someone else's, then lied for thirty years."

Sandra chuckled. "Well, boy, give yourself time. You might be an underachiever now, but there's always the chance you'll catch up."

Chapter Nineteen

Megan didn't expect to see Drew at the hospital, especially after their ill-fated phone conversation. So when she came out of Liam's room on her way to the vending machines, she was surprised into speechlessness when she almost walked directly into his chest.

"I … oh." She skidded to a stop right before ramming into him, and fixed her gaze on his chest so she wouldn't have to meet his eyes. Sandra was with him, and she rolled her eyes extravagantly at Megan's reaction. Megan could feel her cheeks begin to burn with a blush.

"I was just … There are vending machines down the hall, and I …"

"Well, nobody's stopping you, girl," Sandra said when Drew couldn't seem to respond. "Get me one of them Kit Kats while you're at it, would you?"

"Sure."

"How's Liam?" Drew asked before she could leave, having finally found his voice.

"He's okay. Scared, but he won't show it. You know Liam."

"Well, I'll say I do," Sandra put in. "My guess is, he's about to rip the head off anybody who comes his way."

"That's about right," Megan said.

"Well, you first," Sandra said, giving Drew a little nudge toward the door of Liam's room.

If Liam was surprised or irritated to see Drew there, he didn't give any sign of it, possibly because he was engaged in an ill-tempered rant.

Ryan was standing next to the bed, and while he seemed to be listening good-naturedly, he also looked relieved when Drew and Sandra showed up.

"They've got the goddamned cooking channel on the TV, and the fuckin' remote doesn't work. Do I look like I want to learn how to make"—he looked at Ryan—"what was it again?"

"Béchamel sauce," Ryan supplied.

"Right. Do I look like I want to learn to make a fuckin' béchamel sauce?"

It was unclear whether he was addressing Drew or Sandra, but Sandra was the one who answered.

"Well, I figure the day you learn to cook anything that doesn't come out of a can, I'm going to be checking the sky for flying alligators."

"They're about to cut my goddamned leg off. Would a little baseball be too much to ask for?"

"Well, I guess it's wouldn't." Sandra went to Liam's bedside and took his left hand into both of hers. "Now, I know you're scared, but I don't figure they're really going to cut your leg off, son."

Liam frowned at her. "I didn't say I was scared. I said I'd like some damned baseball." He glanced grudgingly at the TV, where a chef was whisking something. "And some food. I haven't eaten anything since last night."

"The surgery—" Ryan began.

"Yeah, yeah, the surgery, blah, blah, blah," Liam groused. "Where's Megan?"

"Vending machines," Drew said.

"Actually, she's hiding out from you," Ryan said to Liam. "You wuss."

As the scheduled time for the surgery drew near, more family members and friends filtered in and out. Colin and Julia came, and then Breanna showed up with the boys, and then Orin made an appearance and reminisced about the surgeries he'd had in his lifetime: an appendectomy, a gall bladder removal, and during his long-ago childhood, the removal of his tonsils.

Megan returned and sat with Liam for a while, as did a couple of the ranch hands and a few guys Liam liked to drink with down at Ted's.

To avoid turning the whole thing into an impromptu party that would put undue stress on the hospital staff, they filtered in and out a few at a time while the others milled around in waiting rooms, in the cafeteria, and in the lobby.

Drew wondered if the big turnout indicated that Liam was in more danger than was immediately apparent. He wandered over to Colin, who was standing in the corner of the surgical waiting room, talking on his cell phone to somebody in Los Angeles about something having to do with the tax implications of a property sale.

When he was done and had tucked his phone into his back pocket, Drew said, "He's going to be okay, right? I mean, it's a broken leg."

Colin didn't offer immediate reassurance the way Drew had expected him to.

"I saw the X-rays," he said. "Looked like somebody stepped on a pretzel."

"Oh. Shit," Drew said.

"I mean, he's going to live. But that leg …" Colin shook his head and left the thought out there.

Suddenly, Drew started to get scared for Liam. He didn't like the guy—probably would never like the guy—but that didn't mean Drew wanted any harm to come to him. It didn't mean the man should end up permanently broken.

Across the room, Megan was talking to Julia. Drew watched her, the way her face lit with animation in response to something Julia was saying. He watched the way her hair fell into her eyes and she brushed it away. He watched her smile about something, watched the little space between her brows wrinkle in concern about something else.

There was a world of stories and emotions and possibility, just in that face.

When she finished with Julia and walked out of the room, back to Liam, maybe, or to somewhere else unknown, Drew wanted nothing more than to follow her.

But Liam needed her right now, he figured.

"She's not even standing there anymore, and you're still staring at the place where she's been," Sandra said to him under her breath. He hadn't even seen her walk up.

"What?" He'd barely heard her.

"You'd better pull yourself together, boy."

Drew had told himself that he would leave once Liam went into surgery, since there was nothing of practical use that he could do here. But when the time came—when Liam had been wheeled off by a couple of guys in scrubs—Drew couldn't seem to go.

So he settled in at a bank of chairs in the waiting room, feeling awkward. His long legs were stretched out in front of him, crossed at the ankles, and his hands were knotted together in his lap. There were Delaneys everywhere—in this room, in the hall-way, down at the coffee cart.

He was wrapped up in his thoughts—about Liam, his mother, Sandra, his inheritance, and everything—when Megan came into the room and quietly sat beside him.

They sat side by side in companionable silence for a while, until she said, "About me and Liam …"

Drew shook his head and then gave her a faint smile. "He needs you right now," he said.

They left it at that, and waited for news.

The surgery took several hours, amounting to numerous coffee runs, games of cards, reminiscences by the Delaneys of Liam's most memorable mishaps and injuries, and sitcom episodes on the TV mounted high in the corner of the waiting room.

Finally, when the sky outside the windows was dark and most of the hospital had quieted down, the surgeon came into the room to report that Liam's procedure had gone as planned. The bones had been repaired using a considerable amount of hardware, and he was expected to regain full function—though not without a good deal of recovery time and physical therapy.

The mood among the group went from anxious forced cheer to giddy relief. Liam would no doubt be a pain in the ass during his recovery, but he *would* recover. With that established, everyone's focus shifted to the practical matters of how to get Liam through the coming months, how to fully staff the ranch while Liam was out of commission, and how to proceed with the wedding with the minimum possible disruption.

"Well, I suppose I'm going to have to come out of semi-retirement for a while," Orin said, scratching his chin thoughtfully. They were all standing around, at loose ends while they waited for Liam to come out of the anesthetic so a few key family members—including his parents—could see him.

"No, Orin, you're not going to do that," Sandra said in a scolding tone. "You've got the thing with your back, plus your blood pressure. We've got plenty of sons ought to be able to pick up the slack."

"Sure," Ryan agreed. "And I can hire a couple more hands."

It didn't escape Drew's notice that it would take "a couple" of ranch hands to replace one of Liam. Possibly, he'd underestimated the man's skills and his worth.

"Maybe Drew here can pitch in." Colin slapped Drew on the back.

The suggestion took Drew by surprise. "I don't know anything about ranching."

"Neither does anybody, when they first get started. You'll learn."

Colin seemed altogether too pleased with himself for Drew's taste.

"But …"

"What else have you got to do the next few days?" Sandra asked, squinting at him in that way of hers that made you feel like she had X-ray vision of all of your inner workings.

"Well …" He struggled to come up with something, then seized on the one thing that came to mind: "Place cards."

Sandra scoffed, and it almost looked for a moment like she might smile. "Well, that's fine. You help your mama with the place cards. And when that fifteen minutes is up, well, I figure you can help out on the ranch."

By the time the chitchat, the obligatory visits to Liam's room, and the travel arrangements of who would ride with whom back to the ranch were settled, Drew was pretty much locked in, with no way to escape other than fleeing in the dead of night.

The thought did occur to him, more than once.

Chapter Twenty

Colin hadn't been much of a rancher, either, until a couple of years before, when he'd moved to Montana to be with Julia and had taken over the family's operation out there. Colin was a Harvard-educated lawyer, and his strong point was real estate—the buying of it, the selling of it, the managing of it, and the making of astronomical profit from it. But with all of the pre-wedding events except the rehearsal and rehearsal dinner having been canceled, even he put on his boots and his hat and got his hands dirty after Liam's surgery.

Drew was paired up with Colin the next day as they rode out into the pasture to check on the stock.

Drew knew how to ride—he'd been raised in Montana, after all—but it had been awhile, and his ass started to ache before the first half hour passed. That was the first indication that it was going to be a long day.

The second was when they found another pregnant heifer who seemed off, and Colin said she might be ready to deliver.

"We'd better bring her into the barn so we can keep an eye on her," Colin said.

"Isn't that how Liam got hurt?" Drew asked.

"No, Liam got hurt because he couldn't stay in the saddle. You do that, you won't have any problems."

"Sure," Drew said, trying to sound agreeable.

The morning was shrouded in a low fog, and the pasture, the rolling hills in the distance, and the cattle themselves all looked soft and gauzy in the diffuse early light. A cool breeze off the ocean did a little to cut the smell of cow shit and sweaty horse, but Drew still longed for the scent of sawdust in his workshop.

This time, there was no difficulty roping the heifer and leading her back to the barn. The difficulty came in when the labor didn't progress the way it was supposed to.

About an hour after they'd moved her into a calving stall, the amniotic sac had begun to emerge—a sight Drew was fairly sure would haunt his nightmares well into the foreseeable future.

When an hour passed and nothing else happened, except for the cow—and Drew, for that matter—becoming increasingly uncomfortable, Colin called Ryan to the barn, since Ryan had more experience with this sort of thing.

When he got there, Ryan took a look at the heifer's backside, then washed his hands, cleaned the back of the cow with some kind of solution, and put on a long plastic sleeve over his arm.

"Please tell me you're not going to do what I think you're going to do," Drew said, feeling increasingly queasy.

"I've got to check the calf," Ryan replied, as though he'd done this sort of thing all of his life. Which, of course, he had. "We should have seen two hooves and a nose by now."

He slathered the sleeved arm with some sort of lubricant and then, acting as though it were the most normal thing in the world, violated the cow in a way that Drew found objectionable not only morally, but aesthetically.

"Oh, God," Drew moaned.

"Hang in there, champ," Ryan said conversationally. "I've

just gotta—uh oh.”

Drew couldn't imagine what might be worse than seeing Ryan up to his shoulder in cow genitalia, but he had to ask anyway.

“ 'Uh oh,' what?” His knees felt a little weak, but he valiantly remained upright.

“The calf's breech. If I can just …” He rooted around in there while the cow—whose head was secured at one end of the stall, presumably to keep her from bolting or kicking the shit out of Ryan—shifted on her feet and mooed mournfully. “Well, shit.”

“What?”

“It's not gonna work. The calf's positioned ass first.” Ryan pulled out his arm, which was now coated with some type of goo that didn't bear thinking about.

“So, what does that mean?” Drew asked, feeling a little wobbly on his feet.

“It means that calf's not coming out on its own. Call the vet, would you?”

As Colin got out his cell phone to call Megan, Drew tried to steady himself. “Why the hell did you want me out here, anyway?” he asked.

“I figured it was time you saw what we do here.”

“You stick your arm up a cow's ass?”

Ryan chuckled at him from where he stood at the cow's hind end. “If you think a calf comes out of the cow's ass, then we've got more work to do than I thought.”

Drew almost forgot his mixed feelings about seeing Megan again, amid his terror about what she might have to do to the cow once she got there. It turned out that his concern was justified. The cow needed a C-section, which was something Drew didn't even know people did on cows.

She didn't waste time once she arrived with her vet tech in tow—the poorly positioned calf was, apparently, an emergency—and before he knew what was happening, Megan made the first incision and Drew's world went all soft and black.

He'd never thought of himself as a fainter, but then again, the question had never been tested by this particular scenario.

As blurry color started to return to his vision, he was aware of Ryan and Colin supporting his weight and leading him to another part of the barn, making gentle fun of him as they did it.

They set Drew down well away from the carnage with his back propped against a wall, and Colin handed him a bottle of water.

"I just … haven't eaten. That's all," Drew said weakly, sipping from the water bottle.

Colin laughed at him—the bastard actually laughed.

"That's what they all say," he remarked, slapping Drew on the shoulder. Then he went back to see how Megan was coming along, leaving Drew to continue his recovery.

He wasn't sure how long he sat there, but eventually everybody came out of the stall, with Megan, the tech, and the two Delaney brothers all looking to be in good spirits. Drew figured that meant things must have gone well—or as well as could be expected, anyway.

He got himself to his feet just as Megan got to him.

"So … how'd it go?" he asked. He was pleased that his voice sounded reasonably steady.

"Good, I think. The calf looks good." She'd stripped off her gown and hat and booties and was wearing jeans and a T-shirt, looking reasonably put-together, given the circumstances. "You guys will have to watch the mother for a few days, give her antibiotics."

"Okay." He nodded. He was sure Ryan and Colin already knew all of this, but he wanted to act like he had some useful role to play.

She came to stand beside him and peered at him with an amused look on her face. "Don't feel bad," she said. "I've seen experienced ranch hands go down like they've been shot."

"So … what happens now?"

"The guys and Ellie—that's my tech—are moving the mother and the calf to a clean stall. Then I imagine one of the ranch hands is going to have some cleaning up to do."

The thought of some poor guy having to hose out blood and amniotic fluid and who knew what else made him feel woozy again, so he sat down on a stool he'd found nearby and took a few deep breaths.

"Are you okay?" she asked him.

"Yeah. Still a little shaky, though." He hated to admit that he lacked the fortitude to handle the sight and, indeed, the very thought of blood and bovine internal organs, but there it was.

Colin came over while they were talking.

"Is he okay?" he asked Megan, as though Drew weren't there.

"Still a little unsteady," she said. Drew had the uncomfortable sensation of being one of her patients.

"Yeah, looks like it," Colin remarked. "I'd better get him back to the house."

"I can do that," Megan said. Her voice was casual and offhand, but Drew's heart was beginning to speed up. The idea of being alone with her, even for the few minutes it would take to walk to the house, was bringing him around.

"But you're busy." It would just be good manners to protest a little.

"We've got to stay around awhile anyway to keep an eye on the animals," Megan said. "Ellie can do that until I get back."

So Drew grabbed his water bottle and took another sip, and the two of them walked out of the barn and into the late afternoon sunlight. A cool breeze blew in off of the ocean, and it felt good on Drew's skin, making him more steady and alert.

"That was … I've never seen anything like that," he told her as they walked up the path toward the house. "Are they going to be okay?"

"Should be," Megan said. "I've had C-sections go wrong—where things seem okay at the time, but then the animal doesn't make it. But usually, they recover just fine. That one went smoothly, so … We'll see."

"Those guys are never going to let me live this down," Drew said.

She smiled. "Oh … I think they get that this isn't your usual milieu."

The fact that she'd just saved two lives, combined with the fact that she'd used the word *milieu,* made him want to kiss her. He wanted it so much, in fact, that he would gladly endure what he'd seen in the barn again if he could be with her at the end of it.

But he couldn't get past the image of her holding Liam's hand and looking at him with love.

"How are things between you and Liam?" he asked, because getting her onto that topic might push the thought of kissing her out of his head.

She looked down at the ground in front of them and shook her head. Their feet crunched on the dirt path.

"I'm not in love with him," she said. "But I can't stop caring about him. Not now. Not while he's hurt. I just—"

And that was what did it. Hearing that she wasn't in love

with Liam—hearing it confirmed—broke his resolve. He closed the distance between the two of them, pulled her to him, and kissed her.

Megan knew she shouldn't be doing this. But all rational thought was extinguished by the sudden sensation that she had pure, crackling electricity running through her veins.

She had loved Liam—or at least, she'd thought she had. But she'd never felt this all-consuming passion for him, this desire like some kind of wild beast inside her. She wrapped herself around Drew, let her body melt against him, her hands gripping fistfuls of his hair. His embrace lifted her off her feet as he claimed her with his mouth.

After a time that felt both endless and not nearly long enough, he was the one to pull away.

He took hold of her shoulders and held her at arm's length.

"This was a mistake." His voice sounded rough.

"But ..."

"You'd better head back to the barn." He let go of her, turned, and walked toward the house, leaving her shaken and trembling.

They'd started their walk toward the house with Drew feeling unsteady on his feet. Now Megan was the one who thought her knees just might give out.

Chapter Twenty-One

After the C-section, Megan went home to feed her pets, clean Mr. Wiggles's litter box, and take Bobby and Sunshine for their walk. Then she drove out to the hospital to see Liam, feeling restless and irritable. Everything in her life was in upheaval. She'd closed her clinic for the week to accommodate the wedding schedule, so she didn't even have the comfort of her usual routine to soothe her.

Being with Liam was hard, with her guilt and her changed feelings toward him, and her growing and uncontrollable feelings for Drew. And yet, she had to be with Liam right now, until the crisis of his injury passed. If she didn't, she'd never be able to live with herself.

Not that it was easy to do that now, with the memory of her afternoon of passion with Drew still fresh—*very* fresh—in her mind.

And then he had to go and kiss her.

How had things gotten so out of control? How had her life taken this turn?

No.

Her life hadn't just magically taken a turn. She'd made choices, taken actions, and those actions had brought her here.

She wasn't some victim of circumstance. If anyone was a

victim here, it was Liam.

God, Liam.

Liam with his sweet core buried under so many layers of defensiveness and bravado. It had been hard for him to love her in the first place, hard for him to leave himself vulnerable enough to let her in.

And now, what had she done with that trust? She'd fallen in love with another man.

To think that Liam had even been prepared to marry her.

With a jolt, she remembered that Liam had been planning to propose at the wedding. She smacked the steering wheel with her palm as she drove east on Route 46.

She'd been planning to end things earlier rather than later so it wouldn't come to that. But then he'd been hurt, and she'd nearly forgotten that she had a deadline for coming clean.

Well, not *completely* clean. She needed to tell him how she felt, but that didn't mean he needed to know about Drew. Not yet. Not until the shock of the breakup wore off.

The phone rang, coming through her truck's Bluetooth.

"Hey," Breanna said, her voice filtered through the speaker system. "You're coming to the rehearsal dinner, right? Mom wanted me to ask you, since Liam isn't coming, obviously, and you were going to be his date. … Actually, she didn't tell me to ask you. She said to tell you you're coming, and not to take no for an answer."

The rehearsal dinner was scheduled for the following evening, and Megan hadn't given any thought to whether she would go without Liam. Drew would be there, which raised a whole host of issues that she'd rather not deal with, especially in front of the entire Delaney family. But when Sandra said she wouldn't take no for an answer …

"Geez, Bree, I don't know."

"You don't know what? There's going to be food, and you have to eat."

"Yes, but …"

"But what?"

"It's just … complicated."

"Dinner isn't complicated. Food isn't complicated. Well, I guess some of that fancy French stuff is, but …"

"You know what I mean."

Breanna let out a slow sigh, like a tire with a minute leak. "You mean Drew."

"Well, yes! What am I supposed to do, Bree? Am I supposed to sit there eating pot roast next to him, at a big table with the whole family around us, and try to act like nothing's going on? Like everything's fine?"

"Eggplant parmesan."

The non sequitur had Megan momentarily disoriented. "I … what?"

"We're not having pot roast. It's eggplant parmesan. Apparently, that's Julia's favorite, so …"

"Bree? Can we focus, please?"

"No, I don't think I will. I think I'll recite facts about the menu until I bore you into submission and you agree to come. The side dishes will be caprese salad, a really nice garlic bread, oh, and these roasted tomato tarts that Isabelle wanted, even though I think they're a little frou-frou …"

"Breanna!"

"Look, Megan, just come to the dinner, okay? I want you there. We all want you there."

Instead of responding with her plans for the dinner, Megan blurted out the main thing that had been troubling her since the moment she'd left Drew at his hotel the day of the accident.

"I don't know what I'm going to do, Bree."

Breanna knew Megan wasn't talking about the dinner invitation.

"About Drew, or about Liam?" she said.

"Either. Both. I'm on my way to the hospital now. How can I tell him? Especially now that he's hurt. But ... how can I *not* tell him?"

"You've gotten yourself into a mess, all right," Breanna agreed.

That wasn't an answer—not that Megan expected Breanna to have any solutions for her.

"He said he was going to propose at the wedding," Megan said. "You don't think he's still going to do that, do you?" The idea was the worst-case scenario. No, the worst-case scenario would be Liam finding out about her and Drew at the wedding, and pummeling Drew into unconsciousness. She guessed that with Liam in a wheelchair or on crutches, at least that was one thing she could cross off her list of worries.

"Okay. Okay. I'd better hang up. I'm getting close to the hospital now, and I have to get myself psyched up before I see him."

"Psyched up," Breanna repeated.

"Yes. You know, I have to get myself into the right frame of mind to pretend that everything's okay. When it's really, really not okay."

"All right," Breanna said. "But what should I tell Mom about the dinner?"

"Tell her"—she blew out a breath—"tell her I'll be there." Regardless of the state of things between her and Liam, the Delaneys were like family to her. You showed up for family. She hoped to God she wouldn't lose that part of her family when the truth came to light.

***

Liam was sitting up in his hospital bed, his bandaged and immobilized leg stretched out in front of him, his ever-present scowl—so much like his mother's—firmly affixed to his face.

"Hey," Megan said tentatively, waving the fingers of her right hand at him as she came through the door.

"Oh. Hey. I still can't get this damned remote to work." He pressed some buttons with more force than strictly required, while waving the thing at the television. "Goddamn it. If I have to be stuck here, you'd think I could at least watch some decent TV."

"You want me to see if I can get somebody to come and replace it?" she offered.

"Ah … no. I guess not. Screw it." He tossed the remote onto the table beside his bed.

Megan pulled up a chair next to the bed and sat down, her purse in her lap. "How are you feeling?"

"Not too bad, I guess." He rubbed at his face, which hadn't been shaved since before the accident. "Considering. They've cut back on the pain meds, but I still feel okay, so I guess that's gotta be good."

"Sounds like it. Have they told you when you can go home?"

"Tomorrow, I guess, unless my leg falls off or something."

"You'll be able to come to the wedding," she said.

"Yeah. But Colin's going to have to get another grooms-man, I guess, because I don't think I'll be up to standing for the length of a wedding ceremony."

"Oh, he's got that worked out," she said. "He wants you up there, so he's going to give you a chair."

He squinted at her. "He wants to have me up there in front of the whole damned church in a chair, while everybody else is standing?"

"Yeah. He does."

Liam rubbed at the back of his neck with his hand, and a slow grin spread across his face. "Well … Colin's a good guy, I guess." It was as close as Liam was likely to come to saying that he was touched by the gesture.

He reached out and took her hand in his. "Listen, Megan. I've got something special in mind for the reception. I might have to do it on crutches, but I'm still going ahead with it. It might not go exactly as I planned, but …"

Maybe it was the look on her face. Maybe it was the way her hand tensed in his. Or maybe he already knew, and something in her body language confirmed it. Whatever it was, he stopped in the middle of his sentence and looked at her—really looked at her for the first time in a while.

"I thought … I thought you wanted a commitment. That the reason we'd been having problems was because I hadn't—"

"Oh, Liam." Tears shimmered in her eyes.

He let go of her hand and drew his away. "You're not going to marry me, are you?"

She shook her head, and the tears fell.

"Well … why didn't you tell me? If you knew, why …?"

"I didn't want to hurt you." Her voice was a whisper.

He looked away from her, focusing his gaze on the darkened television. "You've wanted out for a while now, I guess."

She nodded. "When you moved out here from Montana to be with me, it was … We'd only been dating a few months. And it was moving so fast. We'd barely gotten to know each other, and you moved all this way, and I—"

"And you didn't want to be the bitch who said, 'Hey, slow down, because I might not want to do this.'"

"Well … yes. It all started happening before anybody even asked me what I thought. What I wanted. And then once it was done …" She shook her head and stared at her hands in her lap. "I thought, well, maybe it'll work. Maybe we really are meant to be together." She looked at him. "I tried, Liam. I wanted it to work."

Lines of tension formed around his mouth, his eyes. "Well, I guess if you have to try that hard to be with me …"

"Liam …"

"I guess you'd better go," he said.

"But … I want to be here for you while you recover, while you—"

"I want you to go."

He wouldn't look at her—instead, he focused on a blank spot on the wall.

She stood up, put the strap of her purse over her shoulder, and walked out of the room, leaving him alone.

She hadn't wanted to do it like this, but at least he knew the truth now.

Part of it, anyway.

At least that was something.

Chapter Twenty-Two

I t wouldn't be like Liam to blurt out to everyone that Megan had dumped him. He was more likely to brood silently until someone pried it out of him. But someone must have pried, because Megan hadn't been home for more than an hour before the phone calls started.

Breanna. Julia. Sandra. And then Drew.

She let them all go to voice mail. The women would want to talk about it, and she couldn't talk about it right now. And Drew would want to be with her, would want to come over. And she didn't think she deserved to be that happy after how she'd made Liam feel.

It was late afternoon by now, and the shadows on the walls of her cottage had begun to lengthen with the waning of the day. She lay huddled on her sofa, a blanket over her, Mr. Wiggles snuggled up beside her. She'd been crying earlier, but not now. Now, she simply lay staring at the wall, feeling the vibration of the cat's purr against her.

It wasn't regret she was feeling, not exactly. The breakup had to happen, and the fact that it had happened sooner rather than later was probably a good thing. But she'd caused pain for someone she cared about, and there was nothing to do but sit with the raw ache of that for a while.

The ache gnawed at her, but under that was something else: a sense of freedom.

She'd felt trapped by her relationship with Liam for so long now. Not trapped by him, exactly, but by her own need to be a good person, to be loyal, to stick. Now that it was over, she needed a moment to regain her equilibrium before hashing it out with anyone.

Especially Drew.

She didn't realize she was holding Mr. Wiggles too tightly until the cat meowed in protest and then wriggled away from her, jumping off the sofa and retreating to safety.

Megan sniffled, then reached out to the box of tissues on the coffee table, plucked one out, and blew her nose. She was grateful that, other than the C-section, she didn't have to work today.

Oh, shit—work.

She'd barely considered what the breakup would do to her veterinary practice. She'd been the go-to vet for the Delaneys since shortly after she'd moved to town, and what was going to happen with that now? Would they stop using her, in solidarity with Liam? And if they didn't, how would that be? What would it feel like when she went to the ranch to care for an animal and had to deal with Liam standing there glaring at her?

And what about the Delaneys? Would they still be her friends—her second family?

What about the wedding? Was she even still invited?

It was all too hard to think about. She hoisted herself off the sofa and went into the kitchen to see if she had any ice cream, because ice cream was the one thing a girl could count on in the event of emotional upheaval.

To her disappointment, all she found was crappy diet ice cream—the kind with unpronounceable marvels of chemistry in the ingredient list instead of actual foods like milk, cream, and sugar.

Deciding it was better than nothing, she pulled out the carton, grabbed a spoon from a kitchen drawer, and dug in.

She was just scraping the last bits from the bottom of the carton when her doorbell rang.

Well, at least she could be sure it wasn't Liam, since he wasn't ambulatory.

She tossed her ice cream carton into the trash, went into the living room, and peeked out the window next to the door, trying not to be obvious when she pulled aside the curtain.

Her heart did a little leap when she saw Drew standing on her doorstep, looking uncertain and impossibly appealing.

She closed her eyes and took a moment to breathe.

What was she supposed to do? If she opened the door, she would fall into his arms and become so consumed with lust that she would forget everything else.

And oh, God, did she want to forget everything else.

But it didn't seem right. Not right for Liam to be nursing a broken leg and a broken heart while Megan was lost in sexual abandon with another man. Not right for her to be so happy while Liam was so miserable. Not right to move on to someone else so soon—so immediately—after leaving a long-term relationship.

"Go away," she said, through the closed window.

At first he didn't seem to know where the voice was coming from. Then he spotted her in the tiny space where the curtain had been pulled back.

"Megan, open up."

"No. You have to leave."

That just seemed to confuse him.

"This is … Come on. Open the door. Please?"

She dropped the curtain, went to the door, and opened it a crack—enough so he could hear her, but not enough that he could pull her into a kiss and break her resolve.

"Drew, I can't let you in. You have to go. Please." She didn't want to look at his face, because that would make it so much harder to turn him away. So instead, she focused on the top button of his shirt.

She was expecting a protest, but instead, he said, "I heard about you and Liam."

When she didn't say anything, he went on, "Liam told Colin, and Colin told Julia, and Julia told me. "I thought we could talk. I thought—"

"We wouldn't," she said.

"Wouldn't what?"

"We wouldn't talk. I'd open the door, and you'd come in, and in under five minutes we'd both be naked and that would be that. I can't imagine much talking in that scenario."

"Well … would that be so bad?"

Indignant, she forgot to look at his button and focused on his face, instead. Which was a mistake, because she wanted to kiss it, touch it.

"Yes!" she said. "Yes, it would be bad! Because poor Liam is in the hospital with his broken leg, and now on top of that he's got to deal with me and the breakup, and … and it just doesn't seem right for us to sleep together with him feeling all of that!"

She watched his face as he processed that. First he seemed puzzled, and then his features smoothed as he seemed to accept it. "Okay. But can't we just talk and not sleep together? That's not wrong or disrespectful to Liam, is it?"

"No. It wouldn't be. Except that if you come in here, we won't just talk."

"You could come out here," he suggested. "We could sit on your porch or take a walk or something."

"No, Drew! Because if I take a walk with you or sit on the porch with you, I'll be happy! And I don't deserve to be happy right now."

He was quiet for a moment while he considered that. Then he said, "How about if you sit down just inside the house, and I'll sit down out here, and we can leave the door open a little …"

"That's dumb," she told him. "That's a really dumb idea."

He nodded. "Well, you might think you deserve to be unhappy, but I don't agree. Still, I don't want you to do anything you're uncomfortable with. I'm just going to go."

He shoved his hands into his pockets, turned, and went down the porch steps toward his car.

She knew that him leaving had been her idea. And yet, she couldn't quite bear to see him go.

"Drew!" she called out to him. He stopped and turned to look at her. "Maybe we could try your idea. Just for a little bit."

Drew sat on the floor of Megan's porch with his back against the wall next to the door, his long legs stretched out in front of him. It wasn't exactly what he'd had in mind when he came over here, but he could hear her talking to him, so it was a damned sight better than going home.

"I didn't mean to do it right then, with him lying there recovering from surgery," she said. "I thought …. I don't know what I thought. I guess I thought I could just get him through this and then deal with everything later. But he must have seen it in my face or something, because he was about to tell me about his plan to propose. And then he just knew I was going to say no."

"That's why he was going to tell you," Drew said. "He

could see that it was just about over, and that was his Hail Mary play."

"So then, before I even knew what was happening, I was telling him that I couldn't marry him, and he was asking me to leave."

Her voice sounded impossibly sad, and he wanted to hold her, or at least hold her hand. Instead, he sat there and listened.

"But it's for the best, right?" he said. "I mean, you were going to do it sooner or later. It just turned out to be sooner."

"Yeah, but I didn't want it to happen like this."

"You weren't doing him any favors stringing him along if it wasn't working," Drew said. "I mean, if he was wasting his time, it's better to know. It's damned frustrating putting your time and effort into a relationship and then finding out later that it was doomed."

He hadn't meant to bring Tessa into the conversation, but suddenly, there she was.

"Do you think your marriage would have worked out if you hadn't gone through everything you did with Redmond and your mother?" Megan asked.

He'd thought about that many times, and he was certain about the answer.

"No. No, it wouldn't have worked. We might still be together, but we'd be on our way to a divorce anyway."

"How can you be sure?"

He took in a deep breath and let it out with a sigh. "Two things. One, if she were the right person for me, she'd never have given up on us. And two"—he turned his face toward her, even though he couldn't see her where she was sitting behind the door—"I'd have met you eventually. And that would be that."

"You'd have left your wife for me," she said, as though she were trying to be sure she understood what he was saying to her.

"I'd have known that she wasn't the one for me. Because you are."

Her hand popped out of the doorway, and he took it in his. They sat that way for a long time, together but not together, holding onto each other but keeping their distance.

"So, what happens now? Between us?" he asked.

She squeezed his hand a little. "What happens is, we wait. A little while. Because I can't be that person who goes from one man to another in the same day."

"All right."

"And then, we see what happens."

"See what happens," he repeated.

"Yes."

They sat together for a long time as the sky darkened and night fell. When it started to get cold, he got up, walked to his car, and drove back to his hotel.

He could wait as long as he had to.

Chapter Twenty-Three

Of course, it was impossible for Megan to attend the rehearsal dinner now that she'd thrown over Liam for another man. Even if the part about the other man wasn't yet public knowledge.

She couldn't face any of the Delaneys, so she texted Breanna to tell her that she wasn't going to come. Breanna tried to call her, but Megan let the call go to voice mail.

Then Julia tried to call, and she let that go to voice mail, too—until she reminded herself that she was in the wedding party, and a bridesmaid couldn't just drop out of the ceremony without at least talking to the bride.

Sitting cross-legged on her sofa with Mr. Wiggles in her lap, she stroked the cat a few times to calm herself and then picked up her cell phone and called Julia back.

"You're still coming to the wedding, right?" Julia said before Megan could even speak. "I mean, I'm really sorry about you and Liam. Really sorry. But you're still going to be a bridesmaid, right?"

Megan didn't know what to say. She felt tears pooling in her eyes and blinked a few times to clear them. "Do you even want me to? Because Liam—"

"Of course I want you to!"

"Oh. I thought that everyone … I thought …" She couldn't finish her sentence through the emotion lying thick in her throat.

"Megan, I get that it might be awkward for you to go ahead with the wedding, with all that's happening between you and Liam," Julia said. "But you're still a part of the family. You're still my friend."

"Oh." She blinked hard and swallowed. "Oh. That's … Thank you. I hope the others feel the same way."

"Liam is probably going to take it hard at first. I mean, of course he is. But I think everyone else saw this coming."

That wasn't what Megan had expected to hear, and her eyebrows scrunched in puzzlement. "They saw what coming? What do you mean?"

Suddenly, Julia seemed to be sorry she'd said anything. "Well, I mean … It's not my place to say, but …"

"Julia, what are you talking about? They saw what coming?"

Julia sighed. "I think everybody knew that you and Liam were on the outs," she said finally. "Well, except Orin and Colin, probably, but they're guys. Guys never know what's going on with women."

"But—"

"And then there's the thing with Drew," she went on.

"Wait. What thing with Drew? Did he say something to you? Because—"

"Megan. God. He didn't have to. When you two are in the same room together, you've got more electricity than the Las Vegas Strip. I'm not blind, and neither is anybody else around here."

Megan felt a sinking sensation in her chest. "Do you think Liam noticed it, too? He wanted to propose out of nowhere, when he knew things between us weren't right …"

"Claiming his territory," Julia mused. "He was perceptive

enough to know he was losing you, I guess, but he's still Liam, so he didn't know how to deal with it."

Megan flopped back against the sofa cushions, Mr. Wiggles curled up beside her. "Yeah. I guess that's right."

"So … what's going on between you and my brother?" Julia said.

"Nothing! He didn't … It's not …"

"Oh, bullshit," Julia said, not unkindly. "The chemistry, remember? It's like a damned electrical storm whenever the two of you are within fifty feet of each other."

"Oh, God," Megan said miserably.

"So? What's the story? Not that it's any of my business, except that I'm his sister and therefore have a right to poke around in his life. Plus, he never tells me anything, so I have no choice but to poke."

Megan had told Breanna about her encounter with Drew, but Breanna was her closest friend. Julia was a friend, certainly, and a good one, but she wasn't certain they were at the level of closeness it would require for Megan to confess about her illicit relationship. Plus, she was Drew's sister, which meant Megan would be telling Julia not only about her own scandalous behavior, but about his, as well.

And there was the fact that the fewer people who knew about her and Drew, the less chance there would be of Liam finding out and being more hurt than he already was.

"There's no story. There's nothing to tell," Megan said.

"Sure. If that's what you want to go with. I'll just get it out of him," Julia said cheerfully. "But you are still going to be in the wedding, right?"

"Yes. Of course."

Julia sounded relieved. "Great. That's great. Really awesome. And if you're going to be in the wedding, that means you have to come to the rehearsal, of course. And if you're coming to the rehearsal, you might as well come to the dinner, too. Liam won't even be there. He's not getting released until tomorrow."

No matter how she tried to spin it, Megan couldn't think of a valid excuse to skip the rehearsal and the dinner, especially since she wouldn't have to face Liam.

"All right."

Megan started to hang up, but then she heard Julia's voice.

"Megan? Don't worry. Liam will be okay. And you will, too. It might not seem like it right now, but you will."

Later that day, as Drew dressed for the rehearsal, he mused over the intense discomfort that was facing him that evening. One, he'd have to be in the same room with the woman he was in love with, without admitting to anyone or showing in any way that he was in love with her. Two, he would have to face the family of the man whose girlfriend he'd slept with. And three, he would have to face his mother.

He'd managed to avoid his mother since he'd seen Redmond's letters, which hadn't been easy, since she seemed to be everywhere. He knew he couldn't avoid her forever, but he just didn't know what to say to her. He'd come to terms—mostly— with the fact that she'd cheated on Drew's dad, and that she'd hidden Drew's true parentage from him for so long. But this new information, that Redmond had wanted to be a part of Drew's life but had been shut out by Isabelle, had been a devastating body blow. How could she have let Drew think his father hadn't wanted him? And how could she have kept a man from knowing his only child?

He feared that if he really took the time to talk to his mother about it, he'd end up saying things that would cause an irreparable rift between them. And while he was more or less willing to do it and let the consequences be whatever they were, he didn't want to do it right now and cause problems for Julia's big day.

He planned to avoid his mother as much as possible over the next couple of days, which shouldn't be hard, given how much would be going on.

Drew was wearing a suit and tie, which he almost never did, and which he wouldn't be doing now if his mother hadn't had very specific ideas about what it should look like for her daughter to marry a billionaire. The Delaneys would have preferred a backyard barbecue, probably, but Isabelle was the driving force behind the planning of this thing, and she wasn't about to let the opportunity go to waste.

Anyone could have a backyard barbecue, but when you were marrying into one of California's most important families, by God, the least people could do was dress up a little, in Isabelle's mind.

So Drew straightened the tie and combed his hair, checked the closeness of his shave, and made sure his shoes were gleaming. He fed Eddie and refilled his water dish. Then he cursed his luck for having a soft-hearted sister who cared about pleasing their mother, and got into his rental car to head for the rehearsal.

The wedding was being held at the Santa Rosa Chapel, a small, white wood building that dated back to 1870, shortly after the Delaneys settled the land where the family still lived.

The way Julia told it, that was the one wedding detail about which Colin had put his foot down. Isabelle had protested that the chapel wasn't big enough to hold all of the couple's 200-plus guests—and she was right, it wasn't. But Colin had argued that the chapel had been a part of his life since his infancy. Though the Delaneys were only casual Catholics, he'd been christened there, he'd attended Christmas concerts there, he'd said goodbye to Redmond there, and he'd witnessed the weddings of his friends there. It was where he wanted to get married, and he'd been unwilling to budge on the point even in the face of Isabelle's pleas.

When Drew walked into the chapel to take his place as a groomsman, Isabelle was loudly complaining about the fact that she'd been forced to invite some of the guests to the reception only, because of the lack of seating inside the tiny building.

"It's just so *rude*," Isabelle was telling Julia and Colin as Drew walked down the aisle to meet the others, who were loosely gathered in the area around the altar. "Imagine telling people that they're not *welcome* at the *ceremony.*" She shook her head and made a judgmental clucking sound with her teeth.

"Oh, I don't know," Colin replied. "I think some of them are grateful they can cut straight to the party."

"I know I would be," Drew said.

Colin greeted him with a smile and extended his hand, shaking Drew's firmly. "Drew. Thanks for putting up with all of this." He extended his free hand to encompass the church, the intense wedding schedule, the clothing they'd all been forced to wear, and all of the myriad inconveniences a wedding represented.

"Put up with it!" Isabelle said. "Why, he's honored! Aren't you, Drew?"

"I am," he agreed, because how could he do anything else when Julia was fairly beaming with happiness? "You look beautiful," he told her.

Julia was wearing a pale pink silk wrap dress, and her hair was swept up into a loose updo, with auburn tendrils trailing down around her neck. Drew didn't think he'd ever seen her looking so lovely, or so content.

"You look pretty good yourself," she said, and reached out

to straighten Drew's tie, which didn't really need straightening.

"Is"—he cleared his throat—"Is everyone else here?" By *everyone else,* he meant Megan, but he couldn't exactly say that directly.

"Well, Liam's not going to make it, of course, and we're still waiting for Megan and Ryan. Everybody else is around here somewhere, I think."

People were, in fact, milling around both inside the church and outside, in the historic cemetery that surrounded it. Mike came in the front door of the church looking acutely uncomfortable in a suit that he'd probably bought for the occasion.

"You sure you don't want a girl for this?" Mike asked Julia.

In a break with tradition, Julia had opted for a Man of Honor rather than a maid or matron. The gruff, fifty-something contractor had been her closest friend for years, and she wasn't about to push him aside on her wedding day just because of gender.

"I want my best friend for this," she said. She reached out and squeezed his hand, and the man actually blushed.

Megan came in a few minutes later, flanked by Ryan and Sandra. Ryan looked like some kind of *GQ* model in his navy blue suit, which came as something of a shock to Drew, who had never seen the man in anything but jeans and flannel button-down shirts. Sandra didn't wear dresses—somehow, it just wasn't in her nature—but she'd traded in her usual Levi's and fuzzy slippers for a pair of black slacks, a silk blouse, and some kind of flowy cardigan that Drew would have bet Isabelle had picked out for her.

As shocking as it was to see the two of them dressed up, Megan was the one who grabbed Drew's attention. She was wearing a sapphire blue dress that hugged her curves in a way that made him instantly lose at least twenty IQ points. The skirt fell to just above her knees, giving him a tantalizing view of her legs, and the top had a kind of keyhole cutout that offered just a peek of smooth cleavage.

It took an embarrassing amount of time for him to realize that Julia was talking to him.

" … get started? Drew?"

Julia's voice was a distant buzz, like the drone of a honeybee.

" … you think, Drew?"

He was vaguely aware of someone talking to him, but he didn't know what they were saying, and he had no sense of it being important. At least, not as important as looking at Megan.

"Focus, you jerk!"

Okay, now *that* was the sister he'd grown up with. He blinked a couple of times and looked at her.

"What? Sorry. I guess I wasn't paying attention."

"I guess you weren't." Julia looked pointedly at Megan, and then at Drew. "I was asking whether you were ready to get started."

"Oh … sure. I guess so. Yeah."

She leaned toward him and whispered into his ear, "If you ruin my wedding …"

"I won't."

"I swear to God …"

"I won't," he said again, more firmly this time.

She glared at him in the way only big sisters do, then gathered everyone together to listen to the priest go through the details of the ceremony.

They all went through the processional while the wedding planner—a slender, crisply dressed woman in her forties with a dark, tight bun—told everybody what to do.

The groomsmen—Drew and Stuart Guthrie, a big, burly guy who'd been Colin's college roommate—lined up at the altar, leaving a space for Liam. Ryan, who was the best man, stood closest to Colin, who waited expectantly for his bride-to-be.

The bridesmaids filed one by one down the aisle: Gen, Breanna, and Megan. Finally, Mike brought up the rear.

When they were all in place, Julia came down the aisle on her mother's arm.

Tears glimmered in Julia's eyes, and Drew knew it wasn't about her happiness to be marrying Colin, though she was happy. She was crying because her father wasn't there.

Suddenly, Drew felt himself choking up a little, too. Andrew McCray, Julia's father and the man Drew had thought was his as well, had been dead for five years, but the wound wasn't any less fresh today than it had been when it happened.

He should be here. It wasn't right that he wasn't here.

When Julia came within range, he reached out and squeezed her hand.

As the priest went through a brief summary of what would be included in the ceremony—I'll say this, and then you say that—Drew couldn't keep his eyes off Megan. Being here, in the context of a wedding, made him feel nervous butterflies—or maybe they were bees—in his stomach.

The sensation wasn't unpleasant. There was a lot to be said for knowing exactly where you were going and what you wanted and with whom, and that was how Drew felt now. As though his future had been laid out neatly for him, as though a bounty of riches and rewards was his, and all he had to do was reach out and take it.

Chapter Twenty-Four

The dinner was being held at Neptune, the most upscale restaurant in Cambria, where Ryan's close friend Jackson Graham was the head chef. They'd rented a private room at the restaurant for the night, an arrangement that had come at not inconsiderable expense. Isabelle and her husband, Matt, were paying. There'd been a delicate series of negotiations regarding who would pay for what, with Colin offering to foot the bill for everything, and Isabelle, not wanting to be entirely outdone, insisting on covering the expense for at least *something*.

Because the rehearsal dinner was on Isabelle's dime, and because it was so important to her that she appear neither cheap nor poor in comparison with the Delaneys, a number of people who weren't in the wedding party were invited to the dinner.

This included Drew's aunt and uncle and their two kids; a couple of the ranch hands from Montana whom Colin had become especially close to; and a handful of others, including friends of Colin and Julia who were here from out of state and a few Cambria fixtures who were close to Orin and Sandra.

The crowd started gathering at Neptune shortly after the rehearsal wrapped up, and people were milling around with cocktails in their hands by around seven p.m.

Drew was drinking a craft beer and chatting with Stuart in a far corner of the room when Megan walked in.

If Drew was trying to pretend that he wasn't waiting for her and hadn't noticed her, he was a complete failure, because Stuart noticed Drew's interest the moment she walked in.

"She's a looker, all right," Stuart commented, as though Drew had said something to which he was merely agreeing. "A damned shame she's hooked up with Colin's brother."

The comment brought him out of his Megan-induced reverie.

"Your news is out of date," he said.

"What do you mean?"

"I mean she broke up with him."

Stuart, who looked like some kind of lawyer-lumberjack hybrid with his beard, his barrel chest, and his crisp suit, seemed taken aback. "What? When did that happen?"

Drew took a long drink of his beer, trying to appear casual. "Today."

Stuart let out a low whistle. "She did it while he's laid up in the hospital? Man, that's cold. Still, if she's free ..." He wiggled his eyebrows to suggest what he might do now that Megan was available.

Drew felt the sudden and almost irrepressible urge to throw the guy to the floor and step on his throat, though it would probably be like trying to wrestle a tree trunk. Instead, he shrugged, feigning a lack of interest.

"You can try, but I don't think she's your type."

"She's a woman and she's hot. That makes her my type."

Because Stuart was paying such close attention to Megan, it didn't escape his notice that she was paying close attention to Drew.

"Man, I think I know who *is* her type. She's looking at you."

"No," Drew said casually, waving a hand to dismiss the

idea.

"Uh … yeah. She's looked over here about a dozen times since she walked in, and I can tell you she's not checking out my ass."

Drew wanted nothing more than to cross the room, sweep Megan into his arms, carry her out of here, and make hot, unrelenting love to her until all thoughts of social propriety and sensitivity were drowned out by their moans of pleasure. Knowing that she was watching him and thinking about him made him want it even more. But since that wasn't an option, he drained his beer, ditched the bottle on a tray positioned nearby for that purpose, flagged down a passing waiter, and ordered another.

It was going to be a long night.

The seating arrangement was merciful—to a point. Drew sat at one end of a long, rectangular table and Megan way down at the other, so that was good. But he was seated with his mother to his left, which was a problem, and Stuart to his right, which was even more of a problem, since the guy wouldn't stop making comments about Megan.

"God, look at that cutout thing on her dress," Stuart said in a stage whisper, referring to the keyhole that exposed a small but tantalizing glimpse of Megan's breasts. "It's like a little portal to an enchanted kingdom with unicorns and fairies and shit. Like *Lord of the Rings,* but with sex."

This guy was a Harvard-educated lawyer? How in the world had that come to pass? And more puzzling, how could it be that he was Colin's friend? Colin was one of the most refined and tasteful guys in Drew's acquaintance, but his college roommate seemed like he ought to be holding a club and dragging a woman around by the hair.

"Could you maybe not talk about her like that?" Drew said.

"Like what?"

"Like she's … I don't know. A sex object for you to ogle at."

"Dude, all I'm saying is, it's a nice dress."

The dinner conversation with his mother didn't go much better, mainly because she was trying to pry into his life the way mothers do, at a time when he was in no mood to let her into his innermost thoughts. Either she didn't realize that he was pissed at her, or she knew, and was trying to defuse the situation by burying his anger in an avalanche of questions, observations, and minutia.

Drew's stepfather, Matt, who'd finally made it to Cambria after wrapping things up at work, tried valiantly to provide a buffer, but it wasn't very effective.

"I just thought, now that you're *well off*"—she pronounced the two words as though they made her tongue tingle—"you might consider putting aside that business with the boats and do something else. Something *meaningful.*"

"Building boats *is* meaningful to him, Iz," Matt said. "He's building something with his hands. Creating something. I wish I could do what he does."

Drew shot his stepfather a smile of gratitude, but he knew Matt's words wouldn't sink in with Isabelle. He was right; they didn't.

"Oh, it's all fine, I guess," she went on. "For a hobby. But now Drew's got a chance to really *do* something! The Delaneys are all over the financial magazines with their philanthropy, and their land deals.… You could be like that, Drew! You could really *be* somebody!"

In just a few short sentences, Isabelle had managed to imply that Drew's work was meaningless and that he was a nobody. An impressive feat, even by her standards.

"Dad taught me boat-building," Drew said mildly.

"Well, yes, but I don't think he meant for it to take the place of a career," she said.

"Isabelle, it *is* a career for Drew," Matt said. "One that makes him feel close to his father. You shouldn't—"

"It's okay, Matt," Drew said, leaning across Isabelle to address him. He appreciated what Matt was trying to do, but it was hopeless; besides, he'd prefer not to engage with Isabelle at all if he could help it. Not now, when Redmond's letters were still fresh in his mind.

Across the table, Mike was leaning toward Julia to mutter something to her—apparently, it was something about the food. He was holding a piece of asparagus between his thick fingers and using it to poke at his fingerling potatoes.

Seated at two o'clock was Drew's aunt, who had heard part of his conversation with Isabelle and was leaning in to add something. "It must be so nice not to have financial worries," she said. "Joe thinks he's going to lose his job after this quarter's reports come out. If we had just a little cushion to help us … but the twins' private school tuition is through the roof, so our savings is next to nothing." She made a *tsk* sound and shook her head mournfully.

Drew guessed he was supposed to volunteer to provide the cushion now that he literally had more money than he knew what to do with. It wasn't the first overture his Aunt Marcy had made to that effect. The interesting thing was that before he'd come into his inheritance, Marcy and Joe had liked to brag to him about how well they were doing.

"The twins could always go to public school," Matt offered.

"And take them away from their friends and the environment they know?" Marcy shuddered. "If only there were some way …"

"Speaking of gold-diggers," Matt said to Drew under his breath, leaning across Isabelle, "have you heard from your ex lately?"

Thinking about his ex-wife made him think about how different she was from Megan. When he looked down the table toward where Megan sat, he caught her eye, just for a moment. He couldn't say how he knew it, but he knew that his relationship with her would be different than what he'd had with Tessa. It wouldn't be a battle, and it wouldn't end badly.

It wouldn't end at all.

He realized Matt was still talking, and he tried to focus.

Megan didn't choose the dress to distract Drew. That would have been shallow, ill-advised, and insensitive toward Liam.

She chose the dress because it was one of the few she owned, and it fit. Of course, now that she was here in the same room with Drew, the fact that the dress did seem to be distracting him felt like a nice bonus.

It felt good that he was watching her. But the fact that it felt good made her feel bad. Basically, all of her emotions were confusing the crap out of her.

She chatted with the people on either side of her—Breanna on one side, Orin on the other—and tried not to look at Drew. But his presence was impossible to ignore, like a light in a darkened room, or a flash of lightning on the horizon. She tried to make convincing conversation over dinner about the wedding, or her latest veterinary patients, or the excellent Neptune food, and she thought she was succeeding admirably. Until Breanna leaned over and whispered in her ear.

"Why don't you just go over there and sit in his lap," she hissed. "It'd be less obvious."

"What are you talking about?" Megan said.

"Oh, come on," Breanna shot back at her. "You two can't stop making moony eyes at each other. "Either stop it or get a room."

Megan looked down at her plate dejectedly. "I'm being stupid," she said.

"I won't argue with you."

Chapter Twenty-Five

If Drew had been asked to predict when the whole house of cards would come down in a scattered mess of queens and jokers, he'd have said it would be at the reception the following day. Surely with the drinking, the dancing, and the emotion of people declaring their eternal love for each other, something was bound to happen.

And something did happen. Just not the thing that Drew expected.

The vows had been said at the chapel, which was aglow with candlelight and fragrant with the smell of roses. Women had cried delicately into white tissues, and Liam, freshly home from the hospital, had sat in his place near the altar, a pair of crutches nearby.

Megan had looked almost impossibly lovely in her blush pink bridesmaid dress, a crown of white flowers woven into her hair.

And Drew had behaved himself—mostly. He couldn't control the longing he felt like a dull ache in his chest, but he did control his own conduct, greeting Megan with the same reserved courtesy he showed everyone else.

Afterward, they'd all gone to a resort in Paso Robles, where Isabelle had booked a ballroom and where many of the out-of-town guests would be staying the night so they could get drunk off their asses without worrying about transportation.

The ballroom, with generous windows and French doors that opened onto a vineyard, was done up with white table linens, arrangements of roses in the same color as Megan's pale pink dress, flickering candles, sparkling crystal, and gold flatware. A five-tiered wedding cake towered over a table at one side of the room, and a five-piece band played classic love songs as people filtered in and gathered around the open bar.

Julia and Colin hadn't arrived in the ballroom yet because they were tied up out in the vineyard with the photographer, who wanted to take advantage of the dusky light.

Megan had already gotten a glass of champagne from the bar and was standing apart from the crowd when Drew walked in, and although he knew he shouldn't do it—knew he should stay as far away from her as possible—he couldn't help himself. He came up silently behind her and spoke so close to her ear that she let out a tiny, intimate gasp of surprise.

"You look incredible," he whispered. "I can't stop thinking about you."

She didn't turn to look at him, but her eyes slipped closed at the sound of his voice.

"This is torture," he said, his voice a low growl. "Seeing you looking like this, but not being able to touch you …"

She downed the champagne in her glass, ditched the glass on the nearest table, and headed for the door. She shot him a look over her shoulder, and the message was clear: *Follow me.*

He left a decent interval for the sake of subterfuge, and went after her.

She went out of the ballroom, down a hallway, through the lobby, and through a door near the reception desk. He followed her through the door and found himself inside a gray concrete stairwell that looked like it existed mainly as a fire exit.

"Where are we going?" he asked her.

"I don't know, but ... there's gotta be ..."

She hurried up a flight of stairs and through another door. Then she looked around and bolted for a door marked HOTEL PERSONNEL ONLY.

He followed her inside a large closet filled with linens, coffee pods, and tiny bottles of toiletries. She closed the door behind them—and then she turned to him and threw herself at him.

In an instant, nothing else existed but her. The towels, the cleaning supplies, the reception below them—all of it vanished into a puff of distant memory as he took her into his arms and devoured her mouth with his.

He maneuvered her around, and her back thumped against the closed door as he pressed up against her, his hands on her body, his tongue exploring the welcoming warmth of her lips, her mouth.

If he'd been thinking clearly, he'd have considered the fact that someone from housekeeping might come in and discover them at any time. But he wasn't thinking clearly—in fact, he wasn't thinking at all.

He slid his hands under her dress, up her thighs, and over the delectable curves of her ass. She was wearing some kind of tiny lacy underwear, and this discovery caused him to grow even more painfully hard than he already was.

He pushed the lacy panties down and slid his hand between her legs.

She was warm and wet and ready for him, and he slipped a finger inside her.

Megan gasped and threw her head back, her lips parted in pleasure. He nipped her throat lightly with his teeth as he explored the hot depths of her with his hand.

"Oh … God." Her words came out breathy and urgent. She clung to his shoulders with her hands.

There was no time for subtlety or nuance—no time, only a desperate need—and so he shoved her panties down the rest of the way, unfastened his tuxedo pants, lifted her up, and thrust into her with her legs wrapped around him and her back pressed against the door.

"Oh! Oh!"

Her cries of pleasure, her closed eyes, the expression of bliss on her face as he took her drove his arousal higher and higher. He had one arm wrapped around her to hold her in place, and with his free hand he pulled the strap of her dress down to expose one of her delicious white breasts. He fastened his mouth over the pink peak, teasing the sensitive nub with his teeth.

They both were getting louder as their passion rose toward its crest, and so, knowing no other way to silence them both, he kissed her hard and kept his mouth on hers as she rose, rose, and then gasped and shuddered with release.

Moments after her, he clutched her to him, pushing her into the door as his own pleasure crashed and exploded like a bomb blast in his brain, blocking out everything but waves and waves of pure bliss.

They stayed that way for a long time, unwilling to move, as their breathing slowly began to calm, their pulses gradually returning to normal. Then he let her go, and she lowered her feet to the floor. They both sank down to the linoleum, sitting with their backs against the wall, stacks of clean white towels surrounding them.

He held her in his arms.

"I didn't … That wasn't …" She seemed to have lost the power of coherent speech.

He pressed a gentle kiss to her forehead.

It wasn't long before their senses returned to them, and they realized they were both partially naked in a hotel utility closet.

Since that didn't seem like an ideal arrangement, they got up and reassembled their clothes. Drew ran a hand through his hair to neaten it, and Megan, figuring her hair was a lost cause, settled for making sure that her panties were on and all of the necessary fasteners on her dress were closed.

He gave her one last kiss, and grasped the doorknob.

Which didn't turn.

"It's locked," Drew said, trying to keep any hint of panic out of his voice. Panic wasn't manly, and he didn't want to embarrass himself.

"It can't be locked," Megan said.

"But it is." He tried the knob again, but it wouldn't budge.

"That doesn't make any sense," Megan said. "It was unlocked when we came in. And … and why would anybody put a doorknob on a utility closet that can't be opened from the inside?" Her voice was beginning to rise in a way that was sexy as hell when they were in the throes of passion, but was somewhat alarming now.

"I don't actually think it's locked," Drew said. "I think it's stuck." He tried to wiggle the knob some more, but it wouldn't wiggle. Even a locked doorknob had some give, but this one didn't. He pushed on the door, hoping that maybe the latch mechanism wasn't fully in place, but the door was sealed.

"Oh, God," Megan moaned. Again, that particular phrase had sounded much better earlier.

"Okay," Drew said, as though he had a solution in mind. "Okay."

"I don't have my cell phone," she said. "Because I have no pockets! Why don't women's clothes have pockets!?"

They could have gotten into the whys and the social implications of Megan's lack of pockets, but instead, Drew reached into his own pocket and was relieved to find that he did have his phone.

Now the question was who to call.

If he called the hotel, they could send somebody up to unjam the door and let them out, but then they'd have to explain what they were doing in the closet in the first place.

If he called someone at the reception, then he wouldn't have to explain what they were doing in the closet—because they'd already know. Then they'd probably still have to get someone from the hotel to open the door.

The hotel it was, then.

Drew brought up the smartphone's browser, Googled the hotel, and dialed the front desk.

"A friend and I are stuck in a closet on the second floor," he told the guy who answered the phone, trying to keep his voice dignified and neutral. "I'd appreciate it if you could send somebody up."

It took longer than one might expect for the hotel maintenance guy to get to them. For one thing, they only had one guy on duty at the moment, and there'd been a problem finding him because he'd slipped out for a cigarette and had left his phone in the building.

And second, there were several utility closets on the second floor, and the guy had to go to all of them before hitting the right one.

By the time he got there, Drew had fielded a call from his mother inquiring about where he was. He'd made up a lame excuse about needing to go to a nearby drugstore for some Tylenol to treat a headache. The funny thing was, he really was starting to get a headache now.

"You in there?" the maintenance guy called through the door.

"We're here," Drew said.

He heard the guy trying the doorknob. "It's jammed," the guy told Drew. "We been having trouble with it for a couple weeks now. Keep meaning to replace it. Guess I put it off too long."

"I guess you did," Drew agreed.

There was the sound of tools and a jiggling of the knob, and in a few minutes, part of the knob came off and fell onto the floor inside the closet. Drew could see the maintenance guy's pants through the hole where the knob had been.

The door opened, and the guy—a middle-aged, balding man in coveralls—smirked at them.

"We were … looking for some extra shampoo," Megan said, grasping a bottle and holding it up triumphantly.

"Uh huh," the guy said, still with the smirk on his face.

"Listen," Drew said, starting to sweat. "I know this is … weird. But if you could … you know … not say anything …"

"Heh. You think you two are the first wedding guests to get it on in a closet? Please."

"So you'll keep quiet?" Megan asked hopefully.

"About twenty bucks ought to do it." The maintenance guy held out his beefy hand.

Chapter Twenty-Six

They had enough sense to go downstairs separately. Drew went first, strolling into the reception just as the bride and groom were having their first dance. Megan came a little bit later, having made a stop in the ladies' room to rearrange her hair and wipe off her smudged lipstick.

The first thing Megan did when she came into the room was check to see where Liam was. She found him sitting at a table with Orin, deep in conversation. His leg, encased in a brace, was stretched out in front of him, his crutches propped up against the table. When she walked into the room, he glanced at her, then looked away.

Breanna, trailed by her two boys, came up to Megan, looking exasperated. "Where were you? You missed the dinner entirely." She turned to her boys. "Why don't you guys go chat with Bailey and Marshal?" She pointed across the room to a couple of kids about her sons' age.

"We want cake," Lucas said, a hint of a whine in his voice.

"They're going to cut the cake later."

"But—"

"Michael, take your brother and go play with Bailey and Marshal."

"But I want—"

"It wasn't a request." Breanna fixed her oldest son with her stern mother look, and the boy slumped away, followed by his brother. Breanna rolled her eyes extravagantly as they went.

"Now, as I was saying …"

"I … was off checking to see if they have a room. For me. In case I drink too much, and … I want to be a safe driver, you know." Megan could feel herself blushing and willed it to stop.

"Really?" Breanna smirked. "I'm assuming they had one, because Drew went with you, and you were gone a long time."

"Oh, my God. Does anyone else know? Did you say anything? Because—"

"No, you jerk, of course I didn't say anything. Who would I tell? And anyway, the last thing we need is Liam bludgeoning Drew to death with a crutch."

Megan accepted a glass of champagne from a passing waiter, and she downed half of it in one gulp.

"So, you did get a room, then?" Breanna prodded her.

"No."

"Then what …"

"A closet," Megan whispered, feeling simultaneously exhilarated and humiliated.

Breanna blinked a few times.

"A storage closet," Megan hissed, *sotto voce*. "We got stuck. A maintenance guy had to get us out. God, I am so embarrassed."

A slow grin spread across Breanna's face. "Don't be. I think I have a new role model."

When Drew came in, he faced a similar confrontation—this one with his sister.

"Are you crazy?" Julia said, after she finished her dance with Colin and had made her way to Drew through the crowd.

"Did you have to sneak off with her during my reception? You couldn't wait until afterward?"

"Now, wait. I didn't—"

"Oh, save it," said Julia, looking like a vision of beauty in acres of ivory tulle. "And try to keep your pants on for the rest of the evening. If you can."

It seemed impossible that Liam didn't know what was going on, since everyone else seemed to. But if he did know, he didn't say anything about it to either of them. Maybe his senses were dulled by the pain medication he was on, and it was making him a little slower on the uptake than he should have been. Or maybe he was intentionally ignoring things he would have preferred not to know about.

Either way, they all made it through the rest of the evening without incident. Couples danced, cake was cut and eaten, photographs were taken, the bouquet was thrown. And Drew and Megan stayed a discreet distance apart from one another, as though that ship hadn't already sailed.

When it was over, Drew, who was sober, volunteered to drive a few of the heavier drinkers back to Cambria. Two of them were Isabelle and Matt, who'd both hit the bar pretty hard and seemed to be feeling the effects of it. The other was Mike, Julia's Man of Honor.

Isabelle was riding shotgun in Drew's rental car, with the men in back. To Drew's relief, Isabelle was still buying the headache story.

"Does your head feel better, honey?" she asked as they headed back toward Cambria on Route 46.

For a minute, he'd forgotten about his cover story. "Uh … Yeah. A couple of Tylenol cleared it right up. I'm good."

"The thing about headaches," Mike said, "is they can really screw you. They screw you hard. They just pound you until you're moaning, 'Oh, God,' am I right? Then when they finally let go, it's sweet relief."

"Are we still talking about headaches?" Matt asked.

Drew made eye contact with Mike in the rearview mirror, and the guy smirked at him. The asshole actually smirked. Clearly, Julia had told him what had happened.

Man of Honor, my ass.

"It wasn't that kind of headache," Drew remarked.

"What was it, honey? A migraine?" Isabelle wanted to know.

"No, it was—"

"Probably the throbbing kind," Mike put in, clearly pleased with himself.

"I think it's coming back," Drew said dryly.

Megan was sober enough at the end of the evening, so she went back to Cambria in her own car. The drive gave her plenty of time to think about what had happened that evening, and what it all meant.

Had she really had sex in a hotel closet at her almost sister-in-law's wedding? Oh, she did that, all right. Not only that, but it had been the most intense erotic experience of her life.

If it weren't for the guilt, she'd be giddy with the afterglow. Oh, screw it. Guilty or not, she was giddy as hell.

She had to tell Liam about her relationship with Drew sooner than later, though. If she didn't, and he found out from someone else, he'd be devastated by the betrayal.

On the other hand, she wondered if she would really have to tell him at all. Drew lived out of state—out of the country, in fact—and he'd be returning there now that the wedding was over. She and he could carry on a long-distance relationship—she could go there instead of him coming here—and because of the vast stretch of miles between them, there was no reason Liam had to know.

Except that *of course* he had to know, because he was Drew's cousin. Eventually, it would come up, especially if she and Drew were together long-term.

Not that she was even thinking about something long-term with a man she'd known for a week. Except she *was* thinking about it, which obviously meant that she'd been driven completely out of her rational mind by the great sex.

Which, really, could happen to anyone.

I'm a coward, that's what I am. A closet-sex-having, insane coward.

Megan had always been a sensible girl, and after that, she'd been a sensible woman. She didn't have tattoos, she didn't have a colorful history of drinking or recreational drug use, she'd never gone skydiving, and she didn't have one-night stands. She wasn't impulsive, and she usually led with her brain rather than her heart. She was a doctor, for God's sake.

But right now, she seemed to be doing foolish, impulsive things left and right. What would be next? A tongue piercing? A sudden career change to exotic dancer or alpaca farmer?

It was as though she didn't even know herself anymore.

But the thing was, this version of Megan had just had better sex than the old Megan had ever imagined was possible.

Maybe it was worth considering just going with the change.

Chapter Twenty-Seven

The next day, with the wedding wrapped up, the Delaney hospitality machine was slowly being dismantled. Out-of-town friends and relatives were packing up their cars and heading either to their homes or to the closest airport; Colin and Julia were sorting through the wedding gifts and preparing to ship them to their home in Montana; and Liam was continuing his recovery at home on the ranch. Megan was seeing furry patients whose health needs had been put off during her vacation.

Drew knew he should say goodbye to Megan and then drive to San Luis Obispo to catch his return flight, but he couldn't bring himself to do it. There were plenty of reasons to go: He had a boat to finish. He could make a clean getaway without having to have a meaningful talk with his mother. And if he went now, he could get out of Cambria before getting pummeled by Liam—who might be able to take him, even on crutches.

But there was one very compelling reason to stay: Megan. How could he leave when he'd just found her? How could he go back to a small island in Canada when Megan wasn't on it?

He was sitting in his hotel room mulling things over when he heard a knock on the door.

Megan.

His heart started beating faster just thinking about her being here, just imagining that she'd come here to see him.

But when he opened the door, the woman standing there was not the one he'd wanted to see.

"Oh. Hi, Mom."

Isabelle, who'd had too much to drink the night before, looked tired and a little bit pale. But she also had a look of determination that Drew was certain didn't bode well for him.

"Drew, may I come in?"

He stood back to allow her to enter.

Even tired and hungover, Isabelle was presenting herself with care, as she always did. Her clothes were neat and freshly pressed; her hair was blow-dried and sprayed; her makeup was carefully applied. Drew sometimes wondered if the makeup and the hair were a form of armor protecting Isabelle from the many and varied dangers of the world.

"Oh, goodness. This place is a mess, isn't it?" She made a tutting noise with her tongue as she perused the unmade bed, the clothes on the floor. "I suppose boys will be boys. And you're planning to check out anyway. Might as well leave it for the maid!"

Drew recognized the chatter for what it was: a delaying tactic meant to smooth the way for the real subject she'd come to talk about.

"What can I do for you, Mom?" He kept his tone polite but formal.

She pulled out the desk chair and sat down, her purse held before her body like a shield.

"I wanted to ask you a question," she said.

"Okay, shoot."

She took a deep, shaky breath, then came out with it.

"What I want to know is, if the Delaneys can forgive me, why can't you?"

Apparently, he hadn't made his decision to leave fast enough.

"Mom …" He rubbed his forehead with his fingers. "We don't have to talk about this."

"Yes, we do." Her lips pressed together in determination, making tiny lines feather the skin around her mouth. "You've barely said two words to me all week, and when you did, it was polite chitchat. I was hoping that this week, we'd be able to talk, to clear the air. But you—"

"You don't want to do this." Anger simmered in his voice. "Believe me. You don't want to go there."

"But *why*? Honey, it's been *years* since you found out about Redmond. I know you were hurt, and you had a right to be. You had a right. But when are you going to move on? When are you going to put it behind you and let me back into your life?"

Until today, he'd managed to maintain a level of cool detachment toward Isabelle. It had been important for him to keep his anger in check, simmering below the surface, for Julia's sake. But she was talking to him now as though he were being somehow petty and immature by taking issue with her. How dare she minimize what she'd done to him? And how dare she suggest that he was the one with the problem?

"I found the letters," he said, his voice hot.

"What letters? I don't know what you're talking about."

"The letters Redmond sent to you, that you returned to him unopened. He saved them, did you know that? He was asking to see me. Asking to be a part of my life. Which you'd know if you'd even bothered to read them." Talking to her about it, finally saying the words that he'd been thinking, was like breaking a dam. All of the anger, all of the hurt, was rushing through him so fast and so hard that he didn't think he could stop it.

Isabelle opened her mouth and then closed it again, like a beached fish gasping for air. "Drew, I—"

"You let me think he didn't want me. That he didn't love me. How could you do that? Do you know how worthless I felt? That's why I didn't get in touch with him; I thought he'd rejected me. And then it was too late."

"Oh, honey." Isabelle's eyes were brimming with tears. The sadness and hurt on her face almost made him feel sorry for her. Almost. "I didn't want to hurt your father. I—"

"That was before. I get that part. I get why you didn't tell me any of it while Dad was alive. But after? Once I knew about Redmond, you still didn't tell me that he'd wanted me." He turned his face away from her so he wouldn't have to watch her cry.

"It just ... it seemed easier," Isabelle said in a small voice.

"Easier for you," he amended.

"Yes. And easier for you. I thought if I opened that door, then you'd always wonder ..."

"So you made the decision for me. You took the choice away from me. And don't tell me you didn't know what was in the letters."

She made a low sniffling noise. "I knew. At least, I was pretty sure what the letters said." She looked up at him with watery eyes. "And I didn't want to risk losing you. He had so much money, the ranch, the land, and I ... I was afraid you'd choose him over me."

It was maybe the most honest thing she'd said to him since any of this had started, and he felt his anger begin to ebb. He didn't even know if he wanted to give up the anger; it had been his companion, hovering in the background of his life, for so long.

"I wish you'd had more faith in me," he said. "I wish you'd trusted me enough to let me make that choice myself."

"Oh, honey. I'm so sorry." She rooted around in her purse and came out with a wad of tissues that she used to dab at her eyes and her reddened nose. "Can you forgive me? Please?"

Could he? Did he have that in him to give to her?

"I don't know, Mom," he said. "I really don't know."

At the veterinary clinic, Megan tried to focus on work, but her heart wasn't in it. Drew was supposed to go home today, and she couldn't stop tormenting herself with the question of whether he was going to get on that plane, and whether she would see him before he did.

She could have just called him, of course, but that didn't seem like the right thing to do. Maybe it was her pride, and maybe it was years of indoctrination in the idea that a woman who calls a man post-sex is desperate and clingy. In any case, she decided to wait to see what he would do.

Deciding to wait was easy enough; the actual waiting was much more difficult.

Megan wasn't the only one anxious to know what Drew's next step would be. At about ten a.m., after Megan had just finished examining a stray cat for the local shelter, Breanna called to see if there had been any news.

"So? Did he call?" The way Breanna was hissing out the question told Megan that she was afraid someone else might hear her. Like maybe Liam.

Megan, her white coat on and her hair back in a sensible ponytail, sighed and leaned her butt back against the examining table. "No. Not yet."

"Well, crap."

"What if he left already? What if he went home without even talking to me?"

"Oh, I doubt that," Breanna stage-whispered. "I'm not sure when his flight's scheduled, but he hasn't said goodbye to my mom yet. Those two seem to get along pretty well, so I'm sure he would have."

"Okay." The reassurance made her feel a little better. "Okay, you're right." She changed the subject. "How's Liam?"

In her normal voice, Breanna said, "A little loopy from the pain meds, and grumpy that he didn't even get to drink last night. He and Mom got into it because he keeps getting up and trying to do things, and she says he needs to take it easy and rest."

Megan rolled her eyes. "I'll bet that's going over well."

"Yeah. 'Fuck rest,' he says." Breanna said the words in an uncanny imitation of her brother's voice. In the background, Megan heard Liam yelling something to Breanna. "He wants to know if you're going to do a follow-up on that heifer—the one who had the C-section," Breanna told her.

"Tell him it's on my schedule for this afternoon." From what the Delaneys were telling her, the heifer was recovering fine, but she still wanted to do a standard post-op exam to see for herself.

"All right. Just give Ryan a call before you come out; he can meet you at the barn."

After they hung up, Megan realized she was looking forward to checking in on the heifer. Work gave her something to think about besides Drew. It gave her something to do that mattered.

Something other than mooning over a man and wondering whether he had skipped town without so much as a goodbye.

Chapter Twenty-Eight

Drew needed to get going for the airport, but he was stalling. Of course he wasn't planning to leave without seeing Megan. But he was beginning to think he didn't want to leave at all.

How could he leave her? She'd revived him, when he'd felt half dead for so long.

But staying was tricky. What if she didn't want him to stay?

Liam had made the decision to move to Cambria to be with her without even consulting her. Drew didn't want to make that same mistake. But he also didn't want to leave in the middle of something life-changing.

The thing to do, he decided, was not to make any sweeping decisions right now. The thing to do was to stall.

Colin and Julia hadn't left yet, and Colin had been pushing him for some time to have a serious talk about his money and what he should do with it.

That talk seemed like as good an excuse as any to stay in town a little longer. And anyway, it was something he really did need to do.

He called the front desk at his hotel, arranged to stay a couple more nights, and headed over to the ranch.

***

Colin seemed both surprised and pleased that Drew wanted to have the talk. They settled in upstairs in Orin's study, a dark, manly room with wood paneling on the walls and a sofa in the center that had seen better days.

Colin, who'd been eagerly awaiting the day when Drew would get his head out of his ass and take some responsibility for his money, had his laptop set up on the coffee table next to a yellow legal pad.

Drew sat across from him in a battered leather chair, fidgeting. What had started as a means to delay his return home was beginning to feel serious, and he wasn't sure what he thought about that.

"It's about time we got into this," Colin said, tapping on the keys of his laptop. "I don't mind telling you, it's been hard for me not to badger you about it."

"You have badgered me about it," Drew reminded him.

"Yeah, but not nearly as much as I wanted to. Now"—he rubbed his hands together—"what investments have you made so far?"

The part where Drew was embarrassed by his ineptitude was coming sooner than he'd hoped.

"Uh ... well ... it's in the bank."

"Right. But in what kind of fund?"

Drew looked at him blankly.

Colin's shoulders slumped. "Don't tell me it's in your checking account."

"Well ... no. I do have a savings account...."

"Oh, for God's sake ..."

Drew, feeling defensive, ran a hand through his hair. "Look, I'm coming to you for help. Don't make me feel like a dumbass."

"You *are* a dumbass." But Colin said it with such good humor that Drew could hardly be mad at him.

"Okay. Then help me stop being one."

"I thought you'd never ask. Literally—I thought you would never ask."

With the ribbing out of the way, they got down to business. The two of them went over Drew's assets, including cash, property, and his shares in the Delaney corporation. Because the subject was vast—as were Drew's assets—it was impossible to cover everything in one sitting.

Instead, they ended the session with a preliminary to-do list for Drew. Number one on the list was hiring a financial adviser. Colin provided him with a list of names to consider.

"Can't I just hire you?" Drew asked.

Colin shook his head. "That's not a good idea. I represent the corporation, and what's best for the corporation isn't always going to be what's best for you. A lot of the time it will be, but … I can't foresee every circumstance. You need somebody whose main obligation is to you." He gestured toward a piece of paper in Drew's hand. "Everybody on that list is good, and they're all trustworthy. If you want to look at somebody who's not on the list, run it by me, and I'll check them out first. A lot of 'financial advisers' out there are just scam artists, so you want to be aware."

"Yeah. I've managed to figure out that much on my own." Drew fielded about two calls per week from so-called financial advisers with ideas about what he should do with his fortune—mainly, put it into their pockets. It was probably time to get some legitimate help.

Colin started to close his laptop and gather up his things. "This is just the beginning, you know. Just the first step. You need to educate yourself about what's in your portfolio. And you need to keep learning about the ranch. You got a start the other day. You need to build on that."

Drew nodded. "I know you're right. It's just been overwhelming."

"I'm sure it has been. But it's time to stop being overwhelmed and start being proactive." He picked up his things, stood up, and clapped Drew on the back. "You're my brother-in-law now, I want to see you do well."

"Yeah." Somehow, the statement made Drew feel a little bit embarrassed. "Thanks."

"You know, if you're not in a hurry, you could spend some more time on the ranch today," Colin suggested.

Colin was offering him an excellent excuse for delaying his departure—which was exactly what he'd been hoping for.

"Okay. What did you have in mind?"

What he had in mind was for Drew to shadow Ryan for the afternoon, the way he'd done with Colin before.

Colin called Ryan and set it up, and before he knew it, Drew was mounted atop a big chestnut mare, following Ryan out into a golden brown pasture.

The fences in the northeast pasture needed checking, and they'd been doing that for the better part of an hour when Ryan got a call on his cell phone that Megan was here, wanting to examine the heifer.

Ryan told her he'd meet her, and he turned his horse around to head back toward the barn.

"I'll go," Drew offered, trying not to sound obvious. "I mean, if you want. It'd give you a chance to finish with the fences."

Ryan looked at him appraisingly. "You don't know much about cattle," he observed mildly.

"I don't know anything about cattle," Drew said. "But I figure Megan knows enough for both of us. All I have to do is be there, right?"

"Well, I guess that's about right," Ryan said.

"I can call you if anything comes up. If there's a problem." To himself, he sounded like a thirteen-year-old making a case for why he was old enough to babysit his younger brother.

After a moment, Ryan nodded. "All right, then. I wouldn't mind finishing up with this. It'll save me having to come back out here later."

As Drew rode back toward the barn, he felt the giddy anticipation of seeing Megan again. The events that took place inside the utility closet the day before ran over and over in his mind—which made sitting in the saddle a little uncomfortable.

He still didn't know what he was going to tell her about his plans, though. He decided to stay flexible until he spoke to her. He would pack up his place on Salt Spring Island and move down here without hesitation if she wanted him to. But things between them were so new, he wasn't sure that was what she wanted.

He'd have to feel her out—hopefully, in more ways than one.

When he got to the barn, she was already there with her veterinary bag in her hand, looking ridiculously sexy in jeans, battered boots, and a T-shirt that hugged the same curves he'd so recently become intimately acquainted with.

She'd been expecting to see Ryan, so when Drew came into the barn instead, her eyes widened.

"Where's Ryan?" she said.

"He's out in the pasture. He sent me."

A slow grin spread across her face. "Really."

"Really. You'll just have to make do."

He didn't even pretend to be there for the sake of the post-operative cow. Instead, he went to her and laid his hands lightly on her hips.

"I was wondering when I'd get to see you," he said, his voice low.

He leaned in for a kiss, and she melted into him as though she'd done it a thousand times, as though her body were made for it.

Neither of them was aware of anything but each other. If they had been, they'd have heard the sound of someone coming into the barn—or, more accurately, someone hobbling into the barn on crutches.

"We can find another goddamned vet if you can't keep your mind on the job."

At the sound of Liam's voice, Drew and Megan pulled apart as though they'd been electrocuted. Megan stared at Liam, and her hand flew to cover her mouth.

"Liam."

He turned around on the crutches and went back out the door and into the bright afternoon.

"Oh, no," Megan moaned, and ran out the door after him.

Only then did Drew notice Orin standing just inside the barn door. Of course Liam wasn't alone; he'd have needed someone to drive him here from the house.

"Well," Orin said. He rubbed the back of his neck with his thick hands and looked at Drew with more than a little discomfort. "This doesn't look good, son."

When Megan got to Liam, he was sitting in the passenger seat of Orin's truck, concentrating on the task of not looking at her. She ran to his side of the truck and pleaded with him through the open window, her hands grasping the door frame.

"Liam. I can explain."

Even as she said it, she felt like a fool. How exactly could she explain what he'd just seen? Was there anything—truth or fiction—she could say that would make him feel better about seeing her kissing Drew?

"How are you gonna explain that?" he said, as though he'd read her thoughts. "You're gonna tell me he wasn't really kissing you? And you weren't really kissing him back? You had something in your eye maybe, and he was just trying to help? Is that what you're going to tell me, Megan?" He still refused to look at her, focusing instead on a spot on the dashboard.

Her eyes filled with hot tears. "No."

She'd thought that if he found out about her and Drew, he'd react with explosive anger, that he would yell or throw things, or try to hit Drew. Instead, he just sat there speaking to her in a tone that was cold and controlled. His face looked stricken, and that was so much worse than the anger would have been.

"I suppose you're also going to tell me that this didn't start until after we broke up." He finally turned his cold gaze on her. "Don't you dare say that, Megan. Because it's bullshit, and we both know it."

The tears that had been gathering in her eyes began to fall.

Orin came out, climbed into the driver's side of the truck, and started the engine.

"You're gonna want to step back from the truck, Dr. Scott," Orin said.

She did, and he drove away from the barn and back toward the house, a cloud of dust rising up behind them.

Dr. Scott.

She'd thought of the Delaneys as her family—had thought of Orin as a kind of second father. Hearing him address her that way made her realize just how much damage she'd done.

Chapter Twenty-Nine

Drew had never much liked Liam. Everybody knew that; it was pretty much accepted as a fact of life.

But he hadn't meant for Liam to see what he'd seen, and he hadn't meant for the man to feel the way he probably felt.

He got back to the house a little after Liam to find Orin sitting in his usual chair by the fireplace, staring grimly at the wall, and Liam nowhere in sight.

"Where is he?" Drew said.

Sandra came out of the kitchen, and the stern look she gave him told him that Orin had already filled her in.

"I don't think he much wants to see you right now, boy," she said.

"I know that. Don't you think I know that?" He ran a hand through his hair, making it stick up at odd angles. "I need to talk to him. I need to make it right."

Orin scoffed. "You move in on a man's girl, there's no way to make that right." He still didn't make eye contact with Drew.

"Sandra, where is he?" Drew said.

She crossed her arms over her chest and grunted, then gestured with her chin toward the back hallway. "Downstairs bedroom, first door on the right."

"Now, Sandra ..." Orin started to protest.

"The boy wants to face him like a man. I figure he's got a right to do that, and Liam's got a right to have his say." She looked at Drew. "Go on, now."

Drew's heart was hammering when he came to the door. He knocked softly, and when there was no answer, he eased open the door and peeked in.

"What the fuck do you want?" Liam barked at him. He was stretched out on a twin-sized bed in a small bedroom that was sparsely furnished with a bookcase and a chest of drawers.

Drew had come here determined to talk to Liam, but now that he was here, he didn't know what to say.

What strategy had he planned for this moment? An excuse? An explanation? Some sort of rationale for why Liam hadn't really seen what he thought he'd seen?

He figured there was only one thing Liam really needed to hear.

"I'm sorry," he said.

Liam glared at him from his spot on the bed, his injured leg stretched out in front of him, his head propped up on a pillow.

"Ah, just ... fuck off."

Drew stood there a moment, then went out and started to close the door. It was almost closed when Liam said, "I knew it. I fuckin' knew it."

Drew opened the door again and waited.

"Ryan called to tell Dad that you and Megan were out in the barn. Wanted him to check on you, make sure you had things under control with the heifer." He let out an angry puff of air through his teeth. "I was pretty sure what I'd see if I went out there. And I was goddamned right." He shot a glare at Drew. "Predictable son of a bitch."

Drew blinked in surprise. "You knew?"

"Of course I goddamned knew. Everybody knew. I'm not blind or stupid."

Drew felt like a fool, and more than that, he felt the shame of having been needlessly cruel.

"Liam … "

"Just get the hell out." Liam leaned back and put his forearm over his eyes, a clear signal that this conversation was over.

Drew didn't know what he was going to do now, but he figured he wasn't welcome in the Delaney house at the moment. He headed through the front room and out the door without talking to anyone.

He was all the way down the front steps and halfway to his car when Sandra called to him from the front porch.

"Drew."

He turned around and faced her without a word.

"Well, it looks like you've made a mess of things," she said.

"Looks like."

"Where the hell do you think you're going?"

If she was suggesting that he shouldn't leave, that he shouldn't drive away from the ranch and never come back, then there was no accounting for it.

"I figure I'm pretty unwanted here around now," he told her.

"Oh, that's so much bullshit, and you know it." She came down the porch stairs and stood in front of him, her hands on her narrow hips, face tight and hard like a fist. "I won't pretend you didn't make things harder for yourself with Liam, because by God, you did. But if you're planning to run out of here and flee back to Canada, then you're not the man I thought you were."

He rubbed his eyes with his fingers. "Sandra …"

"Don't pretend you weren't thinking it. You run and hide—it's what you do. But Liam's your family, and family doesn't stop just because you're off hiding out in a hole somewhere."

"I wasn't—"

"And what do you think's going to happen between you and Megan if you run away like a scared rabbit?" She grunted. "You may be willing to pretend you never knew any of us, but are you going to do the same thing with her?"

"I … no." The truth was, he hadn't known what he was going to do when he rushed out of the house moments before. His first instinct had been to head to the airport and get on a plane.

"I thought …" He sighed and looked at the brown earth that stood between him and Sandra. "I really thought it was time to make peace with everything. I was going to try. But Liam …"

"Liam's hurt and angry, and he's got his pride," Sandra said, her voice softer now. "But he knew things weren't working between him and Megan, son. He already knew that much."

"He's never going to forgive me," Drew said.

Sandra grunted. "Well, he might not. But he didn't throw a lamp at your head. I figure that's gotta count for something."

Megan knew better than to try to talk to Liam this soon after what had happened. So she spent a couple of minutes crying about it in the barn, and then she wiped her face and got on with the job she'd come here to do.

The heifer was being kept in a stall until her incision healed, and Megan went in, determined to focus on her work.

She was pleased with what she saw. The animal was up and allowing her calf to nurse. The incision looked good, with no signs of infection.

Megan went through the steps of a post-op exam, then crossed to the sink at one end of the big barn and washed her hands.

Where was Drew?

She wanted to think that he wouldn't run away after what had happened, but she knew he had a history of hiding out when things got difficult. She wasn't one hundred percent confident that he would stay to work things out. And that realization made her wonder—not for the first time—if she'd lost her mind, falling for him so quickly.

She loaded her veterinary bag into her truck and thought about what to do. She couldn't talk to Liam, not yet. But what about Drew? Should she call him? Should she try to find him, maybe at his hotel?

She thought about it as she drove off of the ranch property and back toward town. She was still contemplating her choices when a call came in over the Bluetooth in her truck.

When Megan answered the call, Breanna launched into it.

"Holy crap, Megan. What happened? Liam's got himself closed up in the downstairs room, Dad's pissed, and Mom is walking around grumbling and banging pots. Nobody's talking, but I got the sense it's got something to do with you."

"It does." Megan turned the truck onto Highway 1 south toward Main Street. As she drove, she told Breanna about what had happened at the barn.

"Oh, crap." Breanna sounded equal parts horrified and impressed at the sheer size of the shitstorm Megan and Drew had created.

"And now I don't know what to do!" Megan moaned. "I can't talk to Liam yet, because he's probably too hurt and pissed. And I'm not even sure what to do about Drew! He's going to run, I just know it. He's going to hop on a plane without even saying goodbye, and he's going to disappear into the wilds of British Columbia, never to be heard from again."

"Oh, come on. I'm sure he won't—"

"It's what he does!" Megan wailed. "When he found out about Redmond, he ran away! And then, when Colin found him and told him about the inheritance, he got out of here as fast as he could and didn't come back for two years! He wouldn't have ever come back if it hadn't been for Julia and the wedding. He runs! When he feels trapped, or confused, or overwhelmed … he hides like a rabbit in a damned burrow!"

Saying it all out loud, Megan realized maybe for the first time how true it was—and how much it didn't bode well for any future relationship.

Breanna let out a sigh. "I want to tell you you're wrong, but … you're not."

"I'm not! I know I'm not!"

As she drove toward her clinic, Megan suddenly understood what she had to do.

Nothing.

If Drew was going to run away from Cambria, from the Delaneys—from *her*, it was better to know now than later. Better to understand that he wouldn't stick right now, before she up-ended her life for him any more than she already had.

Otherwise, they might be living together or even married before something came up—an argument over money, or living arrangements, or exes, or children—that would prompt him to go back into his hole and leave her alone and devastated.

It was better to know now. It was better to stand back quietly and wait to see what he was going to do.

"Megan? You got quiet," Breanna said. "Are you okay?"

"Yeah," she said finally. "Yes. I'm okay. This sucks, but I'm okay."

"What are you going to do about Drew?" Breanna asked. "I mean … do you really think he's going to just leave? Just like that?"

"We'll see."

"Oh, boy," Breanna said, her voice full of dread.

Chapter Thirty

Julia heard about what Drew thought of as The Barn Incident sooner than he'd expected. He'd thought she would be somewhat out of the loop because of the inevitable post-wedding fog, but he'd been wrong.

She called him just as he was getting back to his hotel. He thought about ignoring the call, but she would just keep calling until he picked up. Might as well get it over with now.

"You idiot," she said. "Damn it, Drew."

"You heard," he said mildly.

"Yes, I heard! I heard that you got caught making out with Liam's girlfriend, and now my whole new family of in-laws is upset, and this is not what I had in mind as I pack for my honeymoon!"

His shoulders slumped as he let himself into his room. "I'm sorry, Jules."

"Are you? Are you really? Because I'm pretty sure I warned you that something like this was going to happen."

"I don't think you did, actually."

"Well, I was thinking it!"

What she'd told him was to keep his pants on at the reception—which he hadn't done. But what she'd meant was, *Don't do anything stupid*. If failing to be stupid had been his goal, then he'd failed spectacularly.

He sat down heavily on the bed, the phone to his ear.

"Listen, Julia …"

He'd meant to reassure her somehow, to give her reasons why she need not be alarmed by the blowup between him and her new family. But the reasons wouldn't come. When it came time to offer them, he had nothing.

"What?" she demanded. "What, Drew?"

"Hell, I don't know." He lay back on the bed, feeling defeated.

"What are you going to do?" she said. "Are you and Megan a couple now? How are you going to face Liam? You two already didn't get along. Did you know that his last girlfriend—the one before Megan—cheated on him? And he caught her with somebody else? That was *years* ago, Drew, and he *still* hasn't gotten over it! But he trusted Megan. And now this."

She sounded as disgusted with him as he felt with himself.

"I'm sorry, Julia."

Her voice softened a little, probably in response to how miserable he sounded.

"You should probably spend less time being sorry and more time figuring out how you're going to fix all this."

"I don't know that it can be fixed."

"I don't either. But you're going to try."

The thing was, it would make so much more sense to deal with this after everything settled down. Right now, emotions were high. Feelings were raw. People were going to be irrational. But if he gave it a little time—a couple of months, say—then everyone would have gained some perspective.

That's what they all needed: some perspective.

The argument made sense to him as he packed his stuff and loaded Eddie into his cat carrier. Drew had a client waiting for a boat, after all. He couldn't just abandon the project. He had a life on Salt Spring Island. He had obligations.

He'd missed his flight when he'd decided to stay around to bond with the Delaneys—and look how well *that* had turned out—but he figured if he went to the airport, he could catch the next one available.

And if that didn't work out, he could always keep the rental car for a couple more days and drive.

All he knew right now was that he needed some space, some time to think. He needed to separate himself from the anger and hurt he'd caused. He needed to get away from the chaos of his relationships with the Delaneys, and from the uncertainty that had pervaded his life since they'd come into it.

He just needed to get away from here and back to his home, where nobody thought he was a terrible person, and nobody was looking to him to fix some colossal mess that he'd made.

Home was quiet, and it was simple. He ate, he slept, he ran his errands, and he built his boats, and when he got lonely, he had Eddie to keep him company.

Easy.

He drove to the airport trying not to think about what he was leaving behind, or about how everyone had been right about him.

Megan waited for Drew to call, and when he didn't, she tried to tell herself to be patient.

Of course he would call. Everything that had happened between them had been magical, electric. There was no way he could walk away from that.

Unless she was the only one who'd felt it.

Unless he'd only said he did, to get her out of her under-pants in the utility closet at the hotel.

She went about the rest of her day feeling more than a little pathetic, and more than a little like a cliché. Was she fifteen again? Because that was how it felt—letting a guy kiss you behind the bleachers and then wondering if he was going to laugh about it to his friends. Wondering if you were ever going to hear from him again, or if you'd see him near the lockers with his arm around another girl.

It was remarkably like that, except Megan had let him do a lot more than kiss her.

She ran through it all in her head as she examined Mrs. O'Neal's Weimaraner for cervical spondylomyelopathy. She tried to focus on the alignment of the dog's spine instead of on her love life, and she thought she was doing a fine job of it until she realized Mrs. O'Neal was talking to her and she hadn't heard a word of it.

" … should check."

Megan raised her head from where she'd been bent over the dog.

"What? I'm sorry … What were you saying?"

Mrs. O'Neal was visibly irritated. "I said, she's been walking normally, but my friend Opal's Weimaraner had this problem, so I thought I should check."

"Oh. Of course. I'm a little bit distracted today."

"Distracted!" Mrs. O'Neal gave Megan a haughty glare. "Do I have to find a different vet?"

"No, of course not." Megan attempted to look as efficient, focused, and doctorly as possible. "I assure you I'll give Bela my full attention."

"Well, I hope so." Mrs. O'Neal sniffed.

The truth was, there was nothing wrong with Bela other than the fact that she was saddled with an overly anxious owner. Megan wondered if she should do some X-rays anyway, just to reassure Mrs. O'Neal that she knew what she was doing.

Ethically, though, she couldn't justify the expense or the annoyance to the poor dog, who appeared to be in perfect health.

She informed Mrs. O'Neal that Bela had neither cervical spondylomyelopathy nor any other detectable health condition, and received exactly the response she expected—judgment and disdain.

"Why, you didn't even perform any tests!"

"Testing for a condition your dog doesn't have would be expensive and unnecessary, Mrs. O'Neal," Megan said. "But if she starts to show any symptoms …"

"Symptoms! I came in today so we could catch this *before* she shows symptoms."

"But—"

"I should think you'd want to be proactive, as a medical professional …"

"But I—"

"Come on, Bela." Mrs. O'Neal snapped on the dog's leash and led her out of the exam room, pausing briefly at the reception desk to write a check for the exam while grumbling loudly about distracted doctors, poor, suffering animals, and the sorry state of veterinary care.

Ellie, Megan's vet tech, who also worked as receptionist as the need arose, watched Mrs. O'Neal with raised eyebrows as the woman went outside to her car.

"Well, she was pissed."

"Yeah." Megan propped an elbow on the reception desk and slumped. "I had the nerve to tell her that her dog was healthy."

"Usually, that's considered good news."

"Usually."

Bela was the last appointment on her schedule today, but there was still half an hour until closing time. Megan thought about all of the useful things she could do: updating patient files, sending out vaccination reminders, cleaning out the storage room, accounting. She needed to place an order with her pharmaceutical supplier, and she needed to restock the supply drawers in the exam rooms.

She had Ellie until closing time; between the two of them, they could get a lot done if they put their minds to it.

But Megan's heart wasn't in it, and she knew any attempt to focus and be productive would be futile.

"Why don't you just go home early, Ellie? We're not expecting anybody else, and any emergency calls will ring my cell."

"Sounds good." Ellie, a woman in her midthirties with ash-blond hair, piercing blue eyes, and a commendable ability to make friends with even the most irritable of the animals who came into the clinic, peered at Megan with concern. "Is everything okay?"

"Yes, of course." Then Megan gave up the pretense, and her shoulders slumped. "Well ... no. Not really."

"What's wrong? Can I help?"

"Thanks, but no. You can't. Unless you can psychically will a particular man to call me, or text me, or send me a freaking smoke signal to let me know what the hell he's thinking."

She hadn't meant to unload like that, but now that she had, she felt a little better.

Ellie leaned forward conspiratorially. "I heard you got caught in the barn making out with Liam's cousin." She made a face. "Yikes."

Megan drew back in surprise. "You heard that? How?" The incident was only a few hours old, and there'd been no one here in the clinic except their scheduled clients. Had one of them already heard? And if so, who'd told them and when?

"I have ways," Ellie said. "Mysterious ways."

In a way, it was helpful that Ellie knew, because that meant Megan could seek her advice.

"If you make out with a guy in a barn, and let's just say for the sake of argument that it wasn't your first time doing … things … with the guy, and you get caught by the guy's cousin who's also your ex, wouldn't you expect the guy to at least call afterward for a debriefing? The first guy, I mean. Not the ex."

"You might," Ellie agreed thoughtfully. "Or, because you're an adult woman with autonomy and access to a phone, you might call *him* instead of waiting for him to take the initiative."

Megan considered that. She'd resolved not to call him—and for good reasons. But now, that resolve was beginning to crumble.

"You're right. I'm an adult woman. I'm independent. I'm fully capable of taking action instead of being passive. Why wouldn't I call him? Am I so indoctrinated in the traditional gender roles that I believe he has to be the one to make contact? Am I that much of a …" She searched for a word. "… a *sheep*?"

Ellie wrinkled her nose. "Kinda seems like it."

"Well … crap."

Ellie was right. Megan needed to just call him. She needed to just ask him the questions that were on her mind: *Did you talk to Liam? Are we a thing now? Are you going to run away? Do you feel the same way about me as I do about you? What are we going to do?*

Instead of calling him, she decided this was a conversation they should have in person.

He certainly wouldn't be at the Delaney Ranch right now, after all that had happened with Liam. Some people in this situation might stay there and try to work things out, but that wasn't Drew. Drew would retreat to think things over.

So, it made sense to try his hotel.

She locked up the clinic, said goodbye to Ellie, and climbed into her truck for the short drive to Moonstone Beach.

"He isn't here," the middle-aged woman at the hotel reception desk informed Megan.

When Megan had arrived, she'd knocked on the door of Drew's room, and some other guy had answered. Foolishly, she'd thought he must have changed rooms.

"Did he go out?" she asked stupidly. "I can wait."

"He checked out, honey," the clerk said. "A couple of hours ago."

"He … he checked out?" Somehow, the words weren't making as much sense as they should have.

"That's right. He told me this morning he'd be staying a couple more days, but I guess he changed his mind. Too bad, too. I had to charge him for late checkout. I hated to do that, but it's the owner's policy."

"Oh."

"I can't give you his contact information—against policy. Sorry about that. But if he calls in for any reason, I can—"

"I have his number," she said numbly.

"Oh. Well, then you can just give him a call," the woman said, as though it were just that simple. As though it were not an issue that he'd apparently left town without even saying goodbye. As though that didn't hurt at all.

Chapter Thirty-One

In the rationalizations Drew constructed for himself, he wasn't abandoning Megan. He wasn't running away. He wasn't even avoiding his problems.

He was simply doing what he'd planned to do from the beginning—going home after the wedding was over. And if that meant that everyone involved could avoid the inevitable conflicts and confrontations, well, so much the better.

He could call Megan later and tell her why he'd left. He could explain it all to her, how he was saving everyone unnecessary strain and discomfort. And then he could figure out when and how they were going to see each other again.

Surely there had to be a way for them to be together without all of the misery and drama.

He just had to think about what it was.

He turned in his rental car at the San Luis Obispo airport, then took a shuttle to the terminal. He carried his cat and his luggage to the Delta desk to see if he could get a flight.

The first one available wasn't leaving until the next morning. He booked the flight, and then caught a cab to a nearby Motel 6 he'd found on his phone.

At the motel, he checked in, moved his stuff into the room, and then took Eddie outside to a little patch of grass near the pool where he could walk around and pee.

As Drew stood there watching the cat sniff at a patch of weeds, he didn't feel well. He felt tired, lonely, and sick, as though some unnameable virus had attacked both his body and his mind. Nothing in his world was where it was supposed to be. He felt as though all of the pieces in his personal life puzzle had been shaken and scattered, some never to be found again.

It's the Delaneys. Redmond and Liam … all of it.

He felt certain that if he could just get home, get back to Salt Spring Island and his cottage with its workshop full of saw-dust and tools and his partially built boat, he'd be okay. He'd be able to focus and shake off this unsettled feeling.

He lay back on the bed—ignoring any thoughts of where the bedspread might have been and under whom—and stared at the ceiling. While he lay there, a text came in from Tessa: *Can't we please just talk?* He deleted that one. She hadn't wanted to talk to him when he'd been broke and alone. She hadn't been much interested in anything he'd had to say then.

He checked his voice mail and found messages from a lux-ury car dealer, a charity he'd never heard of, and a Realtor hop-ing to tell him about a piece of property that would make a won-derful investment.

He deleted them all, feeling more alone than he could re-member feeling since the day Tessa had left him.

Eddie curled up on the bed next to him, and Drew stroked his head and thought about Megan.

The thought of Megan made him feel so many conflicting things that he didn't know how to begin to sort them out. He felt warm and excited, and also scared out of his mind. He want-ed her, but he was afraid to want her. He yearned for her from within the deepest parts of himself, and yet that yearning was all mixed up with his feelings about Tessa. About having loved someone, and then having been abandoned.

He needed some perspective, that was all. He needed time to think.

He was still fully dressed and lying atop the bedspread when he fell into a restless sleep. Drew was just starting to dream— something about wandering through an abandoned house with a maze of too many rooms—when his phone rang.

He checked the display: Julia.

Drew's first instinct was to turn off the phone without answering, but he'd come far enough in the past couple of years, at least, to know that he had to resist the impulse.

He accepted the call.

"Jules."

"Where are you?"

"Don't start."

"Don't start what? It was a simple question. You were here in Cambria, and now you're not. Where are you?" Her voice had started out calm enough, but it was gaining volume as she went.

"I just thought it would be better if I left."

"Better for who? For who, Drew?"

"For everybody."

She was quiet for a moment, and he could practically see her face, the frustration and judgment.

"You need to stop doing this." And now her voice wasn't angry or shrill. It was just sad.

"Doing what?" But he knew. He knew what he was doing.

"Running away, Drew. Taking off and hiding when life gets hard. Life is hard! Get used to it! Mom lied to you about who your father was, and that sucks. It really does. But now you've got money, and a new family who want to get to know you, and a really great woman who's falling for you ... and okay, let's put aside the fact that she was Liam's girlfriend. The point is, you've got a lot to be happy about, but you're not!"

He sighed and closed his eyes and felt the world slipping away from him. "Tessa was a really great woman who fell for me once. And look how that turned out."

"*That's* what this is about? Tessa? About you being afraid of getting dumped again? God, Drew ..."

"She wants to get back together, did I tell you that? Now that I'm rich, apparently whatever flaws I had are suddenly tolerable."

"Oh ... no. You're not going to—"

"Of course not. I'm not stupid."

"Well ..."

"Okay, I'm not *that* stupid. But ... how do I know it won't happen again? With Megan?"

Julia's voice turned tender. "You don't. You can't. But you have to at least try, or you'll never know what could have been."

They sat in silence, together over the phone line, while he thought about that.

"Everyone's pissed at me," he said.

"It wouldn't be the first time," Julia said. "You'll survive."

He hung up the phone, got undressed, and got under the covers. Then, with Eddie beside him, he stared at the ceiling until finally, he slept.

Megan didn't want to cry over a man. She didn't want to be that kind of woman, especially when the man in question was someone she'd known for all of a week.

But the fact was, when you felt something so irresistibly compelling with someone that you threw out all of your principles and behaved in ways that you normally wouldn't, and that person left without saying a word to you, it hurt. It hurt so much that a little crying didn't seem unreasonable.

That's what Megan was doing—crying in her pajamas, with Bobby on her lap and a glass of wine in her hand—when the doorbell rang.

Of course, her first thought was that it was Drew. That he'd come back for her, that he'd never actually left town without saying goodbye in the first place. There'd been some mistake, that was all. And now she was going to feel stupid to have misjudged him.

That was why she flew off of the sofa, dropping Bobby unceremoniously out of her lap and onto a sofa cushion, as soon as she heard the chime. She composed herself carefully with her hand on the doorknob, not wanting to look too pathetically eager.

Still, she *was* pathetically eager. And her heart, which had soared just moments before, came crashing down painfully when she opened the door and saw Liam standing there on his crutches.

"Oh. Liam. I … You didn't drive here yourself with that leg, did you?"

"Hell, no. My dad's in the car."

He looked embarrassed, angry, and more than a little uncomfortable. She was certain he'd come here to tell her what a horrible person she was for what she'd done to him—and she deserved it. She stepped back to let him in.

"Liam, I'm so …"

"Save it."

Fresh tears started to flow, so she grabbed some tissues from the box on the coffee table and snuffled into them.

"Go ahead." She threw her arms up into the air. "Go on. Tell me I'm a miserable excuse for a human being. You can say it. Have at it!" She plunked down onto the sofa, the wadded-up tissues in her hand.

He came the rest of the way into the house and shoved the door closed behind him with a crutch. "That's not what I came for, but now that you mention it."

She blew her nose and looked up at him through reddened eyes. "It's not?"

"Ah ..." He lowered himself into a chair, set his crutches aside, and rubbed his face with his hands. "No. I just ... I thought we should talk about, you know ... everything. It all happened pretty suddenly, and I feel like my damned head's about to pop off."

"Okay." She nodded her head and sniffled.

She knew she looked awful with her puffy, red eyes, her Hello Kitty pajamas, and her hair piled messily atop her head, loose strands flying everywhere. But her appearance was the least of her worries. She deserved to look like shit.

"Megan ... How long have things been going on between you and that guy? Did you start seeing him before we broke up?"

She nodded mutely, and fresh tears flowed onto her cheeks. She wiped at them with the wad of tissues.

"Really." He seemed to be saying it more to himself than to her.

"I never meant for this to happen." But that was what everyone said, wasn't it? It was the all-purpose cliché excuse. *I never meant to do it.* She couldn't imagine that it offered much solace to anybody.

"Well ... what the hell?" Liam seemed more puzzled and hurt than angry. "Were you that miserable with me?"

"No! No. I mean ... I knew that things weren't right between us. And I knew we needed to end it, because I just wasn't ready for marriage, or living together, or ... or any of it." She looked at her hands in her lap. "But that's not why I got involved with Drew."

"All right. Then why did you? Explain it to me, because I don't understand. Why did you have to start up with him before we were even through? And why my cousin, of all people? Why him?"

How could she explain the immediate, undeniable chemistry she'd felt with Drew? How could she make Liam understand that she hadn't had a choice? What could she say to make him see that things with Drew had taken on a life of their own, out of her control, from the moment they'd met?

She couldn't. So instead, she said one word.

"Love."

"*Love?* Are you kidding me? Fucking *love?* You've known him, what, a week?"

Liam seemed outraged, and she got that. Outrage was the only logical response to what she'd told him.

"I always thought love at first sight was a myth," she said. "I thought it was something from Disney princess movies and romance novels. But it's real, Liam. I can't explain it. Okay, maybe it wasn't the *first* time I saw him, but it was really soon after that. I knew. I just … knew."

"You knew," he said.

"Yes."

He let out a sigh and looked at the ceiling. "You know how much that sounds like pure bullshit?"

"Yes. I do."

He let out a harsh, humorless laugh.

"I never meant to hurt you, Liam."

"Yeah, well. You did."

"I know."

They sat there for a moment, together but apart, considering the scope of human heartbreak.

"Well ... where is he, then, if you two are in *love*?" He said the word scornfully, as though the very thought of it were offensive.

Megan shrugged and laughed bitterly before dissolving into tears again. "Who knows?"

Liam's forehead creased in either confusion or concern. "What do you mean, 'Who knows'?"

"I mean, he's gone. He checked out of his hotel. I guess he went home."

"You guess? Didn't you talk to him?"

"No!" she wailed. "I went to his hotel after ... after what happened in the barn ... because I thought we should talk! I thought we should discuss what happened, and how to deal with it, and where things are going from here! But he was already gone."

"Wait. Wait just a fuckin' minute. Are you telling me that you fell for this guy—really fell for him—and he just skipped town without even a goddamned *word* to you about it?"

Megan nodded miserably. "That's what I'm telling you."

Liam stood up, grabbed his crutches, and hobbled toward the door, muttering words that sounded like *asshole* and *dickhead* and *kick his goddamned ass.*

"Liam? Where are you going? What are you going to do?" She jumped up from the sofa and followed him toward the door.

"Don't worry about it."

"What do you mean, 'Don't worry about it'? Where are you going?"

"I'll see you later." He went out the door and clomped down the porch steps. For once, Megan was glad that nobody knew where Drew was, because if Liam found him, things were likely to get bad fast.

"Oh, God," Megan said. She closed the door and leaned back against it, wondering how she'd gotten herself into this.

Love sucked.

Chapter Thirty-Two

It had taken Liam just ten minutes on the Internet to find out that the next flight to anywhere that connected to Vancouver didn't leave until the next morning. After that, it took just fifteen minutes on the phone to find out that Drew was staying at the Motel 6 in San Luis Obispo. He might not have found him if Drew had decided to drive up to San Jose and fly out from there, or if he was taking a road trip all the way to Canada.

But he hadn't done those things, and so locating him was easy. It was harder to persuade his father to drive him down to SLO to confront the man, so he went to work on Ryan.

"Just give me a goddamned ride, would you?" he said to his brother on the front porch of Ryan's house on the Delaney Ranch property. "Or do you have something better to do?"

"I do, actually," Ryan said mildly. "I do, indeed, have something better to do than driving you halfway across the county just to get beaten to a pulp."

Liam scoffed. "What the hell are you talking about? When have I ever lost a goddamned fight?"

"Never, when you've had use of both your legs. But in your current condition, I figure he might have the upper hand."

"Don't you worry about that," Liam said, his face set in determination. "You just let me worry about that."

Ryan considered that for a moment, then went inside the house and came back outside with his jacket. "Well, I guess it's probably better if I'm there for this. You're gonna need somebody to drive you to the hospital afterward."

It was late by the time Drew heard the knock on his motel room door. He hadn't told anyone he'd be here, and it was a Motel 6, after all. A late-night knock at a Motel 6 usually didn't mean anything good.

"Who is it?" he called through the locked door. He peeked through the peephole and saw Liam and Ryan standing there in the glow of the parking lot lights.

"Open the door, asswipe," Liam said.

Drew's adrenaline surged. Refuse to open the door? Open it and end up fighting Liam? Call the front desk and ask them to send somebody to roust Liam from the property?

There were two of them and only one of him, but he'd never known Ryan to be violent.

"Drew, open up," Ryan said. "I figure Liam has a right to have his say."

That was fine, if he only planned to talk, but somehow Drew doubted that. On the other hand, the guy was dealing with a substantial physical handicap at the moment.

He opened the door just wide enough that he could look them both in the eye. "What are you guys doing here? Go home."

"I figure I'll go home when I'm damned good and ready." Liam put out a crutch and used the rubber tip to shove the door open, then he clomped past Drew and into the room.

"Let's not do this," Drew said.

Instead of responding to that directly, Liam took the conversation in another direction.

"You're an ass," he said. "You're a pussy, and you're a coward."

Drew, feeling a little bit desperate, turned to Ryan. "Are you really going to let him fight me when he's hurt?"

"I figure I'm just here to clean up the mess afterward," Ryan remarked.

"Who said I was going to fight you?" Liam said. "You really think that's what I'm here for? God, you're more of a dick than I thought you were."

Drew's eyebrows rose. "Then …"

"I came here to ask you what the fuck you're thinking." Liam lowered himself to sit down on the bed with some difficulty, then set the crutches down next to him. "A woman like Megan falls in love with you, and instead of being *grateful,* instead of thinking how *incredibly lucky* that makes you, you run out instead of even having the decency to talk to her. If I hadn't broken my goddamned leg I'd kick the shit out of you."

This wasn't at all what Drew was expecting to hear, and so it took him a moment to acclimate.

"You … I …"

"What was your plan?" Liam demanded. "You were gonna, what, get her into bed just to get back at me? Is that it? Then you were gonna dump her like a piece of trash you're finished with?"

Drew looked at Liam, and then at Ryan. "That's what you think?"

Ryan shrugged. "That sure is what it looks like."

"No. God … no." Drew sank into the desk chair and rubbed at the back of his neck. Only now did he realize he wasn't wearing anything but his boxer shorts. He'd been sleeping when they got here, after all. "That's not what happened."

"Then what did happen?" Ryan said. He leaned against a wall, his arms crossed over his chest, legs crossed at the ankles.

Drew rubbed his chin with his hands. "It wasn't to get back at you. It wasn't about you at all. In fact ..." He sighed heavily. "In fact, I wish you hadn't been a part of this at all. I didn't set out to hurt anybody."

Ryan sat on the bed a couple of feet from Liam. "Well, I figure we've got all night if you want to set us straight."

Drew didn't owe them an explanation for what had happened between him and Megan, and the explanation, such as it was, seemed unlikely to make anybody feel better.

Still, they weren't here to beat him up, so he guessed they deserved something.

He turned to Liam. "Look ... The first thing I want to say is that Megan cares about you, man. Despite how things might look. She really does care."

"Don't tell me about Megan," Liam grumbled. "I know Megan. Don't tell me about her like you know her and I don't."

"All right."

So instead of talking about Megan, he talked about himself. How he'd been intrigued by her from the first time he saw her. How he'd told himself not to get involved, because he wanted to make some kind of peace with the Delaneys, and he knew falling for Megan wasn't going to get him there. How once he'd let the idea of her into his head, he couldn't stop thinking about her. How something inside him just seemed to know her before he even knew her. Like they'd maybe been together in another life, as stupid as that seemed.

He told them how he knew, in his heart, that she was *the one*, and yes, it was damned inconvenient that *the one* also happened to be involved with Liam. But *the one* only happened once, and a person couldn't ignore it when it happened, no matter how inconvenient it might be.

"I'm sorry you got hurt. But I'm not sorry that I met Megan, or that she has feelings for me. I can't be sorry about that."

When he was done with his speech, which had turned out to be longer and more heartfelt than he'd expected it to be, he fell quiet and waited.

Ryan was looking at him appraisingly, and Liam had the kind of pissed-off expression on his face that would scare small children.

"So, what the hell are you doing in a Motel 6 with your damned cat?" Liam wanted to know.

Eddie, as though he knew they were talking about him, went behind an end table to hide.

Drew, embarrassed, looked at a cigarette burn on the carpet.

"I just thought … after what happened in the barn … that maybe I wouldn't be welcome anymore. It seemed like it would be better if I just left."

Drew looked up just in time to see one of Liam's crutches flying at his head. He put up his arms to shield him, and the aluminum crutch bounced off his forearm and landed on the floor.

"You goddamned fuckin' … you shithead," Liam said.

"Like I said, it's better if I go," Drew told him.

"Do you know Megan's crying over you right now? That's right, she is. Crying because you didn't call her after the thing in the barn, and then she went to your hotel and found out that you'd left. That you'd checked out without even saying goodbye to her, or fuck off, or anything else. You claim to have all these *feelings*." He put air quotes around the word *feelings*. "But if you had any damned feelings at all, you wouldn't have done that to her, you worthless piece of shit."

Drew blinked a few times, surprised by the direction the conversation was heading. "I was going to call her once I got home."

"Once you were already gone and there was no danger of you actually getting into a meaningful relationship," Ryan observed.

"No, that's …" Drew waved his hands in front of him as though that might clear the air among them.

"Look. You wanted to run off and hide up there in Canada after you found out about Redmond, fine," Liam said. "You wanted to go hide some more after getting your inheritance. That's fine, too—no skin off my ass. But now you've got Megan in love with you, and you're gonna, what? Hide from her, too? She doesn't deserve to be something you hide from."

Drew felt a distinct sense of disorientation brought on by the fact that Liam seemed to be, in his own way, urging him to stay. "You … Are you saying you actually *want* me to be with Megan?"

"Ah, fuck you," Liam said, without much heat. "I care who you date about as much as I care about learning to speak Mandarin."

"Which is not at all," Ryan clarified.

"But I do care about Megan," Liam said. "And she wants you, for some damned reason. So the least you can do is man up and stay here long enough to talk to her."

They were all quiet for a while as Drew digested what Liam had to say. Then he rubbed his eyes and ran his hands through his hair. "All right. I'll come back to Cambria in the morning, and I'll go to see Megan."

"Like hell," Liam said, and stood up carefully with the aid of the one crutch he still had. "Pack your stuff and get your ass in the car."

Chapter Thirty-Three

It was past eleven p.m., so Drew expected Ryan to drive him back to the Delaney Ranch. Instead, Ryan drove to Happy Hill, pulled his car up to the curb outside Megan's house, and put Drew's suitcase and his cat carrier on the sidewalk before getting back into the driver's seat.

"Get out of the car," Liam told him.

"Wait. You're not going to—"

"Get out of the damned car," Liam said.

He got out and stood next to his things, and Ryan drove off without saying another word.

Drew turned and looked at Megan's house. The lights were on, so that was something.

Eddie meowed mournfully from inside the carrier.

Drew was still standing there when the curtain in the front window moved. A moment later, Megan was on the front porch looking down at him.

"Drew? What are you doing here?"

"I … uh … Ryan brought me."

"Ryan? But …"

"Can I come up and talk to you?" Then, in something of a non sequitur: "Eddie's here."

Instead of inviting him inside, she grabbed a sweater from a hook inside the door, pulled it on, and came down the steps to stand before him. The neighborhood had no street lights, and most of the neighbors had turned off their porch lights by now. The street was dark except for the light from Megan's window. The ocean air was cool, and a slight breeze ruffled Drew's hair.

"You didn't leave," she said. "I thought …"

"I did, though." He put his hands in his pockets. "I did. I went to the airport, but I couldn't get a flight. Then Liam came and got me."

"Liam? Why would he—"

"I'm sorry." He could tell her the rest later, but he had to tell her that now. "I shouldn't have run away. I told myself I was going because after what happened, nobody would want me here. But really, I was scared."

"Well … so am I!" She threw her hands up in frustration. "I'm scared, too! We're all scared, all the time! You'd better figure out a way to get used to it!" Her voice broke, and she shivered a little in the evening chill. He put his arms around her, and at first she wouldn't embrace him. At first, she kept her arms wrapped around herself, a tight bundle of resistance.

Then, a little at a time, she relaxed and held him back.

"I shouldn't have left," he whispered into her hair.

"You can't do that again, unless I know you're coming back. You can't."

"I won't."

He kissed her, and then they walked together, with Eddie, to the house.

She took him into her bed, but they didn't make love. Instead, they lay side by side and held hands and looked at the ceiling, and talked about it: why he'd left, what it meant that he'd come back, and where they would go from here.

"I was scared," he told her. "Scared that the Delaneys would reject me for a second time. Scared that you might choose Liam after all."

"Scared that it might work out between us, and then I might leave you the way your ex-wife did," she said.

"Yes." That, most of all.

"You can't judge me based on what she did, Drew. It isn't fair."

He squeezed her hand and scooted an inch closer, so that their hips touched. "I know it's not. It was just ... instinct, I guess."

There was something else, too. Since he'd received his inheritance, he'd been so inundated by people who wanted to get close to him because of his wealth, that he no longer knew who was real and who wasn't. But if Megan had been all about the money, she could have married Liam. She could have had her own piece of the Delaney fortune by now. But she'd given that up to take a chance on Drew.

"She wants to come back," he said. "Tessa, I mean. Because of the money. I guess whatever it was she couldn't stand about me, it's a lot more bearable when you add a few hundred million dollars."

"It's a lot to deal with, I imagine. That kind of money."

"Was it ever an issue with you and Liam?"

She turned on one side to look at him. "You mean, the fact that he's rich and I'm not?"

"Well, yeah."

She shrugged. "It must have occurred to him at some point to wonder about my motives. But if it did, he never mentioned it."

He turned, too, so they were lying face to face.

"You know, I was thinking. I could move down here, and—"

"No."

He froze in midsentence.

"No?"

"No."

He felt a deep sense of dread like cold water running through his veins. He'd screwed up, he knew that. By trying to run away from this, from her, he'd made an enormous mistake. But when she'd brought him inside, to her bedroom, he'd thought there could be forgiveness. He'd thought she would give him a second chance. But now, she was saying no to him. No to their future together.

"Does that mean … Megan, I know I was an ass to leave. I know that hurt you. But if you'll let me make it up to you …"

She laid one hand on his cheek and looked into his eyes. "I want you to make it up to me. But I don't want you to move here until you do."

"But …"

"Drew. Liam moved here from Montana when we'd barely been seeing each other for a couple of months. And look how that worked out. When you move here for me, I want it to be because we know each other—really know each other. And because we want a life together. And getting to that point takes time. I do want you—so much. But I have to know that it's right. And I have to know that you won't run away again." She pressed a brief kiss to his lips. "It's okay that you're scared. But I don't want you moving down here for me until you're not scared anymore."

A half grin tugged at his lips. "So, we date? Long-distance?"

"Why not?" She gave him a smile, the first since he'd come here tonight, and it warmed and soothed him. "You'll come here, and I'll go there. And we'll give it time and just see what happens."

He raised his eyebrows. "Might there be sex while we're seeing what happens?"

"That might be one of the things that happens," she agreed.

"I hope so."

He pulled her into his arms and they lay there wrapped up in each other for a long time.

"Does this mean I have to go home?" he said.

"Oh … in a while. There's nothing that says you can't stay around for a bit so we can start all that dating."

"Well, I might do that, then."

After a while, she said, "And while you're here, it would be a good idea to try to patch things up with Liam."

He didn't answer her, but he knew she was right. He needed to patch things up with all of the Delaneys.

"He's the one who brought me here tonight, you know."

"He did? But you said Ryan—"

"Ryan drove. But it was Liam's idea."

She sat up and stared at him. "That doesn't make sense."

"Yeah, it does."

"How?"

Drew lay on the bed with his hands behind his head, looking up at her. "Because he loves you. A lot. Enough that when he saw you crying tonight, he just wanted to make it stop, even if that meant the two of us being together. Even if it meant letting you go."

"Oh." Tears glimmered in her eyes. "Oh."

"Damn it," Drew said.

"What?"

He shrugged. "I wanted to hate the guy, but now I really can't."

"Give him a chance," she said. "You'll like him."

"Yeah, well, maybe."

Eddie mewed and scratched at the inside of his carrier, which they'd brought into the bedroom to keep him safe from Megan's various pets.

"You want to let him out?" she asked.

Drew sat up on the bed. "Yeah, he'd like that."

"Well, if you're going to be coming over here a lot, I guess we'd better introduce him to the gang."

"You think your dogs will like him okay?" Drew said skeptically.

"Only one way to know."

She opened Eddie's carrier, then opened the bedroom door. Then they both winced as Eddie bolted under the bed with Bobby, Sunshine, and Mr. Wiggles chasing him in a cacophony of barking and hissing.

"I guess they're going to need a little time, too," Megan said.

Chapter Thirty-Four

Drew went to the Delaney Ranch the next day to talk to Liam. He no longer had his rental car, so he asked Megan to drive him out there and drop him off.

He reminded himself to lose the defensive attitude, regardless of how Liam might choose to greet him. Liam might have a habit of acting out in anger, but there was something underneath that, something that was actually pretty damned noble.

He found Liam out in the stables, hobbling around on his crutches and cooing to his horse. He was stroking the animal's muzzle and softly whispering to it as though the two were sharing a particularly interesting secret.

When Drew came in, Liam looked up briefly, then turned his attention back to the horse without a word to Drew.

"Hey," Drew said.

"What do you want?" Liam said. There was no hostility in his voice, just tired resignation.

"I wanted to apologize."

"You did that last night."

"Yeah."

Liam still didn't look at him, focusing instead on the horse's big, dark eyes.

"I figured I should do it again," Drew said. "For what I did to you ... and for hurting Megan."

"Yeah, whatever," Liam said. For the first time since Drew had come into the stables, Liam turned to face him. "You hurt her again, I swear to God I'll kick the shit out of you."

Drew considered that. "If I hurt her again, I'll let you."

They faced off for a moment, and then Liam nodded. "Well, all right, then."

With everything said that needed to be said, Drew turned to go.

"McCray," Liam said.

Drew turned to look at him.

"Not for nothing, but you're a goddamned hypocrite."

"Why is that?" Drew said.

"Because you won't forgive your mother for the same damned thing you did yourself. You both fell for the wrong person, acted on it, and got yourselves into a mess. When it's you, everybody's supposed to understand. But when it's your mom? You barely talked to her all week, and when you did, you seemed pissed off. Like I said: You're a hypocrite."

"That's different."

"How?"

"Because she lied."

Liam turned back to the horse and began stroking its forehead. "Yeah. She did," he said. "She lied, you lied. We're all liars at one time or another. But she's your mother, and you only get one of those."

Drew thought about defending himself, then didn't see the point.

Why defend himself, when Liam was right?

He walked out of the stables and headed back toward the house.

***

When he got to the house, Sandra, Colin, and Julia were there. Colin and Julia were finishing boxing up their wedding gifts for shipping, and Sandra was helping, sealing up a big cardboard box with packing tape.

All of them fell quiet when Drew walked in.

"Is Mom still in town?" Drew asked Julia.

"Yeah. She is. But I didn't think you were," Julia said.

"I figure I ought to talk to her."

Julia's eyebrows rose in surprise. "You should," she said. "Should I come with you? It might help to have a little backup."

"Nah. I mean, thanks. But that's all right."

"Okay."

And as long as he was facing his fears—his fear of a real relationship, his fear of rejection, his fear of a true reconciliation with his mother—he figured he might as well deal with his fear of the many and awesome responsibilities of wealth.

He turned to his brother-in-law. "Colin? Are you two going to be around for a while? Because I thought we could talk about …" He cleared his throat. "I wanted help picking one of those financial advisers."

Colin looked vaguely stunned. "Uh … yeah. Later this afternoon?"

"Good."

He walked outside, thinking to get a little air before figuring out how he was going to get to his mother's hotel without a car.

He was standing on the porch thinking about everything when Sandra came out and stood beside him.

"I don't know what happened over the past twelve hours, but I'm thinking it was a lot," she said.

Drew nodded. "Yeah. It was." He told her what had happened with Liam—how Drew had tried to flee the country and had been dragged back to work things out with Megan.

"I figure it's about time you faced up to things, instead of holding on to all that anger," Sandra said, poking him in the chest with one finger.

"Me too," he said.

"*Hmph*. You want a place in this family, boy, I figure you've got one. I know you haven't always wanted it, but it's yours, nonetheless."

Impulsively, he reached out and hugged her, and she let out a little sound of surprise. Then she hugged him back.

"I was wondering if I could maybe stay here a while," he said. "To learn about the ranch."

"And to be close to Megan, I'm figuring?"

"Well … yeah."

She nodded crisply. "I'll fix up a room."

"And, Sandra?"

"Mm?"

"Is there any way I could borrow a car?"

Isabelle was in the breakfast room of her hotel when Drew got there. He knocked on the door of her room, and when he didn't get an answer, he found her sitting at a little table with a cup of coffee and a muffin.

When she saw him, her first expression was surprise—followed by her quickly composing her features into a polite smile.

"Mind if I sit down?" he said.

"Please. The breakfast is supposed to be for registered guests, but I'm sure if we offer to pay, we can—"

"That's okay," he told her. "I'm not hungry. I just thought we could talk."

"Oh."

"Where's Matt?"

Isabelle made a tutting sound. "He wanted to take one more walk on Moonstone Beach before we leave. He's quite charmed with Cambria."

Drew nodded.

Isabelle stirred her coffee carefully. "What was it you wanted to talk about?" The tension in her face told him she was steeling herself for whatever he had to say.

"I just … I thought we could spend some time together. If you and Matt are going back today, then maybe … I don't know. I could visit you in Montana."

Isabelle's eyes welled up with tears. Then she reached out her hand and squeezed his.

"I'd like that."

"Yeah. I would, too."

"Honey?" she said, her voice quavering.

"Yeah?"

"I've missed you."

And all at once, he realized he'd missed her, too. All of the time he'd spent angry, all of the time he'd spent hiding—it was all time wasted in a relationship that wouldn't last forever. She wasn't young anymore, and he'd already lost so much when he'd lost his fathers.

He didn't want to lose any more.

When Liam came back to the house, his mother was waiting for him.

Colin and Julia were off at the post office to ship their things, and the front room was empty except for them.

Sandra waited for Liam to settle himself into a chair, his leg extended in front of him, his crutches set to the side. She sat down on the coffee table facing him.

"You're a good man, Liam," she said.

He gaped at her in surprise. "Well, hell. What's this about?"

"You know what it's about." She patted his good knee with her hand.

"I guess I do," he grumbled.

"I think you feel the most of any of my boys," she said. "And that can't be easy. It's why you had such a hard time with Redmond's death. And it's why you're so angry." Her eyes grew a little pink, and her tight mouth moved as she thought about what to say. "You've got a good heart, Liam. You try to hide it, but sometimes it just shows anyway."

She stood up and kissed his forehead before bustling off to the kitchen.

"Well, hell," Liam said.

Made in the USA
Columbia, SC
14 August 2020